THE GIRL WHO FELL THROUGH TIME

THE GIRL WHO FELL THROUGH TIME

BOOK ONE
BEGINNINGS

Kevin A. Reynolds

nanamaru

The characters and events portrayed in this book are fictitious. Any similarity to real persons, living or dead, is coincidental and not intended by the author.

No part of this book may be reproduced, or stored in a retrieval system, or transmitted in any form or by any means, electronic, mechanical, photocopying, recording, or otherwise, without express written permission of the publisher.

"Only two things are infinite, the universe and human stupidity, and I'm not sure about the former."
Albert Einstein

"Causality Paradox: When the future becomes the past, the past becomes the future, and the present does not exist."
Creation and Controllability of Stable Einstein-Rosen Bridges.
Peter Walker, Tokyo, October 2019

Japan: Then & Now

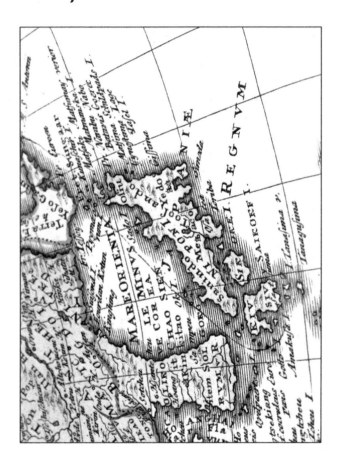

No Death in Vain

Deep in the heart of Japan, halfway between the cities of Nagoya and Kyoto, lie the bones of thousands of samurai. They died in battle, as men of their era did time and time again, shouting and screaming, tearing and slashing at each other with the finest swords, their body armour ragged and bloody, their eyes locked in fierce defiance.

The mountains at Sekigahara are quiet now, silent witnesses to the long-forgotten agony that had continued for centuries as the great dynasties fought each other for control of the land and its people, for their believed historical right to govern, to lead, to conquer, to divide, but most of all to survive. For if they were defeated then all honour would be lost, and death would be their only escape.

Such loss, such heartache, such bravery.

And yet modern Japan was forged from the flames that fired the swordsmiths' kilns, and the Earth itself would be a different, lesser place without those geniuses of the martial arts, the Sony Walkman, Origami and Karaoke.

Indeed, the world is as it is today because everything that ever happened, happened as it did. You might not like it, and you might argue that the tragedies of the twentieth century were a heavy price to pay, and all that pain and loss could have been avoided if the leaders of that time had chosen a different road. Yet without Pearl Harbour and all that followed, we may well have sunk into that abyss of a new dark age that Churchill so rightly feared.

Hiroshima and Nagasaki brought an end to that conflict, but who can say the world has been at peace since? Nine-eleven, financial turmoil, nuclear meltdowns, environmental destruction, and giant tsunamis washing away the dreams of thousands of innocent souls. And war, ongoing, never ending. Korea, Vietnam, Iraq, Afghanistan. Wars on drugs, on cancer, on viruses, on religion.

Churchill had a point.

But what if it didn't have to be that way? What if it could be changed? What if past mistakes could be corrected, and mankind guided back on to the true path of its beautiful destiny? If you thought you could do that, if you had the power, you might try. You might not be overly concerned about the owners of the bones buried under the battlefields of feudal Japan, but didn't you owe that to the millions who had needlessly suffered and perished in these so-called modern, enlightened times?

And what about those who were unconvinced about the climate changes impacting the planet? If only they knew what you know now. If you could guide them, advise them, help them learn from their mistakes so they never had to make them in the first place, then we would all soon be living in a 'new age of light.'

Yes, if you thought there was a way to save all mankind from its own folly, you might well try.

But, then again, what if you were wrong…

Part One:

Present

Nene

This is death, the world between worlds.

The light is so bright I can barely open my eyes. And that terrible sound that roars like a thousand waterfalls scares me so. I can hardly hear my own thoughts as I am spun around and around, like a child's toy, without mercy.

Where is the tunnel taking me? To heaven, it must be. Not hell, let it not be hell. In hell there is no light, and everything here is light.

Father! Where are you? I was with you. There was a fire. We were at dinner. Someone else was there, too.

The visitor!

He reached out for me, but his hand was beyond my grasp as a I fell into the tunnel. Not fell. I was dragged, pulled in, sucked down into the whirlpool of light.

Father, how will you survive on your own? I am so sorry to leave you, but I am gone to mother. Yes, I will be with mother again. I cannot recall her face; I was so young. But I will know her, I am sure.

It is calmer now. I float like a cherry blossom on a gentle morning breeze, carried along by fate. The dreadful sound is gone. I feel peace, tranquility. Death is surely nothing to be afraid of. Leaving those we love behind, that is hard to do.

There was something, a memory of a world.

I cannot grasp, cannot think.

The light is so much brighter.

Someone is there. Mother, is that you?

A shape at the end of the tunnel.

A door! It opens, now shuts.

Where am I? The floor is hard, like stone.

Is this heaven? No, it cannot be. There must be light in heaven, here there is only darkness.

"Mother!"

Why doesn't she answer? She cannot, because this is hell.

Yet I still breathe, and I feel solid rock beneath me.

No, this is not my death, not unless... yes!

He said he would come, and I should wait for him. I remember!

But his face... why can't I remember his face? His name? It is gone. Like the world before, lost.

Please come soon. I am waiting for you.

So scared, so afraid.

So alone in the dark.

One

Peter Walker stepped out of exit 13 of Tameike-sanno station and headed towards Ark Hills.

He'd used the stairs rather than the escalator, as he elected to do wherever possible, partly to serve as a form of exercise, but mainly because he disliked standing still behind others who had decided to stand still. He didn't consider himself to be a fitness fanatic, far from it, but he knew that looking after his physical self would have demonstrable benefits on the clarity of his mind and the ability of that tired old clunker-brain of his to think useful thoughts. The data on that was clear, as was the data on how making even the simplest choices on the smallest things in life results in positive outcomes in the larger things. Starting with choices such as making your own way up the stairs, rather than having the stairs doing that for you.

Things?

That was far from a rigorous analysis, but 'things' was good enough. And if he was being honest with himself, he hadn't actually read any papers regarding the psychological aspects of decision making, but there were enough people on YouTube who had and Peter trusted a few of them, even if he did seem to spend half of his time watching flat-earth videos and wondering how people could be so moronic.

But as the whole world knew all brains work better with caffeine, and the Ark Hills Starbucks provided plenty of that, along with a table by the window and free 5GHz. *Pete's Tokyo office*, as he liked to think of it, although one of these days he might have to try one of those AnyWork hot desk set-ups. On the other hand, if he did that it would imply he had failed to achieve his primary objective of getting his sorry arse back to Europe, a failure that would have the undoubted benefit of providing him all the time he needed to continue his research, but without the resources at the Hadron Collider he wouldn't be able to prove anything beyond the theoretical.

Failure, as someone famous had once said, was not an option.

Even if he were right, nobody was going to believe him without hard evidence, and even then he doubted they'd be convinced. He was having a hard time convincing himself, but Peter was pretty adept at the mathematical theory of space-time and even better at thinking beyond the limitations that his fellow physicists placed on themselves, and he had a hunch that he was right. No, not a hunch, more of a conviction supported by a new interpretation of the Schwarzschild metric that resolved the exotic matter requirements for the negative energy required to stabilize-

"Ohayo, Peter-san."

Shit. He'd been so wrapped up in his own thoughts he'd arrived at the counter without realizing it. He didn't even remember coming in through the main entrance.

"Ohayo," he replied to Mika, who was always there on Monday mornings, smiling sweetly for him. For everyone, actually, but especially for him.

"Same as usual, Peter?" Mika asked, in her New York accented English. She'd spent ten years there during her father's assignment to one of the big banks - he could never remember which - and had come back more American than Japanese. Her next stop was a tour of Australia, just as soon as she'd finished her degree, which was something along the lines of artificial intelligence applications in quantum computing, making her one of his favourite people along with Madam Curie and Sabine Hossenfelder. Although it would take a lot to knock Herr Albert off the top of that particular list. The fact that she was small and extraordinarily cute had nothing to do with it.

"Yes, please, Mika. Thank you," he replied. "And a cheese ham roll thing too, heated up, if you don't mind."

"Sure," she replied. "Seven ninety, please."

Peter paid, then checked his watch as Mika popped his breakfast in the microwave and made his Grande coffee of the day. It was ten twenty-seven, and with any luck his corner table would become available at precisely ten-thirty when the tall-guy went up to his office; provided he was following his usual morning ritual of coffee, emails, eBook and iTunes. Peter leaned forward to check around the pillar. The fellow was tidying up his things, getting ready to go upstairs.

"Here you go," said Mika.

"Thanks," Peter replied, then headed for his table, arriving at the exact moment it was available.

"There you go," said the tall-guy.

"Thanks," Peter said, promising himself that one of these days he'd start a conversation, especially now that he could see the man's Kindle was open at The Theory of Everything by Stephen Hawking, his personal favourite of his old professor's books.

Peter planted himself down, took his MacBook Pro and a jumble of documents out from his rucksack and settled in for the morning shift. The first order of the day was International Standard. He logged onto the wi-fi and squirrelled his way into the IS network, where, after opening a few doors he had discreetly left there the previous week, he typed:

> Peter Walker was here, October 22, 10:47. I'll be around later to hand you the bill.

He was being cheeky, if not rude, but the head of IT was adamant that their firewall was impenetrable, yet here was Peter Walker-san with a cheese and ham thing in one hand and a coffee in the other, snooping around and dropping little markers for the slightly arrogant and self-important Yoshida-san to find right where Peter would tell him to go looking for them, which he had set his Outlook to do at exactly 11:11. It wasn't the only marker either, but IS was his biggest client and he wanted to be invited back to show them where the others were hiding. What's more, Peter didn't think much of his own hacking skills. Someone who really knew what they were doing could walk away with the entire Japan customer list along with the supposedly secret files on that new product range that had taken him no more than ten minutes to find on his first day at their offices.

"So much for your brilliant firewall, gentlemen," he muttered as he logged out.

Perhaps he wasn't such a bad hacker himself.

Abe-Sensei was the next item on his list, which Peter kept in his head, as he did with things important, unlike the names of Japanese Banks in New York, which didn't qualify.

Shit, where was it?

He'd put everything in order at home before he came into town, so the hard copy should be at the top of the pile. The fact that he now found it in the middle of said pile didn't faze him, but it did make Peter wonder what he'd been doing when he was sorting out the day's proceedings over his morning tea. That wasn't like him, not like him at all.

Yes it is, you oaf. It's just like you.

He smiled at the thought of his brother, God rest his soul. Except there was no God, or none that Peter had ever found. How could there be? Michael would still be here if there was, Peter was sure of that. In any case, it was beyond proof, unlike his own work and that of Professor Abe, whose article 'An Introduction to Quantum Entanglement' was now firmly in his hand. It was going to run as part of a science supplement in the Japan Times, so naturally Peter was supportive, although he didn't fully agree with the contents. Or, rather, his own research had gone beyond that of Abe-Sensei, but he was too polite to say anything. Too British, perhaps, and thus the red ink marks on each of the three pages were merely grammar and phrasing corrections, with a few notes on 'how about putting it like this...' Peter didn't want to embarrass his good friend and mentor by saying, 'yes, but...'

He picked up his iPhone and tapped Abe-Sensei's name on the recent callers list.

"*Ohayo Gozaimasu*, Sensei, it's Peter here. I've finished checking your article, and I thought some areas could be expressed a little easier, especially for the non-scientific reader. So, I've made a few suggestions, which I'd be happy to discuss when you get back from Shanghai. So, well, have a safe trip, and see you in a few days."

Good, he was done. Although if he'd had a few more customers he wouldn't quite be done and could afford that hot desk, but then he wouldn't have time for the next item on his list.

My life's work is hardly an 'item'.

He'd almost said it out loud. He had a habit of muttering and while it didn't bother him per se, there were those who thought he was either going mad or was in fact already mad and it was all far too late. Well, they were his friends and so he didn't mind, partly because they were just as nuts as he was, but mainly because none of them could explain who exactly was talking to whom. It wasn't an easy question to answer.

'If I am having a nightmare,' Peter had once argued, *'and I wake up sweating, then who was actually giving me the nightmare, and who was actually waking up sweating? Which one of them is the real Peter? In other words, who is the observer observing the dream? Was the thinker having the thoughts, or were the thoughts having the thinker? Where is consciousness, and how can you measure it?'*

That jolly discussion in his Cambridge lodgings had continued for hours with no conclusion, other than the need for more beer. It was bordering on unsolvable anyway. Einstein had famously said, *'Imagination is more important than knowledge,'* but as far as Peter was aware Herr Albert had never solved the mystery of where intuition came from. Peter certainly hadn't. Indeed, he was sure he couldn't if he tried. Far better minds than his had yet to figure that one out, though he suspected the answer lay somewhere in the realm of random quantum fluctuations within the brain's microtubules, but it was only a suspicion, and he was anyway more interested in where those thoughts would lead than where they came from.

So, the long and short of it was that he didn't care if he talked to himself. It made for a reasonably interesting conversation, and with any luck those conversations would lead him to Geneva.

Peter returned Abe-Sensei's article to his rucksack, along with the other documents that he hadn't really needed to bring with him, leaving just one on the table with the title staring up at him: 'Creation and Controllability of stable Einstein-Rosen Bridges.'

His life's work, in a Starbucks, next to his cheese and ham thing and his coffee, with a tea stain on the cover, and on page six that incomplete and unstable sub-quantum kinetic extrapolation that now required his attention. He was going to solve that today, if he could, right where he sat. Assuming it *could* be fixed, that was.

His iPhone buzzed.

His heart skipped a beat at the notification. He opened Facebook on his laptop anyway; he couldn't help himself. The first item in his feed was by Mariko, who was *'Off to Amsterdam for my new job!'* Twenty-two of her friends - their friends - had hit 'like'. So, she had finally made the move, and that little story was over. Well, he'd just have to get on with things, there wasn't much else for it.

He opened the simulation and ran the numbers. A tornado-like graphic whirred all over the Mac like a berserk spinning top, before flinging itself apart in a giant explosion of light. Giant, that was, on the six million-odd pixels in front of him. It shouldn't be happening - his wormholes weren't supposed to blow themselves to pieces like that - so the fault was either in some sub-routine somewhere, which he could fix easily, or in the underlying mathematics, which was a harder fix, or, heaven forbid, somewhere deep in the whole concept itself, which would be a way harder fix and would mean he wouldn't be able to sort it out today, even with three Grandes' worth of caffeine flowing through his veins.

Please let it be the sub-routine.

Peter opened the de-bugger and got to work.

***

"Sumimasen."

Peter didn't realize the voice was directed his way. In fact, it hadn't even registered.

"Sumimasen."

He heard that one, chiefly because the accompanying tap on his shoulder had succeeded in snapping him away from a stack of intransigent protocols that refused to behave themselves. He looked towards the source of the tap. A grey-haired old man with a broad smile was pointing over Peter's other shoulder.

"Mado no soto de dare ka ga yondemasu yo."

Peter's eyes followed the *ojisan's* finger. The fellow was right, although 'somebody outside is calling for you' wasn't doing it justice. It was Jane, jumping and waving her arms around as if swatting a thousand flies.

"Arigato gozaimasu," Peter said, then waved for her to come and join him, which she did by entering through the small side door marked 'exit-only.'

"Hello stranger!" she said, giving Peter a hefty hug.

Peter reciprocated. "I thought you weren't back 'til next week," he said. "Or was it the week after next?"

"Slight change of plans. So, I thought I would drop in and see you."

Jane was shorter than him, a lot rounder, and with frizzier hair to boot. She was also full of that tough-love stuff that had an occasional tendency to rub him up the wrong way, but in all the years he had known her they'd maintained an almost brother and sister like connection. Which might explain how she had found him. But then again it might not.

"How did you know I was here?" he asked.

"Female intuition."

"Ah, coincidence, you mean."

"Plus the fact you bloody live here."

"My clients do occasionally like to see me, you know."

"They'd see a lot more of you if you moved closer in. So would I, come to think of it." Jane pointed at the empty seat next to his. "That taken?"

"Go ahead."

Jane plonked herself down as if she'd just scaled Mount Fuji. Peter did the same, but she missed his less-than subtle fun-poking gesture.

"I like it where I live. It's quiet," Peter said. "Besides, you're not that far away. When you're at home, that is."

Jane smiled.

"So, how was Auz?" Peter asked, fully aware that he already had a good idea of the answer.

Jane grinned. "Three months in Sydney, absolutely lovely jovely. Now, if I could just persuade Sydney to spend another three months in me, perfect."

"You're going to have to introduce me to this guy one day, you know."

"All in good time, Petey-wetey, all in good time. Gotta get through the bonking-like-rabbits stage first before I decide whether he is worthy of an introduction."

"Doctor Pearson, what are you like?"

"It's me hormones, chuck. I can't control 'em."

Jane glanced at Peter's Mac. He'd already closed the simulation - it wasn't yet ready for public consumption - but had left his browser untouched with Facebook still open at Mariko's post.

Jane gave him one of her sisterly-but-disapproving looks. "And nor can you, apparently," she said.

"I was just looking."

"You'd be better off looking for the next one, if you ask me."

"If there is a next one," Peter said, trying to be matter-of-fact.

Jane wasn't fooled. "There will be, mister dreamy-blue-eyes, though she'd have to be something special to poke up with you."

Jane being Jane, as always.

"Oh, I dunno, Jane," he said. "Maybe I'm better off on my own, you know. Just focus on my work. No distractions. Which would be quite nice, actually."

"Get a life, Walker, will you, for God's sake!"

"I've got one, thank you," Peter retorted.

"Says who?"

"Says me, that's who."

"Well, *me*, hasn't the foggiest idea, now, does he?"

"Did you really come all the way here just to tell me that?" he said.

"I came here because Syd's at work, and I've nothing else to do. And besides, he only lives up the road."

"Have you actually moved in, then?"

"Working on it. Still got the place in Hach-my-groji. Going back at the weekend, *actually*. Gotta meet the landlord, tidy up, you know, give it a clean, get ready to end the contract, that sort of thing. Syd's got a trip to Hokkaido and can't take me along, for whatever reason. So, you know, may as well use the time wisely."

She meant Hachioji, but Peter had long given up on trying to get her to say it correctly.

"So, you are moving in, then?" he said.

"Yeah, I suppose I am," Jane replied. "Anyway, enough about moi. What's the story with you?"

Jane picked up his research paper from the table before Peter had even begun to figure out a response.

"'Creation and controllability of stable Einstein-Rosen Bridges.' What a mouthful. And what's that supposed to mean?"

"It means getting a proper job, preferably in Geneva."

"I mean, what's an Einstein thingy whatsit?"

"Most people call them wormholes, you know, as in tunnels through space time. But an Einstein-Rosen Bridge is the correct terminology."

"Oh, an Einstein-Rosen Bridge is the correct terminology, professor 'iggins." Jane flicked through pages of complex equations. "How anyone can understand all this bollocks is beyond me. Oh look, there's a bit about you."

This should be good.

"The question remains," Jane read in her best BBC voice, "can we in fact travel through time and manipulate history, or is there some natural law of the universe that prevents us from doing so?"

"And that's about me?"

"Yeah. If there's any unresolved paradoxes around here, you're it."

"Is that supposed to be funny, Jane?"

"I thought so."

"Really? Mind I have that?"

Peter made a grab for his paper. Jane held on playfully, then let go, saying, "What's in Geneva?"

As if she didn't know. "A big round thing that smashes protons to pieces."

"Oh, yeah, that. I thought you liked it here."

"I do, but I can't stay forever. Plus, all the action is happening there. If I can get this thing published, it might help me get back home."

"And leave me here all by myself?"

"I'm sure Sydney will look after you."

"Wear me out, you mean. I should be calling him mister Incredibonk. Anyway, hold the fort will you, I'm busting for the loo, after which I expect a full update on all things weird and wonderful."

Jane stood up, having only been sitting for a few moments, and walked away. No, not walked. Jane never walked anywhere. For her it was always somewhere between a stomp and a charge. Peter barely had time to close Facebook before she came storming back.

"Forget me bleedin' head in a minute," Jane said, as she grabbed her handbag from her chair before thundering off to the ladies. At last, time for him to recover before the next onslaught. Peter smiled; he wouldn't have it any other way.

She'd left her copy of the Japan Times behind, though. The smaller of the two headlines on the front page caught his eye:

Unlimited Power? Ministry Announces Next Generation Reactor Research.

He picked up the paper and started to read.

Two

The weird and wonderful conversation with Jane lasted two hours and thirty-seven minutes and was likely overheard by everyone in the thirty-storey building, let alone their fellow patrons in the Starbucks. Still, Jane was Jane, and so that was par for the course, so much so that Peter had only just made it on time for the meeting with Yoshida-san at International Standard, and now that he had an extended contract his finances would survive the next six months; enough time for either getting a few more clients, or, hopefully, bagging that role at CERN.

Hopefully?

"Definitely,' he said it out loud, as if that would make it so, although it did make the young girl on the seat in front of him wonder who he was talking to. Peter smiled at her. She looked away shyly as their train trundled onwards.

Peter's thoughts returned to Starbucks. Jane hadn't much liked it when he'd hit her with his idea of no free will. He hadn't been completely serious, but it was one of the potential consequences of his emerging theories and so he'd grabbed the opportunity to try explaining it to a non-specialist in his field, one who was certainly capable of understanding the rationality, if not the underlying irrational mathematics. He ran it over in his mind, looking for gaps in his logic.

"Think of it like this," he had said to Jane as she started her second latte. "You go back in time and meet yourself, age twelve."

"Ugh," Jane had said. "Not that spotty-faced twerp."

"Yes, the one who'd just moved in next door. Remember that day?"

"I do, indeed," Jane had replied.

"So, you're there, twenty years ago, the now Jane, having a cup of tea with the then Jane."

"Hang on, which one's me?"

"Both. But let's say you are you, she is Jane. OK?"

"Got it. But Jane didn't drink tea. She's only twelve."

"Orange juice, then. So, anyway, you start telling Jane about the next twenty years of her life. You know, her army of cats, that day she crashed her bike into a tree, that bloke at school who kept tugging her ponytail, the day she poohed the bed when she had the flu."

"God, you don't remember that, do you?"

Peter had nodded. "Not an easy thing to forget. Anyway, Jane got straight A's, went to medical school, did this, did that, including coming to Cambridge for my twenty-first and throwing-up in my wastepaper basket, which stank for months, thank you."

"You're welcome."

"So, she graduated, somehow, did her residency, went to Africa for the Ebola thing, and then came here, plus or minus a few adventures in between."

"Is there a point to this?" Jane had asked. "Apart from reminding me I can't hold my drink."

"Look at it like this. You, now, here today, know the story of your life. You know every twist and turn, every decision, every clever thought and every daft idea, if you can remember them all. All the things that happened in the past twenty years, you, the now Jane, sitting there, know them all. Theoretically."

"So?"

"The young Jane doesn't. For her the future is open, nothing is yet decided. She doesn't even know she wants to be a doctor."

"So?"

"Don't you see? From your viewpoint sitting here now, at this luxury table pour deux, twelve-year-old Jane's whole future is already decided. Her whole life is mapped out. Everything she will ever think, say or do, is already done."

"So, what you're saying is-"

"Her future is already decided, yes."

Jane had frowned. "That wasn't was I was going to say."

"But you see it, right?" Peter had replied. "We might think we have free will, but there's an argument that we don't, that our whole future is already decided, done, finished, all planned out, depending on which way you look at it. And that's my point. Time travel negates the whole concept of free will. Possibly."

"Oooh, I don't much like the sound of that." Jane had said.

"I'm not sure I much do either," Peter said it out loud.

The young girl on the seat opposite looked at him again. Peter smiled again, and for the second time she glanced away.

He'd simplified things with Jane. Not because she wouldn't understand a more complex argument - in many ways she was just as smart as he was - but because he agreed with Herr Albert that everything should be made as simple as possible, but no simpler. And in any case, he didn't believe in no free will, far from it, but it was an interesting thought experiment and he liked to see people's response to that particular conundrum, especially since most were already familiar with that over-used idea of going back in time to shoot your grandfather when he was a child, thereby dooming yourself to non-existence and the impossibility of being alive to go back in time in the first place. That was a different argument, though, more along the lines of creating a paradox than the abolition of free will.

Whichever way you looked at it, you'd need a working time-machine to prove it, and as far as he knew there was only one double-PhD on the planet who believed it was actually possible. Even his old professor had expressed his doubts, especially after no-one turned up to the party he had held for time-travellers, the one he had announced *after* the party was held.

Nope, only Peter Walker-san thought it could be done. Primarily because nobody *did* attend that party.

***

The train pulled to a halt at Hachioji station, where most passengers disembarked. Peter was still only half-way home. Jane had a point; he lived bloody miles away, but at least the rent was taken care of – for a while.

His iPhone buzzed from its holder on his belt; an update on the typhoon that was passing south of the Japanese archipelago. It would miss Honshu, but those on the small islands that stretched into the Pacific needed to take precautions. Peter didn't even know they were inhabited, but it seemed they possibly were. Obviously were, in fact.

Holding his iPhone prompted him to open Safari and re-read the Japan Times article.

'Next Generation Reactor Research' implied a fusion device. It wouldn't be surprising, given Japan's reluctance to re-start its fission-based nuclear power industry, which had been moth-balled since the 2011 tsunami. Was Abe-Sensei involved in the project? He might be, in fact there was a good chance that he was. It was something Peter himself would have been tempted by a few years back, but his interests had moved on since then. On the other hand, a fusion reactor might come in handy for his own little project.

Speaking of which.

Peter opened his rucksack and exchanged the iPhone for his Mac. He ran the simulation again, with the same result; a wild, unstable vortex that tore itself apart all over his nice new retina screen. He opened the underlying program and ran through the code for the thousandth time. So much for fixing it today, or tomorrow, or next Friday for that matter. Jane had interrupted him, but that wasn't a good enough excuse.

And what did 'fix' mean anyway? He could trick it into submission by adjusting three of the thirty-two parameters into non-accurate inputs, most notably the fine-structure constant, that resulted in a nice, polite tornado that behaved itself. But that was a fudge, and he didn't much like fudge, plus it would imply that antimatter would react to gravity the opposite way normal matter did. Things would fall up, in other words. Maybe that was the whole point; instead of figuring out the physics of wormhole generation he was inadvertently providing the basis for designing a working UFO.

He laughed. Thankfully, his part of the carriage was empty and there was no one around to wonder what had gotten into this weird gaijin.

"I'll figure it out," he muttered to himself. "Eventually."

And, with any luck by the end of the day he should have the physical evidence he needed to make people sit up and listen.

***

Ninety-two minutes later Peter picked up his mountain bike from the small cycle-park at Mitsutoge station and headed down the aptly named 'Fuji-michi' - 'Mount Fuji road' - although today the promised view was obscured by the low cloud that marked the extreme northern reach of the typhoon.

He stopped at the local convenience store to buy dinner, which turned out to be a rather unappetizing o-bento, as all the decent ones had already been snapped up. He'd have to do better than that, but both food shopping and cooking were far from the top of his personal capability list.

Peter exited the store and mounted his bike, taking the longer route that ran past the little river that led to his house. He liked this part of the journey, which itself was a form of time-travel. The mountains, rice fields and old farmhouses that punctuated the landscape made the area as near to Totoro-country as you could get. In fact, there wasn't much of the modern era to it at all, apart from the expressway that ran down one side of the valley and the single-track train line that ran down the other. Time had not exactly stood still - there were a few base-stations around - but the world hadn't yet managed to catch up. For that you'd either need to turn around and head back towards Tokyo, or keep heading west until you'd arrived at Fuji-Yoshida, and even then you'd only be a few years ahead, despite the pioneering Kadota research center at the edge of town, where Peter had once had an actual office with a real job and some sort of future.

Both worlds were gone now. One the victim of time-limited budgets, and the other, well, good luck in Amsterdam, that's all he could say.

It started to rain. Not the typhoon-downpour that was deluging the small chain of islands that extended two hundred kilometers into the Pacific Ocean south of Tokyo, but enough to make Peter sprint the remaining eight hundred meters home.

***

Peter arrived at the single-storey farmhouse just as the rain changed from enthusiastic drizzle to raging shower. How it could do so in such a short space of time was one of life's little mysteries, but with the combination of the mountains lining the valley, the river basin that ran through it, the micro-climate inducing Mount Fuji less that fifteen kilometers away and the typhoon itself, it wasn't too surprising.

So, not so mysterious then, is it.

"Nope."

Peter opened the small door to the American style mailbox at the front gate. For the second time that day his heart skipped a beat. Inside the box was a single white envelope. The fact that it was thin, with a blue CERN logo on the front and was post-marked 'Geneva' was a giant clue what the contents were, as was the fact it was a letter and not a cheery email from Tom.

"Shit," he said, looking around as if there were answers lying hidden somewhere, just waiting to be discovered.

Standing there getting splattered by rain all afternoon wasn't going to achieve anything, so he set his bike in its stand under the car shade and went into the house, where Pebbles came to greet him, rubbing her neck on his calves as she always did when he came home.

"Hey girl," he said, picking her up, then putting her down again. She padded off to her seat by the window.

Peter dropped his half-sodden rucksack to the floor and planted himself at the kitchen table.

"Shit," he said again, tapping the letter onto the palm of his left hand. He'd been so sure. He could be wrong; it might not be bad news. He should check, as it was unlike him to jump to conclusions without first examining all the available evidence.

He opened the envelope. He wasn't wrong.

"Fuckkity, fuck, fuck, fuck."

Pebbles looked across at him.

"Sorry," he said.

Pebbles returned her gaze to the rice fields outside.

The wall-clock showed four twenty-seven. Peter pulled the o-bento from his rucksack, followed by his Mac. He opened Zoom and hit the instant-meeting button. His friend answered immediately.

"Professore!" said Tom, with his usual joviality. "Good morning, or good afternoon, whichever it is. How's things?"

How's things? Better for you than for me, Peter was about to say, but found the control to hold back. Which wasn't easy considering the view behind Tom was the concentric ring system of a giant Hadron Collider detector. Although it wasn't a live image, instead it was a virtual background that Tom used to remind everyone where he was and where everyone else wasn't.

Peter waved the letter. "How do you think?" he said.

"Ah, yes. Sorry about that one, Pete. A bit out of my hands, it was."

"I thought you said you could swing it for me, Tom."

"I said I would try. But there were forty-two other applications, most of whom don't need the bother of relocating. You could try going for some of the lower grade jobs, you know, it'd get your foot in the door."

"I wanted this one," Peter said.

"I know, but, I mean, Director of Directed Research. Big job. But is it really your, thing Pete?"

"Right now, yes, it is."

"Well, you can try again in April, if you want. There's a new project getting under way, something might open up."

"April's a long wait, Tom. The buggers cut my funding. I'm now masquerading as an 'independent IT consultant.' An ex-Professore."

"Yes, I am aware of that, and... well, what can I say. I'm sorry, Pete. Really, I am. It would have been great to have that unusual mind of yours on the team."

"Did you give them my paper?"

"Ah... no."

Peter let that sink in. "And may I inquire as to why not?" he said after a deliberately awkward pause.

"Why not? Because Peter is being Peter again, that's why not."

"Should I be being someone else?"

"I think be being Peter is quite enough." Tom picked up a document from his desk and waved it at the camera. "I mean, according to this masterpiece, not only is our understanding of particle physics flawed, which granted could be true, but it also seems the big bang couldn't have happened the way we think it did because space-time is not what we think it is. Which would make the hiring committee a tad doubtful, I expect. And then by page, where is it?"

Tom flicked through the document.

"Page five and a half, you're now saying that creating Einstein-Rosen Bridges is surprisingly easy. All you need is a dab of negative energy, a drop of exotic matter and a couple of gazigawatts, all coupled to a bunch of super-cooled super-conducting magnets, of which we have several here, and Bob's your uncle. Or maybe your grandad, because according to this, you could zoom about freely in time and visit the old bugger being born. In fact, you could even be the old bugger himself. Not exactly the sort of non-CERN CERN stuff they'd want their next director to be touting, don't you think? So, to protect you from yourself, which is the firm yet unobtainable goal of my entire existence on planet Earth, I kept the thing safely hidden under a coffee cup on my desk."

Peter sat back. He'd expected this kind of response, which was why he was months away from publication, years even. Maybe he shouldn't have sent it in, but what was done was done. It didn't make him wrong, though.

"OK," he conceded. "Possibly I did go a bit overboard, but I can prove it, starting with messers Einstein and Rosen.

"Ah, with that..." Tom turned the page. "'Harmonic space-time oscillation detector' contraption of yours. Whatever that's supposed to be."

"It's a prototype, not a contraption. And today's the day, right?"

"Indeed it is."

Tom put on his Google glasses, disabled the virtual background and switched to the frame-mounted mini-camera. He walked over to the window, through which Peter could now clearly see the enormous detection equipment that stood poised to make history.

"The on-going quest for the answer to life, the universe and everything else resumes at thirteen fifteen GMT precisely. God, would you just look at that bloody great thing. Beautiful, just beautiful."

Peter stared at the image. It was beautiful, the most beautiful thing he had ever seen. And like such things always seemed to be for him, it lay a million miles beyond his reach.

"But I don't think we're creating any wormholes here Pete," Tom said. "And even if we are, they'll be tiny little things, just a couple of nanometers across, hardly capable of stretching themselves all the way to Japan."

"You'll see."

"Well, I am skeptical, obviously, but remain open to the persuasion of incontestably irrefutable evidence, of which I expect you'll find absolutely none whatsoever."

Peter heard voices. Tom swivelled his head, bringing three helmeted colleagues into view.

"We're on, Tom," said one of them, a Japanese woman whom Peter half-recognized from somewhere. There were hundreds, if not thousands of people there, so it was likely he knew some beyond Tom and the four others from his graduation ceremony.

"Ah, I think that's my cue, Pete. If you do figure out quantum gravity by teatime, let me know, there's a good chap."

"Tom, before you drop off, could you review my method on the sub-quantum kinetic extrapolations—"

"Gotta go!" Tom said as he disconnected.

Peter closed the box on Zoom to end the meeting.

"Gotta go," he echoed.

***

Peter sat for ten minutes while the rain pummelled the roof. It was getting dark, the thick clouds obscuring what was left of the late afternoon sun. If the typhoon had changed direction and was moving north, then he'd have to wait for it to pass.

He checked the weather app on his phone. In an hour or two the skies would clear, and everything would be ready for him to catch the start. Timing, he thought, was everything. If he could demonstrate the effect, then they'd have to consider his work as legitimate. Shit, if he could do that he wouldn't even need to apply for a position, they'd come begging for him to join. Yes, that's what he would do; he'd gather incontestably irrefutable evidence and prove himself right. Wasn't that his plan all along anyway, to mix the theoretical with the actual?

Peter headed for the small bedroom that had served as his study from the day he moved in. He slid back the door to reveal the reason he hadn't moved nearer Tokyo, the reason Mariko had given up on them – and the reason he was so bloody broke.

Set firmly against the wall and reinforced by anti-earthquake bracing, modern computer-racking was stacked, not with highly advanced network switching devices, but instead with row upon row of thermionic valves and exposed copper wiring. It looked like something from the fifties, or even the forties, so much so that if you didn't know any better you'd swear it was a replica of Colossus, the world's first programmable, electronic, digital computer, as used in Bletchley Park to intercept and decode German communications in the second world war.

It wasn't, of course. But Tom was right – it was little more than a contraption, cobbled together at minimum cost and maximum labour, a combination that almost bankrupted him physically as well as financially. On the other hand, if Tom had bothered to ask, then he could have explained why it had to be valves and not semiconductors, although there were plenty of those in the guts of the machine. He didn't even know if it would work. Apart from switching it on to make sure it functioned from a technical, electronic perspective, he'd never had the opportunity to test whether it did what it was supposed to do; detect harmonic space-time oscillations. Wormholes, in other words. Even then it would amount to inferring the existence of a tornado in Texas by sensing the wing-flap of a butterfly on the slope of an Indonesian mountain, all from an old wooden farmhouse in the middle of a rice field in Japan.

Piece of cake.

The rain stopped. Pebbles came into the room and rubbed her neck on his calves for the second time, her purr saying, 'feed me.'

***

Peter went outside to check the connectors, leaving Pebbles happily munching at her *Nya Dai-Suki!* cat food. Sticking the translation, 'Pussy loves it' in English on the packet would have raised eyebrows and lowered sales anywhere else but Japan. But this was Japan, so that kind of thing didn't matter.

Pebbles certainly didn't care, Peter thought, as he edged through the gap between his bike and his Mini Convertible. The car had been one of Mariko's insistences to which he'd reluctantly agreed. *Not so,* Peter reminded himself; he'd been just as enthusiastic as she had. It was being the one who footed the bill that had gotten to him. Maybe it was better this way, now that she was gone; his dwindling inheritance wouldn't have stood the strain much longer. Mind you, neither would he if couldn't get some sort of result tonight.

Now I'm thinking like a bloody soccer coach.

Peter went through to the garden. Of all the reasons he had agreed to live here and not in a more modern apartment near the research center, it was the plot of land he was now standing on. Japanese city homes may have been renowned world-wide for being small and surrounded by concrete, but that didn't apply to farmhouses, especially remote ones at the foot of small mountains. The land had been in Abe-Sensei's family for generations, and now that there were no more generations who were willing to do the work, the rice fields had been sold to neighbouring farmers, the house had been reformed and the garden made into something vaguely English – all in preparation for being sold-off sometime in the near future as a *besso,* a 'place in the country', Japanese-style, with a magnificent view of Mount Fuji, even if that magnificent view was occasionally obscured by clouds, as it was today.

But the landscape wasn't why Peter had readily agreed to move in. Instead it was the space, and Sensei's kind permission, even support, for him to assemble the two amateur radio antennae that now stood tall and proud at the east and west corners of the allotment: his own private monitoring station.

What the neighbours thought was, well, their business. The nearest one was a hundred meters away, so he was hardly inconveniencing anyone. As long as Peter took everything down when he left Japan, then it wouldn't matter. He was far more concerned by the thought of a typhoon knocking everything over, which explained the numerous restraining wires and other reinforcing bits of metal and rope, all of which Abe-Sensei had insisted on, as if Peter had needed convincing. But with the latest super-storm hundreds of kilometers away, that was one thing he wouldn't have to worry about. Not this day, at least. And as long as Abe-Sensei kept the rent ridiculously low, then all would be well.

He crouched at the base of the east antenna and tugged on the bundled of cables attached to the scaffold-like structure. The connection was secure. He checked the west antenna; also, secure. He followed both cables back to the air-conditioner pipe-inlet point on the south wall, where a year earlier he'd removed the clay-like packaging, pushed the cables through the space, then filled it in again with new putty.

Peter's simple solution to the problem of how to bring the hard-wired signal into the house hadn't impressed Mariko. That was the day the end had really begun, though he'd never been able to figure out why she had been so upset. Something to do with him thinking more about his work than he did about the two of them, apparently.

Fair enough.

Satisfied that everything was as it should be, Peter turned to head back indoors just as a gap in the clouds revealed the summit of Fuji-san, fifteen kilometers away. A good omen, although he didn't much care for those near-superstitious lines of thought.

Then why think it?

"Good question," he said, as he squeezed his way back between bike and car.

Three

At exactly nine o'clock that evening Peter switched on his contraption, followed by the air-conditioner. Those valves would run hot in that confined space and fire was certainly a risk, albeit a small one. He went into the lounge, which was more a central family area than a defined living room, and sat at the desk where his contraption controller waited silently for instructions.

"It's not a contraption," he reminded himself as he checked the readings on the user interface, which resembled a cross between an oscilloscope and a seismograph, all software driven. A series of parallel sine waves pulsed across his Mac, representing zero-event detection; provided the thing worked, that was. The fact that he was trying to detect wormholes generated half-way across the planet with equipment that he had no idea would do its job, and was de facto being prototyped that very day, didn't augur well.

LIGO, the 'Laser Interferometer Gravitational-Wave Observatory', had cost millions, billions even, and could detect a mirror-wobble of less than a ten-thousandth the diameter of a proton, all generated by spinning black holes thousands of light years away. And here was Peter Walker, in the middle of a rice field, trying to do something similar with nothing more than a room full of Russian military-grade vacuum glass tubes with strips of hot metal inside.

"OK, so maybe it is a contraption," he said to Pebbles, who had just jumped on his lap. "But, who knows, it might just work."

He preferred not to think about what he'd do if it didn't.

***

Four past nine.

There wasn't much else to do but sit, wait, and watch for signs of… something, anything. A blip, a flutter, even an infinitesimal quiver would give him enough data to analyze, to dissect, to scrutinize down to its furthest extremes. And if, just if, there was a major movement of those sine waves, if interference patterns formed and danced their way across his screen, then he'd have something to show the world.

He'd be as famous as Albert!

"It's not about that," he said, although Pebbles had already curled herself up into a vibrating ball on his thighs and was no longer listening.

Peter's hands were shaking. Everything he had ever done, all his research, his years slogging through the impossible maths behind his even more impossible re-interpretation of the science, his willingness to distance himself from the mainstream, to position himself outside the accepted norms of the soon-to-be-antiquated flow of the current rational; all hung on the next few minutes.

Eleven past nine.

Four more minutes. Not long now.

Fourteen past nine.

The moment of truth was sixty seconds away. As soon as the Hadron Collider fired up, the initial ripples would flow through the solid rock of the Earth at near light speed, impact the peacock-feather arrangement of the antennae arms in the garden and create a readable fluctuation that the thermionic values would amplify in a way that no semiconductor could.

That was the whole point, Tom.

Everything was moving, the entire system was being affected. It had to be physical, not just at the electronic, sub-quantum level. Space-time itself was harmonically pulsating. The trick was the clever signal pattern set-up in the antennae by those even cleverer algorithms of his. Without those, it won't work. LIGO wouldn't detect anything, or if it did no-one would understand the implications.

Only me and my contraption would know.

Nine-fifteen. Nothing. Not the slightest murmur, not even the feeblest hint of movement.

Nine-twenty. Still nothing. Could the start have been delayed?

Nine-thirty. He'd keep watching, keep waiting. What else could he do?

Nine forty-five. Maybe there was a technical problem in Geneva and the whole thing had been called-off.

A chat box opened. It was Tom.

Find anything?

Peter stared at the message for a full minute before typing.

Not a lot.

Tom wrote back immediately.

Better luck next time, lol.

Peter closed the chat box. Now what was he going to do?

He gently set Pebbles down on the floor and went into the kitchen to get his last beer from the fridge. He stuffed the empty o-bento box that he'd left on the table into the over-full rubbish bin and wandered back into the main lounge, where he sat on the sofa and stared at his whiteboard. It was covered in a mess of rehashed thoughts and unresolved quantum equations – a hardcopy of the junk that formed the organized chaos of his mind. He got up and erased the anarchy.

Beer still in hand, Peter returned to the sofa and lay down to contemplate the ceiling. How could he have been so stupid, so wrong, so misguided? Now Tom thought he was a fool. And if Tom thought that, so would everybody else.

"Fuck," he said.

There really was no other word to describe it.

***

The incessant beeping finally managed to burrow its way through the fog of a dream within a dream.

Peter woke so abruptly that he wasn't sure if he was awake or not. For a moment he didn't even know where he was, or even *that* he was. But the shrill cry quickly snapped some awareness into him.

An event! He half-fell, half-stumbled the short distance from the sofa to the desk, where his Mac was going wild with excitement. Peter shut off the alarm, which had been set to make the most obnoxious sound at the highest possible volume. If his stereo had been on the entire valley would have heard it, which at three minutes past one in the morning wouldn't have impressed anyone.

The message wasn't what he'd expected.

<u>Event Detected</u>
Time: 01:02:54
Bearing: -58.09 degrees true
Distance: 74,234 +/-22 m
Duration: 7.03s
Re-calculate: Y/N?

"What?"

Peter hit the "Y" key. The tool recalculated and displayed the same result. An event, 74.2 kilometers away? Not the 9,650 or so great circle kilometers to Geneva, which would be correspondingly less if you took a direct line through the planet, a figure he'd never bothered to calculate.

Where on earth was that supposed to be?

Peter opened Google maps, selected his home location, and traced out a 74-kilometer line at near-enough 60 degrees west of true north. The line ended in the Southern Japanese Alps. He scrambled in a draw for a protractor and re-positioned the line at exactly 58 degrees west – not exactly a cartographer-approved method, but if there was a way of doing it in the app he hadn't found it. The end point of the line was right on top of Mount Nyukasa, a place he'd never heard of. Why should he? Mount Fuji - or *Fuji-san* as the Japanese would say - was all he'd ever had to concern himself with.

He switched to the satellite view and zoomed in closer. The answer was staring him in the face.

A short distance from the flat mountain summit stood the Japan Aerospace Exploration Agency Optical Observatory, according to Google Translate. But it was the building a hundred meters away, at the exact summit, that was the culprit, and Peter didn't need Google's help to figure that one out. The large parabolic antenna was a heck of a giveaway.

Pebbles jumped up on to his lap.

"We detected a weather station, Pebbles," he said. "Well, an echo of one, seventy-four kilometers from here, in Japan-land, and not the Hadron Collider, which is in switziland, and isn't a weather station, either, apparently. And it's all because we are just too dumb to get our contraption to tell the difference between wormholes and microwaves. Well, we'll just have to try again next time, won't we."

Pebbles sniffed Peter's face and kissed him, in the way that cats do.

Four

Peter stopped at the tall, overly ornate iron gates to say a brief hello to Tanaka-san, the longest serving guard at the Hachioji campus of the Tokyo University of Technology, who, just as he had since Peter first walked through that impressive entrance three years earlier, was enjoying the 'It's fine day, today.'

"Indeed it is, Tanaka-san," Peter replied, before driving on through to the visitor carpark.

It was 'indeed' a sunny day and the roof of the Mini was down, as it should be in late October, giving him the sense of freedom and, to some extent, control of his own destiny, no doubt enhanced by the rush of wind blasting through his hair on the fifty-minute journey over. Except that, after the failure of his detector to live up to its purpose, control of his own destiny was firmly at the bottom of his personal capability list. Which was partly why he had come to see Abe-Sensei, though Peter doubted there would be any news about research funding unexpectedly becoming available.

He parked, closed the roof, grabbed his rucksack, and headed for the main building.

In the four days since the incident Peter had left his equipment on all day and half the night, testing those Russian valves to their limit. They'd held true, not least because they were well designed and well made, but mainly because they didn't have much to do apart from being 'on.' He'd detected nothing, not a murmur, not even the whisper of an event, which had made him wonder if the microwave incident at Mount Nyukasa was just a system burp that was nothing more than a reflection of his own incompetence.

Or, worse than that, what if the whole concept itself was fatally flawed, and there was nothing for him to discover? No harmonic oscillations of spacetime; no pulses of sub-space energy propagating through the universe; no career defining, world-changing, paradigm-upending, Nobel prize winning moment for this sorry fool on a hill.

It had given him plenty of thinking time, though. Time which, to his surprise, had magically resulted in Kadota Industries calling him out of the blue and saying 'yes' to that proposal he'd submitted six months earlier and had entirely forgotten about. With Kadota and International Standard, he would have enough income to survive another year. But surviving wasn't thriving, and he'd need double that to continue his research and build that newly designed detector he had in mind. Then again, if he had twice as many customers to look after, where would he find the time to actually do his research?

No, 'control of own destiny' wasn't exactly on his character profile card. Not today, at least.

Peter stopped at a door marked 'Professor Y. Abe.' He'd done it again; so lost in his own thoughts he gotten there without realizing it. This was becoming a habit, and not a good one either.

He knocked and opened the door to find Abe-Sensei at his desk.

"Ah, Peter-chan, do come in," said the professor.

***

"You know, I think it is much clearer this way Peter, for the non-specialist mind. Well done. I shall send it off immediately. I have kept them waiting long enough."

Abe-Sensei put the three pages of 'An Introduction to Quantum Entanglement' to one side and sat back in his leather chair.

"Now, how are things with you?" he said. "Are you still intent on returning to Cambridge?"

"There or somewhere in Europe, if I can," Peter replied.

"Ah, yes, CERN. You did say that last time. And Geneva is such a beautiful city, I can well understand. But there may be something of interest for you here in Japan."

"There is?"

Abe-Sensei leaned forward. "Not our research funding, I'm afraid to say. That has gone, completely. But, and this is still confidential, one of my colleagues is involved in next generation reactor design. I could put in a good word for you, Peter. It is very much your kind of thing."

"I think I read something about that a few days ago. It doesn't start for a few years, though, does it?"

Abe-Sensei smiled. "Ah, the press release. Yes, perhaps not so confidential, although I do know a few things that did not make it into those articles. And, yes, the construction is three or four years away, but it is a multi-year project, decades perhaps, although the initial design work is happening now. And that is where I thought you might like to become involved, Peter."

"I'm not sure I can wait that long, Sensei," Peter said. "And fusion, well, lots of people are working on that. By the time the project gets going, it may be too late."

Abe-Sensei sat back and made a church steeple with his fingers, a sure sign the professor was deciding whether to reveal something.

"Actually, I think it will be an experimental matter-antimatter reactor," he said after a prolonged silence.

What!?!

It was all Peter could so to stop himself from jumping out of his chair. "Interesting," he said, as if that simple word could convey his true reaction.

"The location they've chosen is also near where you live. A place called Mount Nyukasa. Not commutable, I think, but not so distant."

"Mount Nyukasa? The one with a weather station on top?"

"That I don't know. But, Peter, it is all most confidential, so please don't let anybody know that I disclosed the type of reactor it will be, if you don't mind."

"No, sure, I understand," said Peter, fighting hard to contain his reaction for the second time. "But, I don't know, Sensei. I'm trying to get back home. Or nearly back. I'll give it some thought. Thank you anyway."

It was a lie, but saying, '*I thought I detected a wormhole there last week, which I assumed was the weather station but now I'm not so sure,*' wouldn't have been the best idea he'd had all day.

"Well, just let me know," Abe-Sensei replied. "Now, shall we head to the canteen, and risk some of their morning tea?"

"I'd love to, Sensei, but I have to get going."

"Next time, then."

"I look forward to it," Peter said. "The visit, I mean. Not the tea."

***

The journey took the full two hours and twenty-nine minutes the GPS said it would, despite Peter doing his best to get a speeding ticket on the Matsumoto-leg of the Chuo Expressway. It seemed the time he'd gained on that section was lost again on the twisty little mountain road that ran from the aptly named town of Fujimi - 'Fuji-View' - to the summit of Mount Nyukasa. If he'd been concentrating, he'd have realized the navigation tool had performed the calculation based on his rather heavy right foot, so the one moment he'd glanced at the arrival time should have been good enough. But Peter's mind wasn't concerned with the accuracy of the Mini's navigation system. Far from it.

An experimental matter-antimatter reactor?

It couldn't be. That was Star Trek level power generation, far beyond the limits of current technology. Abe-Sensei must have gotten that wrong. It must be a fusion reactor, surely, and Sensei had mis-heard or mis-interpreted something his colleague had said.

In which case, Peter asked himself, why was he sitting in his car at the entrance to the Japan Meteorological Agency's Nyukasa weather station? Because five words had skittled around inside his head for the past two hours and twenty-nine minutes like marbles in a pin-ball machine on steroids; *what if it were true?*

What if that's what he had detected? What if his contraption had picked up an echo from a future event, a ripple through the fabric of the universe that had blasted, spacetime independent, through the metal fingers of his antenna straight into the bowels of his Mac? Could it be that maybe, just maybe he was right? Or nearly right. It would be something for him to work on, to investigate, to decipher; to fit in to the maths, the underlying equations, his re-working of current models that Tom had laughed at.

If Peter could show that these kinds of events transcended time, had no time, were measurable across all times instantaneously, for all observers independent of their physical and temporal locations, then he'd have made one of the greatest discoveries in history. But he'd first have to prove to himself that it wasn't microwaves from the Japan Meteorological Agency installation that his equipment had picked up – and from where he sat in the Mini, the evidence was clear.

He got out and walked to the main entrance. The message on the signboard was understandable, even with his limited Japanese, but he needed to be sure. He opened an iPhone app that accessed his camera and auto-translated the *kanji*; the station was closed for refurbishment and would re-open in March of the following year, just as he had thought. Even without that confirmation, the fact that the large parabolic dish no longer had its central sub-reflector was enough to convince him that it hadn't been microwaves from the Doppler radar.

He got back in to the Mini and drove away just as five workmen came out through the front door. It was three thirty in the afternoon; they must have been on their tea break.

***

Five and a half minutes later Peter found a corner with a large run-off area for drivers to stop and enjoy the view of the

Japanese Southern Alps. He parked and sat for a while, roof down, unconcerned by the scenery, to think things through.

Four days ago, he'd detected an event. Since then, nothing. He'd thought it had been microwaves, but now he knew for sure it wasn't. So what? It didn't prove anything. Three years from now a matter-antimatter research project would start - he had decided to no longer doubt Abe-Sensei on that - but how on earth was he going to prove he had detected an event at a location where the device that created the event hadn't even yet been built?

Wasn't that the whole point? The thing was supposed to time-independent — unless it wasn't.

Had work already begun? Could it be that the project had started, and the Japanese government, true to form, had made it look like the reactor wasn't yet under construction, as a way of deflecting press speculation? In which case, why announce anything? Probably because they had to secure 'public understanding' about budget allocation.

Improbable, but not impossible.

Peter glanced to his right. At the apex of the corner, tucked into the side of the mountain, was a decaying wooden hut set next to a padlocked iron gate. The old building looked half-consumed by both age and termites, the once clean glass in the two windows dirtied and broken long ago. A sign on the gate read 立入り禁止 - no entry - in large red kanji. Peter stared at it for a while, wondering what was beyond those iron bars. An abandoned mine? Maybe that was where General McArthur hid all the gold, or found it, or whatever that story was.

He got out of the car, walked over to the gate and tugged at the padlock and its chain, then rattled the bars, as if that would have revealed something. What was he expecting, anyway? Sure, if you were going to build an experimental reactor in the middle of a mountain, what better place could there be than an unused mine complex? All those pre-excavated tunnels would save billions of yen and cut months of construction time.

No – the place was closed, work had not started, there was nothing happening, nothing to see. And why here, anyway? It was more than assumptive of him to think this must have been the place. Move on, Walker-san. Go back home and get a life.

Wormholes? Idiot. You probably detected the last hurrah of that weather station as they tested the dish for the final time before removing the sub-reflector. Yep, that's what it was; no inter-dimensional, sub-space, pan-universe, time-transcendent, cross-pollinating spacetime wobbles here. You were just seeing what you wanted to see, nothing more.

"What on earth was I thinking?" he said, as he headed back to the car.

Five

There wasn't much to the half-village, half-town of Fujimi.
There wasn't even a view of Mount Fuji. At seventy kilometers
away it should have been as clear as day, but the day was no
longer clear, and the mountain was obscured by clouds.

There were, on the other hand, plenty of traffic lights,
most of which Peter thought were unnecessary. Japan hadn't
discovered roundabouts, and so the consequently ubiquitous
traffic control systems were, as he saw it, superfluous to
requirements, like the red ones in front of him.

Peter glanced in his mirror. Mount Nyukasa was directly
behind, dominating the view, although in truth there were so
many peaks he couldn't tell where one started and the next
finished.

Why had he given up so easily?

A polite but sharp toot advised him that the lights had
changed. Peter acknowledged the driver with a wave, then
moved through the intersection. But rather than heading to
the expressway junction, he instead turned into the entrance
of the inaptly named 'Fujimi Shopping Paradise,' and made
his way to the carpark. It was four fifteen, and with the sun
gone behind the clouds it was getting chilly. He put the roof
back up and sat in that enclosed world, that little room of
thought, that space within space, contemplating what to do
next.

He already knew what he was going to do, so there wasn't
much to contemplate, other than to figure out why he was
going to do it. That was the thing; he couldn't explain it. All
he knew was that the mountain was calling out to him, and

Peter didn't want to admit that he was about to do something as irrational as trusting a feeling.

The biggest store in the shopping center was a DIY Center, no doubt the only one in the area, hence its unreasonable size. It would have everything he needed, possibly even a portable electromagnetic radiation detector.

So, what was he waiting for?

He got out of the Mini and headed across the car park.

***

At exactly twenty-eight minutes past six Peter parked at the mountain-view spot across the road from the mine entrance.

It had been dark in the valley below where he'd eaten at the local Denny's, but at 1800 meters elevation it was still light enough to see without the help of the roadside streetlamp, which made him feel rather exposed. It didn't matter, he told himself, there weren't likely to be many cars around at this time of day. And even if there were, people would think he'd just gone for a walk on the mountain, which was near enough what he was going to do, provided you swapped 'in' for 'on.'

Even so, it was nuts.

So why do it?

Because he had to know, he had to be sure, that was why. And because something inside wouldn't let him go home until he found whatever there was to find. Besides, Pebbles could wait for her dinner.

He grabbed the large plastic bag on the passenger seat and removed the contents.

"Electromagnetic radiation detector thing, check. High-power torch, check. Fucking enormous two-handed bolt cutters, check. Worker's construction helmet, check. Can of luminescent spray paint, check."

The DIY store had stocked everything he needed, but this was still nuts, and potentially dangerous.

"Sensible thinking person's brain? Nope, left that behind somewhere."

Peter put the spray paint, torch and EMR detector into his rucksack along with his wallet, keys, and iPhone. There was a half-full bottle of water in a cup-holder, which he put in an external pocket. With rucksack in one hand and fucking enormous bolt cutters in the other, he got out of the car, touched the handle to lock the doors, put on his helmet and walked to the gate armed to the teeth with his collection of cave-robbing tools. He set the rucksack down, then positioned the sharp end of the cutters on the chain. He stayed like that for a full ten seconds before stepping back.

What the hell was he doing?

This was tantamount to breaking and entering. More than that, it was bordering on insanity. Pure, ridiculous, nonsense-level behaviour. Peter looked around. There was nothing and no-one, just him, the chirping insects and his own particular brand of lunacy. He stared at the gate. Even the local bug population thought he had lost his mind. Well, one of them did, according to the rather odd noise it was making, like the pulse of a cardiac monitor in an emergency ward.

Except it was no insect making that sound.

Peter opened his rucksack and removed the EMR detector. It had been pricey, but was the only one left on the shelf and was essentially a hand-held full spectrum analyzer that he'd thought had the rather useful function of both beeping and flashing a red LED whenever it detected a peak signal. Which was exactly what it was doing now.

Peter reduced the volume with the side buttons. The small liquid crystal display showed an EM pulse moving from left to right through the entire frequency range, like a tsunami across an ocean. He changed the scale sensitivity to its broadest setting; the tsunami was still there. He walked around, taking the device in a complete 360 to gauge the source. There was no doubt; the strongest signal was at the cave entrance.

He stopped, transfixed by the flash of the LED. He had read the manual at dinner, so knew the indicator could be set to any level the operator wanted and was still at its default setting, whatever that was. But there was nothing in the manual that could account for the repeating occurrence of that flash: three flashes, a break, one quick flash, another break, one flash, and other break, then four flashes, a break, followed by two more. He counted through five full cycles, just to be sure. It was 3.142 – Pi.

Shit!

The signal was peaking at the rate of the most famous number in mathematical history.

"Well, bugger me sideways."

He snapped the chain clean off the gate, then picked up his rucksack and entered the tunnel, leaving the fucking enormous cutters on the ground along with a mental note to pick them up on the way out.

***

Peter pulled the torch from his rucksack and fired its narrow beam directly ahead. The tunnel was long, straight and from where he stood, seemingly endless. Wide enough for four or five people to walk through side by side, it was carved out of solid rock, with no supporting wooden rafters. It was almost certainly not going to collapse around him, but he was nonetheless pretty much scared shitless.

"Well, this is a good idea, Petey-wetey," he said.

He went forward a few meters, then stopped to let his eyes adjust to the dark – although with the light from the torch, night vision wasn't going to be a critical factor. His EMR detector was still flashing Pi, still showing a tsunami-pulse across the entire spectrum. He had a choice, go ahead, or go back. Courage was in short supply today, but he moved ahead anyway.

A flash of metal caught his eye. He aimed the torch towards the tunnel ceiling; a series of elongated strips ran down the center line. He turned around and followed the wiring back to the tunnel entrance, where he found a breaker box that he'd missed on the way in. It must have been fifty years old at least, but the main switch looked to be in good working order. He pulled it to the "on" position. The neons flashed to life.

"And then there was light."

He set the rucksack down and tied the torch handle to a strap, then removed the can of luminescent spray paint. He should have done that before he came in, but his mind was unused to this level of misadventure. Now he was ready.

"Okey dokey."

He repositioned his rucksack and walked on, nervously confident, spray can in hand, driven by the need to discover, to know, to understand.

But above all, to be right.

***

Acutely aware of the possibility of getting himself lost, Peter sprayed the walls at regular intervals with an arrow pointing towards the exit. Although, as the main tunnel continued uninterrupted, there wasn't much need for that.

After what he estimated to be two hundred meters plus or minus, he came to the first intersection. Two smaller passages split off, one to the left, the other to the right, with the main tunnel continuing straight ahead. He immediately christened it the hen's foot. The EMR detector showed a higher peak signal from the tunnel to the right. Peter sprayed the walls, then headed down that route.

He continued walking for what felt like thirty minutes but was probably less. To keep his mind occupied - which was essentially a way of keeping his fears in check - he tried to analyze the way the tunnel had been dug from the grooves made by chisels and pickaxes, but geotechnical engineering was hardly his field. He wondered when the mine had been in operation; probably hundreds of years before, as a key part of the supply chain that supplied metal ore to the thousands of swordsmiths whose forges spanned the four main islands in the *Sengoku Jidai*, the warring states period that had nearly decimated the country. Which begged the question, how long was he going to keep looking? He couldn't stay there all night. And the further he went, the more chance there was of screwing up and not finding his way out for days, or, even worse, injuring himself and getting stuck there for eternity.

He stopped. The neon lights had come to an end, the last one flashing intermittently above his head. He pulled the torch from its strap and shone it forward. This wasn't the final bulb - the line continued down the tunnel - but they were all out. Peter checked the EMR detector. The signal was stronger than before; he was getting close to the source. He had to keep going, there was nothing else for it.

He moved onwards. The tunnel was now at a more pronounced incline, though not yet a steep slope, and was slowly turning anti-clockwise. He was immensely impressed by whoever had dug through the rock. It must have been back-breaking work, taking teams of men years to complete.

He stopped again.

Or, rather, the tunnel stopped; he'd reached a dead end. It wasn't a true dead end; a large metal door was blocking his progress. Compared to the mine itself it looked recent. There was rust, but not much. Twenty years old? It was just a guess, but someone must have installed the lights not too long ago, so it made sense that the door was done at the same time. Or fifty years ago, whenever it was. Either way, he was getting close. This must be it.

A metal bar was set across the handle and the frame. He pushed the bar up and away and set it down on the floor. The hinges groaned in protest, but he managed to force the door ajar.

He stepped through the narrow opening straight into a complete and utter darkness that his torch could barely illuminate. He pointed the inadequate beam at the far wall, the sides, the floor. Light bounced off stalagmites and stalactites, sprinkling the area with an eerie, surreal reflection that was simultaneously majestic and intimidating.

It was the biggest cave he had ever seen. And it wasn't just big, it was enormous.

"Fucking hell," he said.

There really was no other way to describe it.

Six

His voice echoed around the giant cavern like starlings fleeing from a pack of marauding cats.

"This is the place," he said, softly. "It has to be."

He stepped forward until he came to what he judged to be the center of the cave, though it was hard to be sure exactly where that point was. He stood in awe of mother nature's accomplishment, so much greater than the comparatively feeble attempts of the men who had tried to dig out her secrets, whether they were iron ore or the mysteries of the universe. It would make the perfect place to construct a matter-antimatter reactor; miles from anywhere, deep inside a mountain; safe, remote, hidden. If anything happened and things spiralled out of control, there were several hundred million tons of rock to contain the damage.

He checked the EMR detector; it was silent, the signal gone. He tapped it with a pair of fingers, the ancient tried and trusted method that could not possibly have any effect. Nothing. He adjusted the sensitivity to its maximum setting and increased the volume level. Still nothing.

So, what did that mean?

If he truly was detecting something from a future event, a disturbance that stretched across the boundaries of the spacetime continuum and introduced fluctuations in the Earth's local magnetic field that registered on his EMR device, then it was reasonable to assume that this could be intermittent, not fixed, a repeating, self-reinforcing cycle that-

A sound.

He stopped in mid-thought and listened. There was only silence; the purest, simplest, most complete absence of sound he had ever known.

No, wait. There was something.

"*Ta–*"

A voice! So soft, so weak it was barely audible, yet enough to spike his anxiety level. His heart rate doubled; blood surged through the small capillaries of his inner ear. It was like being inside his own private waterfall. He recognized the dangers and slowed his breathing as best he could.

"Who's there?"

A sound, no more than an exhalation of breath. Was that his own? He couldn't tell. There it was again! He swung the torch to his left.

"Hello?" he called out.

"*Tasukete.*"

He was sure this time – a fragile voice calling for help, in Japanese.

He called back. "Where are you? *Doko desu ka?*"

Silence.

The beam shook with his racing pulse. A flicker of white flashed from behind a stalagmite. He directed the light at the indeterminate shape at the far edge of the cave, which he at first took to be a handkerchief, or a discarded towel. Then he realized it was a sock, a *tabi*, of the kind worn by *Geisha* in Kyoto City. And extending from the *tabi*, as pale as the softest moonlight, was a human leg.

He froze.

***

After several long seconds he concluded it couldn't have been a dead body; cadavers rarely call out for help. He edged forward, controlling his breathing, calming himself as best he could. As he rounded the pillar his torch light shone down on the prostrate form of a woman dressed in a kimono, lying motionless in the narrow beam, her long hair disheveled around her.

"Oh my God."

He removed the rucksack from his back, set it down on the rock floor together with the EMR detector and torch, then knelt beside her.

"Hello," he said.

Her eyes were closed, but she was breathing.

"Are you OK? *Daijobu?*"

The woman opened her eyes but made no reply.

"*Daijobu desu. Watashi wa anata o tasukerimasu.*" He repeated it in English, just in case, "Don't worry. I'm here to help."

A drop of water fell on the back of his neck. Peter immediately concluded she must have positioned herself there accordingly, but how did she get there in the first place? But that, and the thousand other questions now firing through his mind, could wait. Thinking that she must in any case be severely dehydrated, Peter took the water bottle from its rucksack pocket, unscrewed the cap, and lifted her by the shoulders.

"Here, drink this. Slowly, not fast. *Yukuri nonde, ne.*"

Water trickled down her cheek, but she drank.

"Not too fast," Peter said.

She put a hand on his to hold the bottle in place, then pushed it away when she'd finished.

"Good, that's good," said Peter. She was less frail than he had thought, but he still needed to do something. He set the now empty bottle aside.

"We need to get you out of here," he said, unsure how to say it in correct Japanese. He tried anyway. "*Soto e ikimasho. Notte iku yo.*"

The woman nodded, but her eyes closed again when he picked her up, her head falling backwards and her long hair touching the ground. She was light and easy for Peter to carry, but he now had the problem of getting his rucksack on to his back. He set her gently back down on the rock floor.

"Sorry."

He quickly swung the rucksack on to his shoulders, re-tied the torch to the strap and stuck the EMR detector back into the outside pocket. He left the water bottle where it lay.

"One more time," he said as he cradled her again in his arms. This time her eyes opened, and she found the strength to lift her head and lay it on his shoulder.

Their faces were now a short distance apart, but her hair was hanging down so low he would be in danger of tripping over it. He half-knelt, freed up a hand and wrapped it over her like a blanket. As he stood up, she looked at him for a brief second, then closed her eyes.

"OK," he said, hoping that she understood English. "It's a long walk to the car, but I've got you, so there's no need to-"

His torch went out. Everything went totally, completely, frighteningly black.

"Shit."

It couldn't be the battery; he must have somehow hit the off switch. He would need to put her down again to check.

The universe had a different idea.

The EMR began to flash wildly, its red light pulsing itself into a frenzy from within the outside pocket of his rucksack, its cardiac monitor-like buzzer a low volume scream of *something's happening here.*

A glow appeared behind him, soft at first then growing in intensity until it illuminated the whole cave. With the woman still safely in his arms, Peter turned around. The light was neither a projection nor a reflection. It just hung there, in mid-air, a circle of luminescence four meters across and one deep, its bottom edge touching the cave floor, its center area a pond-like ripple of standing waves, translucent yet opaque, existing yet imaginary.

The EMR stopped just as suddenly as it had started.

Peter stood transfixed, completely motionless as the ripple morphed into the slightest of shimmers, the whisper of a haze that revealed another place, another world, another time.

At the center of the image, large metal rings formed concentric circles within circles, much like a particle detector at CERN. A bank of consoles formed a semi-circle in front of the rings. Three figures, no more than human shadows whose indistinct faces were camouflaged by the shimmer, stared back at him. Chaos surrounded them; screens were broken, chairs were scattered like a child's doll house, smoke rose from a destroyed bank of smouldering equipment.

It was a wormhole, open right in front of him, right there, in that place, in real time. And the scene on the other side was one of disarray, of destruction, of devastation.

He took a step forward just as the circle of light snapped shut, returning the cave to total darkness.

"Jesus Christ," he gasped as his torch came back on.

Seven

Nene lay on the strange chair, neither hard nor soft, in the even stranger carriage that moved by itself.

And so fast, so unbelievably fast.

Lights flashed by. How could that be? They were so bright, like the Sun. She had never seen such things, flying past, making a sound she had never heard before. It was frightening. She wanted to escape, to run to freedom, but she was so weak from hunger and thirst she could barely move. She tried desperately to stay awake, tried so hard to not slip back into the darkness. Would she ever return if she did?

This is my death.

But she wasn't dead. She could sense her body, feel the shaking of the carriage, see the rain on the glass of the window. She had never seen that before, not like this. How were they moving? Where were the horses? She couldn't hear their sound. She tried to lift her head to see, but her strength was gone.

And the man in front, his back to her, hidden by the chair, who was he? He spoke English, like Mother and Sakae-Sensei, and some Japanese. How could that be? Had Sensei taught him? Was he from the Netherlands? Portugal? No, he must be an Englishman, like Miura Anjin had been. Had the man arrived at the same time? No, he was still young, and grandmother had known Anjin-san when she was a child; and grandmother had been very, very old.

The cave! The awful, terrifying place. How had he found her? How did he know? She could see his eyes in that small mirror.

Did he put her there? Was it him?

She was being kidnapped!

The tunnel of light!

She tried to remember.

Father! I was there, home with you, but I can't...

She was drifting again, floating between worlds.

Don't sleep! Stay awake! There is danger here!

The carriage faded to black as Nene slipped into unconsciousness.

***

The rain was heavy, but the Tokyo-bound traffic was light; rush-hour had ended hours earlier. Even so, he kept the Mini slow and to the inside lane, with the rear-view mirror angled downwards so he could see the girl in the back seat, who slept throughout the journey, giving him the time and space he needed to work it through.

It also gave his aching arms time to recover – carrying the semiconscious girl through that long tunnel had been hard work, despite her slender frame. And although the trembling in his biceps had subsided, theories were bouncing around his mind like popcorn in an overheated frying pan.

What the fuck was going on?

It had been a wormhole generator; he was certain of that. What's more, the ring-assembly layout was almost identical to the one in the appendix of the paper he had sent to Tom. It was his design! Or, near enough his. Incredible! But something had happened, there had been an event and things must have spiralled out of control, introducing an instability that... no, not an *instability*, that was too small a word. *Catastrophe* was much nearer the mark.

A catastrophic event in the not-too-distant future had ripped a hole in the spacetime continuum and, somehow, in a way he'd have to figure out, the girl had been caught up in it and ended up in the cave.

He knew the ERG, the Einstein-Rosen Generator, can't have been too far ahead in time because the consoles didn't look like they'd come from the Interstellar tesseract.

Advanced, yes, but from another aeon, no. The girl, on the other hand, looked like she'd just stepped out of the Edo Museum in Tokyo. Her hair style, her *nihongami* - Peter was impressed he'd remembered the word - was straight out of a samurai drama, as was her kimono. Well, you could probably walk into any kimono shop in Tokyo and buy something similar, but Peter doubted that was the case. It didn't exclude the possibility of her being an extra in one of those same dramas, but the likelihood of that was extremely low. Zero, in fact, he decided.

So, how the hell did an Edo-period woman get caught up in an unstable wormhole and get herself transported to a cave one hundred and fifty kilometers west of Tokyo, or Edo, or either, since they were different names for the same city. It might not be the Edo period, though, it might be the Meiji. Either way, it demanded an explanation, his explanation.

The cave was the easy part; that's where the ERG was built, presumably powered by that matter-antimatter reactor. Ye gods, it all worked, just as he had thought it would. But screwing up spacetime wasn't something he'd predicted, far from it – and that troubled him, troubled him a lot.

He could work out how the girl had gotten there just by asking her. He's already hypothesized that she had arrived four days previously, when his equipment had detected that event. Ye gods, four days alone in that place, with no food and just that dripping cave water to keep her from compete dehydration. She must have suffered terribly, physically and mentally, not to mention the stress of arriving there in the first place. What had it been like? He hoped she'd be able to tell him; it would only be what she had observed, but that would be a starting point and he wasn't concerned about that. If anything, that would be the easy part.

What troubled him, and what had occupied his mind for the majority of the past three hours, was *why* she was there. Why did the ERG malfunction, why had it ripped a gash in spacetime, why did it slip out of view like that, and what else was going on in other times, other aeons?

A theory was forming in that tiny brain of his, and he didn't like it, didn't like it all.

As he took the Fujiyoshida-Nishikatsura exit, the realization that he'd just made one of the greatest scientific discoveries in history, one that could completely obliterate that same history, scared the crap out of him.

***

Peter carried the girl through the central living area, and straight into his bedroom. She was still either asleep or unconscious, he couldn't tell. He set her carefully down on the bed and covered her with a blanket he took from a cupboard. As he did, their eyes met for the briefest of moments before she slipped back into oblivion.

Peter sat on the chair at the end of the bed where he usually threw his clothes at night. He was staring at the girl, he realized, and turned his gaze through the window to the now clear night sky.

Now what was he supposed to do?

He got up and closed the curtains; at least that was something. Then he turned off the main overhead light and switched on the small lamp by the bed, adjusting it to its dimmest setting. She was safe, comfortable, and wouldn't wake up in darkness. But when she did wake up, what was he going to do then? It had only been a few days, but she had felt so slight and thin, how much weight had she lost? What if it had been a critical amount, and she needed urgent medical attention?

What if she never woke up?

He quietly left the bedroom, sliding the door shut behind him. It was one thirty-five in the morning, but he didn't feel much like sleeping. He paced around the lounge. Not for the first time in his thirty-four years on planet Earth was he stuck in a thought loop.

Jane!

She was at home in Hachioji for the weekend, she had said, which meant she would probably be there Friday night, this night. He found his iPhone and called her, but all he got was a voice telling him to leave a message. Why the hell did Jane never leave the thing on when she slept?

"Fuck," he said, as he ended the call without leaving a message, not realizing that he just had.

Peter grabbed his keys and left the house as quietly as he could.

***

On a good day, the drive to Jane's small apartment on the outskirts of Hachioji took just under fifty minutes. At that time of night there was no traffic, and Peter did it in thirty-two, despite the rain.

He left the Mini parked at the Seven Eleven, dashed across the street and up the stairs to apartment 203, and rang the doorbell four times. No matter how far beneath the covers Jane was, she was bound to wake up.

There was no answer.

Had she changed her plans? He hit the little button for the fifth time. The sleepiest voice on the planet finally answered through the intercom.

"Hello?"

"It's me. I need your help," Peter said, urgently.

"You what?"

"I need your help, now, your professional help."

"Peter, it's half two in the soddin' morning."

"Jane, I don't have time for a debate. I need-"

The door opened.

"Are you all right?"

"Get yourself dressed. I'll explain in the car."

***

Peter waited ten long minutes for Jane to come down the stairs. He opened the passenger door to let her in and accelerated away before she even had a chance to fasten her seat belt.

"Bloody hell, Peter!"

"We need to hurry."

"Hurry for what?"

"You won't believe me, Jane."

"I already don't. What's going on?"

Peter slowed at a red light, checked the road was clear and went straight through.

"Just try to keep an open mind."

"The way you're driving?"

***

"Are you serious?" Jane said. "And could you slow it down, please."

They had been on the expressway for fifteen minutes. At this rate they'd get to Peter's place in no time. Jane hadn't seen him like this for years and was fast becoming concerned he might be having another episode.

"Yes, I'm serious, and no, I can't slow it down," Peter said.

"So, she's wearing a Kimono, inside a cave, half-starved, semi-conscious, having just walked through one of your wormholes a week ago."

"Four days ago, yes."

"Whatever. And now she's in your house. In your bed, in fact."

"Correct."

"Is this a sort of practical joke, Peter? Because if it is, I don't think it's funny."

"It's no joke, Jane, believe me."

Christ, maybe he *was* having an episode.

"Right now, I don't what to bloody believe," she said.

Eight

Peter ushered Jane through the house to the bedroom.

"Now do you believe me?" he said as he slid back the door.

"Oh, dear God, the poor thing. Here, hold this." Jane passed her handbag to Peter. She thrust past him, sat on the bed and held the girl's hand.

"Can you hear me, pet?" Jane said as she gently lifted her eyelids. "Christ, she's out cold." She turned to Peter. "I need some clean clothes, Pete, and some warm wet towels. Not dripping, just damp."

"OK."

At last Peter felt useful. He put Jane's handbag on the kitchen table and went into the bathroom where he took two hand towels from under the sink, put them in the basin and ran the tap warm. He squeezed them dry and returned to the bedroom.

"Here you go," he said.

"Thanks," Jane replied. "And some fresh clothing."

"Sure."

Peter opened the bottom drawer and removed a pair of his winter pajamas. He handed them to Jane.

"Don't you have anything of Mariko's?"

"She took it all with her," he said.

"These'll do."

Jane looked at him for a few seconds.

"Some privacy, Peter, if you wouldn't mind."

"Sorry," Peter said, and turned to leave the bedroom. "Is she going to be all right?" he asked.

"That's why we're here, isn't it, chuck," Jane replied. "Now, close the door on the way out, will you, Pete."

"Sure."

He stood and stared at the closed bedroom door for thirty seconds before sitting down at his desk, where the blank screen of his Mac stared right back at him.

He touched a key – the Mac woke up. He opened his detector monitoring program and retrieved the event data.

Event Detected
Time: 01:02:54
Bearing: -58.09 degrees true
Distance: 74,234 +/-22 m
Duration: 7.03s
Re-calculate: Y/N?

"OK," he said. "What is it you're trying to tell me?"
The answers had to be in there somewhere.

***

Fifteen minutes later Jane opened the bedroom door. She was carrying the girl's kimono, neatly folded.

"Can you find a home for this, Pete? It's in the way here."

As Peter took the kimono he said, "How is she?"

"Between worlds, if you see what I mean. I'll let you know."

"Sure," Peter replied as Jane closed the door, leaving him standing there for the second time.

Holding the kimono gave Peter an avenue to explore. He made space on his desk, set the garment next to his Mac and opened Safari. There were several sites dedicated to the history of Japanese kimono, and although he couldn't say conclusively, he was reasonably convinced that the cloth on the table next to him was from the Edo period. It was the small repeating patterns, white on blue, he reckoned, which were peculiar to women's 江戸小紋, *Edo komon*, of that time – according to Wikipedia, that was. Not exactly rock-solid evidence, but good enough. He was going to need more than this, though.

He went into the study and switched on his detector and the air conditioner. Both would stay on from now, day and night, irrespective of whether he was in the house or not. He should have left the equipment on permanently since the first event, not just when he was at home and awake, so it was possible that he'd missed something. But at least that little mistake was fixed. He'd worry about the size of the electricity bill later.

Peter returned to his Mac and set the detector software to 'live monitoring.' The program showed the same readings as it had done prior to the event; a series of parallel sine waves indicating zero-event detection.

"Okey dokey. Let's see where that gets us," he said.

"Going somewhere?" It was Jane, who had slid open the bedroom door without him noticing. She slid it quietly shut and came over to his desk.

"How is she?" Peter asked from behind his Mac.

"Stable. Sleeping."

"Did she say anything?"

"Not a word. But you and I need to talk, Pete."

"Sure. Want some tea first?"

"Love some."

***

"Here you go."

Peter set Jane's mug on the kitchen table, then sat opposite her.

"Ta." Jane sipped the tea, her asbestos lips impervious to the heat. "Perfect, almost."

Peter had waited long enough. "Well?"

"Well. The good news is she's not in any immediate danger. Weak, and a bit famished, I'd say, but not too seriously dehydrated. But she does need to go to a hospital and get properly checked out. And you need to call the police, too."

"Absolutely. Will do."

"Now, Pete, might be a good idea."

"It's four in the morning, Jane. It can wait."

"No time like the present."

Interesting choice of words, Peter thought. "I think we should wait until she wakes up, give her a chance to rest."

"She'll be fine. Just make the call Pete, will you. My Japanese isn't up to it."

Peter shook his head.

"And what's that supposed to mean?" Jane said.

"Look, I've been thinking about this. If we do that, I mean, can you imagine what they'd do to her? They'll lock her away and, you know, stick needles in her arms, whatever. And then we'll never know."

"Never know what?"

"I know what I saw, Jane."

Jane gave him one of those forced smiles of hers.

"Or do you think I just made it all up?" Peter said.

"I didn't say that, Pete."

"But you're thinking it."

"I'm thinking you should call the police, that's what I'm thinking."

Peter wanted to say that he was thinking that somewhere in time an out-of-control wormhole generator was threatening the existence of everything that ever was or ever will be, but doubted Jane would be open to hearing that trivial little idea.

"I wasn't hallucinating, Jane."

"I didn't say you were. It's just, well, you know, you do have a bit of history there, don't you, chuck."

"That's ancient history. And you know it."

"Yeah but, a dark cave, underground, on your own. The mind can play tricks. You know that."

Peter did know that, but Jane was missing the point. No, not just missing the point; she was completely disregarding everything he had told her.

"I know what I saw, Jane."

"Peter, for Christ's sake!" Jane pointed across the living room to his whiteboard. "You don't actually expect anyone to believe all that bollocks, do you?"

Peter gave her a half-accusing, half-hurt look, neither of which were forced.

"Sorry," Jane said, without being apologetic. "What I mean is, there must be a rational explanation, like some bastard dumped her in that cave. And you found her, which is wonderful, granted. But walking through wormholes? It's just... no. Sorry, but no."

"Wait here."

Peter retrieved his Mac and the girl's kimono from the desk. He sat back down at the kitchen table and set the Mac facing Jane, still on the Wiki page.

"See this?" Peter pointed to a graphic. "It's from the Edo period, three hundred years ago." He held one of the kimono sleeves next to the graphic. "They're practically identical. Edo's the old name for Tokyo, by the way, in case you didn't know."

"I'm not that stupid, Peter. And it looks just like the one in the window of the shop down the road from my flat. So, bang goes that little theory."

"It's not a theory."

"Really? So, she's three hundred years old is what you're saying."

"She could be."

"Doesn't look a day over twenty-five, now, does she?"

Peter sat back. This wasn't what he had been expecting. "Jane, come on," he said.

"Don't 'come on' me, Pete. I'm not in the mood. And you're the one who needs to come on."

"I have to understand what happened Jane. This could be significant."

"Are you intending to keep that poor girl here? Is that what you're saying?"

"What I'm saying is," Peter said, deliberately, "that something is happening, and I need to figure out what it is."

"For God's sake, Peter. This isn't some kind of frog in a jam-jar science project. She's a real person, in distress, and she needs care and protection."

"From me?"

"Not from you, you twit. From whoever put in that cave, that's who."

"And she's just so relieved to have been rescued she's just begging us to call her mum."

"I told you, she's out cold. Probably traumatized by the whole thing."

"Exactly! That's my point, traumatized by coming through a wormhole, and–"

It was Jane's turn to sit back. "Oh, for fuck's sake! Are you going to make that soddin' call, or am I going to have to do it myself?"

As if she could. Jane may have been a good doctor, but languages were hardly her strong point. Nor was supporting him, apparently.

"You know, I thought you might help me out here, Jane," he said. "But instead, you're just irrationalizing everything, like you always do."

"Really? Well, let me tell you something rational, mate. She needs help, not you gawping all over her."

"Jesus, is that what you think I'm doing here? Look, why don't you just sod off home. I'll call you later, and we can-"

Jane was already on her feet. "I cannot believe you are even thinking this, Walker."

"Are you going? It's not even dawn yet."

Jane grabbed her handbag. "You just friggin' told me to. And don't worry, I'll wait for the first train. They do have first trains here, don't they? Or is the whole place full of brainless country idiots who need their fucking heads examined."

Peter tried to block her exit. "Jane, please, I'm sorry."

Jane took a step back. "Peter, listen to me. I don't know what you think you're doing here. No, actually, I do know, and I don't like it one bit. So, here's what we're going to do. You do what you think is right, and I'll do what I think is right, and then everything will be just fine, all right? Now, if you'll excuse me."

Jane brushed past him.

"At least let me give you a lift to the station," Peter said.

Jane opened the front door. "I could do with the bloody walk," she said as she stormed out into the cool morning air.

***

Peter sat at the kitchen table, head in his hands, wondering what had just happened, how he had managed to upset his best friend, and why she wouldn't, couldn't, believe him.

It was so clear, so apparent, so obvious. There was the girl, for God's sake! What more evidence did Jane want? And if Jane had been like that, would others react the same way? He wasn't worried about being a laughingstock, it wouldn't be the first time and he could handle that. Far from it. He was worried about being right, and the implications of that were – shit, he needed to think that through. Possibly he had jumped to too quick a conclusion, and he hadn't even figured out yet how he had come to that conclusion anyway. Going from an unstable wormhole to the end of the universe was a bit of a stretch, even for him.

It was half-four and he hadn't slept a wink, which might have explained why he had been so short with Jane. He regretted the way he had handled it, the almost hostile-witness approach he had taken. He'd make for a terrible lawyer, really he would.

He headed into the living room and slid back the bedroom door. The girl was still asleep, despite the row with Jane.

Now what?

Peter lay himself down on the sofa and stared at the ceiling, trying to clear his mind so he could approach the problem from a new angle.

***

Jane sat in a 24-hour Denny's drinking the same cup of coffee for an hour.

She'd messed up, not only arguing with Pete, but also not realizing the first train to Hachioji wasn't until a quarter past six. She should have made the stupid sod drive her back home, but he was being ridiculous, and blind, and self-absorbed. Even if he was right about all that wormhole rubbish, which she doubted intensely, he had no business keeping the poor girl locked up like that.

What had gotten into him? If anyone found out, Peter could be facing criminal charges. Kidnapping, confinement; you name it, the police would throw it all at him and the 'guilty until proven innocent' Japanese legal system would crush him down to nothing, a tiny human singularity. It would destroy him, and Jane couldn't let that happen.

She had to protect Peter from himself. The question was, what was she going to do about it? She had an idea, but for that she needed mister Incredibonk's help.

It was three minutes past six. Jane paid for her coffee and headed to Mitsutoge station.

Nine

Peter woke with a start from one of those intense dreams that knocks you right back into consciousness, but which you immediately can't remember. Something about a spider walking over his face, he recollected, happy to not be able to recall the rest of it.

It was six past eight. He tumbled off the sofa and slid back the bedroom door. The girl was asleep. Good. He closed the door.

Now what?

First things first.

His Mac was still on the kitchen table. He checked the monitoring interface. Nothing, apart from the familiar sine waves scurrying across the screen.

He needed to pee.

Once that little problem was sorted, he realized that he probably had no food in the house. He rarely did anyway, preferring o-bentos to home cooking; his home cooking, that was. He didn't need to but checked the kitchen cupboards anyway. As expected, there was nothing of value, except for a half-empty box of bran flakes, a loaf of bread and a few tins of mushroom soup. There were a couple of frozen spaghetti meals still in the freezer, but that was unlikely to be the kind of thing the girl would want. She must be hungry, or would be once she woke up. He'd have to get something.

He picked up his keys, phone and wallet, and was about to leave the house when it occurred to him to check on her again. He slid back the bedroom door a few inches. She was still asleep. Good, except he knew that once she woke up things might get a little strange, for both of them. More than a little strange, in fact, and they'd get a lot stranger if Jane decided to contact the police. Would she do that to him? Maybe.

He slid the door closed, then headed for the car.

***

The sound of the door sliding back pulled Nene from one of the deepest, darkest sleeps she had ever known.

She couldn't remember her dreams. Had she had any? She couldn't say, but the memories of the last few days came flooding back like a tsunami, almost overwhelming her; the tunnel of light, the cave, the foreign man who spoke English, the carriage without a horse, the kind woman who nursed her – she spoke English too. Was she his wife?

Nene had said nothing. She didn't dare until she knew where she was, who these people were, and why and how she was here. She was still scared, but not frightened like she had been before.

She was in a bed. She knew about such things, but this was first she had seen, and so different from the futon she had slept on her whole life. The sheets were soft, softer than she had imagined they would be. And this room she was in wasn't like her home, not like her home at all. Tables and chairs and that dresser, all of European design, familiar from books, but again, so different. The walls were the purest white. Was that paper they were covered with? Or cloth? And that thing hanging from the ceiling – was it a lamp? It looked like one. It was unlit, but even so she couldn't see how to light it.

The lamp on the small table next to the bed was alight, but it made no flame, nor smoke, nor smell. Next to the lamp was a small box with unusual green candles, with numbers, in the way that Europeans wrote their characters. She couldn't smell the candle on this either, but it was definitely alight.

A number changed! It was a five, now it was a six! She stared at it, both fascinated and a little more scared. What was it? She did not even know what to call it, but she had seen the same kind of lights in the carriage that moved by itself. She reached out a hand and tentatively touched the box. It felt strange, neither wood nor metal, and she instantly withdrew her fingers. She tried again, this time resting a fingertip on the top. There was no heat, no flame, no candle within.

The number changed again – from a six to a seven. It was now showing four numbers; 'Oh, eight, one, seven.' Other numbers, smaller ones, were changing rapidly: twenty-three, twenty-four, twenty-five.

"Is it a clock?" she said softly to herself, unconsciously using English.

She watched the box. When the smaller numbers reached sixty, the bigger number changed to eight.

"It *is* a clock," she said.

A sound!

The door began to slide open. She lay back down, quickly and quietly, and kept an eye half open, the way children do when they are pretending to sleep.

The Englishman!

She kept perfectly still, watching him through quivering eyelashes. He closed the door. Nene listened to his footsteps across the wooden floor. Another door opened and closed. Had he left the house? A noise came from outside, a strange growl, signifying movement – the carriage, it must be that. The sound went away into the distance.

Was she alone? His wife might still be here, but Nene wasn't afraid of her; it was the man that aroused her concerns. That was the first time she had properly seen his face. He seemed so recognizable, so familiar. She searched her memory but couldn't place him. Had he visited Edo with the Dutch delegation the year before? She couldn't be sure. There was something, though, in the depths of her mind, that spoke of danger.

Nene lay there for ten minutes, listening to the silence. She knew it was ten minutes from the clock. How could anyone have made such a magical thing?

She sat up, placed her feet on the floor and let the dizziness settle, allowing herself to regain balance. With one hand on the table, she slowly stood up.

She could stand, and she could walk.

She went to the door and slid it open a *sun* – an inch, she told herself, realizing that here everything should be in English, even her own thoughts. The gap was wide enough to see the inside of the house. It was one big room, with smaller rooms off to the side, behind other doors.

It didn't look Japanese. Had the tunnel taken her to England? Was it the man who made the tunnel? And why could she remember so little? She was at home with her father, that she could recall; but all else about her journey to the cave was lost to her. Except for the tunnel of light. She would never be able to forget that.

Satisfied that she was alone, Nene slid the door wide open.

***

Peter parked at the 24-hour convenience superstore on the edge of Fuji-Yoshida in the foothills of Mount Fuji.

He'd long thought it was pointless to have such a large 'always open' supermarket in a relatively small town, the nighttime customer traffic couldn't have been enough to make it economically viable. Who would want to buy a pair of shorts at four in the morning? Milk and o-bentos, yes, that made sense. But for that you only needed a normal 24-hour shop, not one with an entire general store attached.

Except it wasn't four in the morning, and the couple leaving with a pair of folding chairs made him realize who the place was for; campers and other visitors to the area who could need anything at any time. And joining them now was someone who needed to feed and properly dress an accidental time-traveler.

Peter stopped at the automatic doors – the incongruity of what he was doing was bordering on the absurd. A few hours before he'd witnessed one of the most significant events in scientific history, one that had simultaneously occurred in the past, the present, and the future; an event that could endanger everything that ever was or will be. He'd even written about it in his paper which Jane had picked up on it that time in Starbucks:

"The question remains," she had read out loud, *"can we in fact travel through time and manipulate history, or is there some natural law of the universe that prevents us from doing so?"*

But it was the next section, the one Jane hadn't read, that was the killer. The sub-heading flashed into his mind:

'Causality Paradox: When the future becomes the past, the past becomes the future, and the present does not exist.'

He'd written that part for effect, to make the reader sit up and take notice, not as an actual prediction. At the time he'd thought it was quite good, almost literary. Now it was a reality, and he'd been presented with the opportunity to prove whether or not you could go back in time and be your own grandfather, or whether doing that would cause a chain reaction that would screw up the entire universe. Shit, maybe he *had* predicted it, but hadn't realized at the time. Which was why he had to understand it now.

Yet here he was, going into a not-so-interesting shop on a not-so-big island on the third planet from the sun on the outskirts of a nothing-special galaxy to buy sandwiches and a change of clothing for a possibly three-hundred-year-old Japanese girl whose name he didn't even know.

At least the universe was still there.

***

Nene moved warily around the house.

The dizziness was still with her, but curiosity drove her onwards, and she could support herself using the chairs and tables that were in the big room.

She had seen the great houses of Europe in paintings that the Dutch envoy from Nagasaki had graciously presented to the Shogun, who in turn had granted three to her father in recognition of his work, although it was Sakae-Sensei who had done the interpretations – he had spoken their language so well. This house was different, foreign yet somehow Japanese at the same time, and there were so many strange, unusual things.

There, in the corner, a flat black... something... standing by itself. She could see her reflection, but it was too dark to be a mirror. What was it? And those metal boxes on the shelf behind; what were they? They shone like a *katana*, yet dull, in a way she had not seen before, and had an English name she did not know: *Sony* – the same as the black mirror. Nene didn't like not knowing, didn't like not having the words to understand what she was seeing; but she was intrigued, so much so her fear and trepidation left her.

She moved to the table near the wall. It was covered in more objects that she could not name, and behind it, on the wall itself, was a large panel, like a *kokuban* in a school, except this was white. It was covered in writing, numbers and mathematical equations, like the ones from *Principia*, the book by the English professor that Sakae-Sensei was translating. And drawings, like whirlpools.

"The tunnel." she whispered.

She was right – the Englishman did know. He had taken her from her home and brought her here, to this place, this house. But why couldn't she remember? She sensed both danger and sanctuary. She would have to be careful, until she understood which it truly was.

A sound! Like an injured bird crying through the forest. It was coming from the big box on the table. Candles that were not candles shone bright red and green, like the clock by the bed. Nene stepped back, startled.

"Nani kore?" she said, slipping back into her native Japanese.

The sound repeated. A hard noise, shrill and loud; not bird-like at all. Then the sound suddenly stopped. Nene stayed where she was.

A voice, from inside the box!

"Hi, this is Peter Walker. Please leave a message or call me on my keitai, or send a fax at the beep."

Nene could hear the words themselves, but she could not comprehend their meaning. Then the box made another sound, just one bird call that wasn't a bird, like a *shakuhachi,* but different. More sounds. Something was moving inside!

Nene stared in awe as a length of the purest white *washi* appeared from inside the box, by itself, as if by magic.

Then everything went quiet, and the candles went out.

Nene kept still.

When she was sure it had ended, she stepped forward and took the *washi*, the paper, from the top of the box. It was covered in *kanji* and *katakana but* written in a style of Japanese she had never seen before. She understood most of it; a merchant's store was selling… something.

"It's a printing press!" she exclaimed, reverting to English. *"Shinjirarenai."*

She had seen one when Sakai Sensei had printed his great dictionary of English and Japanese words, but that one was much larger and needed several people to make it work. This one was miraculous, and it could talk!

Nene grabbed the table; her dizziness had returned. She closed her eyes and centered herself. She must drink water, and eat, too. Feeling better, she opened her eyes. There, that should be the *daidokoro,* the kitchen.

Another sound, from outside, like the carriage, but different; *don, don, don.* It was getting closer, louder, stronger. The house started to shake. Nene ducked low, instinctively. She had never heard such a terrifying noise. Yes, she had – the light tunnel!

A shadow passed by the window. She could see it now, through the glass; a dragon, flying in the sky, its two great arms turned above its head, not flapping like the wings of a bird, its legs stretched downwards.

She couched low, but the dragon flew on, away from the house. The noise lessened, and the house stopped shaking. It was gone. Nene rushed to the window, her curiosity overcoming her fear, her desire to know overcoming her frailty. She watched the dragon disappear over a low mountain ridge.

"A ship," she said, suddenly realizing. "A ship that flies in the sky!"

It was the first time Nene had seen the outside world since awakening. She looked across the rice fields towards the far end of the valley. There, less than half a day's walk away, was Fuji-san; majestic, spiritual, eternal – she was still in Japan.

***

Peter heard the Chinook fly low overhead. He could hardly miss it; the thing was so loud. It wasn't a Cobra either, because the Japanese Army kindly flew over his home at least twice a day, and after three years of interruptions he knew exactly what the whole bloody fleet sounded like.

The girl!

He'd better get moving.

***

Nene moved away from the window.

Where was she? Near Fuji-san, that was clear, but these things, this place, that flying ship – a realization was forming within her mind. The bookshelf! Yes, she would look there. But first, she must drink.

She went into the *daidokoro*. By the window was an *araiba*. It was full of still-dirty plates and drinking cups. Didn't his wife clean things? Unless she was not his wife.

An *ido* - a hand-pumped well - rose from the edge of the *araiba*. It must be a well, she thought, otherwise it wouldn't be dripping water like that. But inside the house? With so many strange and unusual things in this place, at least this was something she could understand.

Nene cupped a hand under the open end from where the drips were falling and pumped the handle.

She leaped backwards with a yelp as water flooded out, hit her hand, the cups and plates in the *araiba*, and splashed all over her chest and legs.

***

Peter rushed to the car. He'd taken way too long in the store, but at least he had come away with a shopping bag full of food and another one full of a pink tracksuit and female underclothing, the kind that Mariko used to wear.

"Will you forget about bloody Mariko," he said as he fastened his seat belt.

He started the engine and sped out of the car park.

***

Nene, her strange clothes still sodden, stood in front of the bookshelf. It was full of titles that made little sense to her, except for one; *The Principia: The Authoritative Translation and Guide: Mathematical Principles of Natural Philosophy - English Edition.* Father had the same book in his library, the one that Sakae-Sensei was translating. That one, however, was in Latin, the language of the Romans.

She continued searching. There must be such a book here, of the type she was looking for. There! *A History of Japan.* Nene was almost afraid to take it off the shelf, but she had to see for herself, she had to know. She carried the book to the kitchen, sat at the table and opened the cover.

The first page she turned to was a drawing, a line that spread across two pages. *'Japan History Timeline'* read the title, and she didn't need to guess the meaning of the word 'timeline.' Her eyes fixed on the 23rd day of the 11th month of the year Hōei 4, known to Europeans as the 16th day of December, the year of Our Lord, 1707.

'The Hoei eruption of Mount Fuji,' it said.

The day she was born.

Three hundred years before the *"Great Tohoku Earthquake,'* of the year 2011, near the far right of the timeline.

***

Peter waited at a set of red lights, wondering if the Chinook had awoken her. He hoped not, but at a couple of hundred meters altitude those things were deafening, and she might be there now, lying awake, scared, still weak, confused as anything.

He shouldn't have left her alone like that. He should have waited until she'd woken up. Even then, what the heck was he going to say anyway? He'd better have that sorted out before he got back.

The lights changed. He moved off, fast.

***

Nene stared at the page, trying to comprehend its meaning, to understand its message. She didn't want to believe, but it was clear to her now – the tunnel had taken her to a new world, one that didn't yet exist, couldn't yet exist. But she was here, and just like Urashima Taro, three days had become three hundred years.

Her mother's words came back to her. *'One day, Nene, you shall see such wonders. Don't be afraid.'* Had Mother known? And how could she not be afraid?

A sound came from outside, like the flying ship, but less so. The carriage! Nene stood and looked through the window. It was him! She grabbed a knife from the *araiba*. It was short and the edge was not sharp, but she knew how to use one; her father had made sure of that since she was a child.

Nene stepped away from the table and readied herself for the door to open.

***

Peter had considered several scenarios during the remainder of the drive home, including revisiting the unlikely possibility that the girl had come from the modern era and was simply dressed that way because she was involved in some kind of drama, or TV show, or movie. He discounted that idea; she would have said something by now, surely.

And if he *was* right, what could he say about time-travel and wormholes to someone who'd never even seen a lightbulb, let alone been schooled in Einsteinian, or even Newtonian physics?

He'd just have to take things one step at a time.

Keeping the clothes bag in one hand, Peter put the food at his feet, pulled his keys from a trouser pocket and unlocked the front door as quietly as he could. He picked up the food and entered the house, heading straight for the kitchen. He set the two bags on the table – and froze.

The girl was standing there, in the lounge, glaring at him, holding a knife. That wasn't one of the scenarios he'd considered.

They stared at each other for a short eternity – he really didn't know what to say. Peter finally figured out something. "Hello," he said.

The girl didn't reply.

Peter tried his not particularly good Japanese. *"Daijōbu. Kizutsuke shinai node, naifu o shita ni oite kudasai."* He repeated it in English, just in case. "It's all right. I won't hurt you. Please, could you put down the knife."

The girl said nothing.

Now what was he going to do? She had one hand on the back of a chair by his desk; she must still be feeling weak. Peter took a step forward.

"Stay there!" she shouted.

Peter stayed where he was.

So, she speaks English.

"Who are you?" she demanded.

"My name is Peter. Peter Walker," he answered.

"What is this place?"

"This is my home. Not far from Hachioji, west of Tokyo, Edo city."

Keep her talking. She's just as apprehensive as he was, and it looked like she knew how to use that knife, too. Maybe not as apprehensive as he was, then.

The girl pointed the sharp end at the kitchen table. "You will sit."

It wasn't a request.

"Sorry?"

"Sit, sit."

Peter sat at the kitchen table, as ordered.

"Do this," she said, putting her hands behind her thighs. "This, like this, with your hands."

"If you say so," Peter replied.

He sat on his hands. On the table in front of him was the Japanese history book that Mariko had bought for his birthday. It was open at the double spread that showed the timeline of major events of the common era. The girl must have found it on his bookshelf – another scenario he hadn't considered.

"You know," he said, "I think I can explain how you came to be here."

Peter moved a hand to pick up the book.

"Do not move!"

"Sorry."

"Sit, like this, again. Both your hands."

Peter sat again on both his hands. The girl released her grip on the chair and came closer, still pointing the knife directly at him. Directly at his heart, he realized.

"It was you who brought me here."

"Well, I found you in a cave," Peter said. "And then I brought you here, remember?"

The girl stared. "I know you," she said.

"Er, no. I'm sure I would remember if we had met before. Definitely."

She came closer still, until she was at the other side of the table. His pajamas were wet, Peter noticed. He was about to ask how that had happened when the girl half-stumbled, grabbing a chair to steady herself.

"Are you all right?" he asked, although it was obvious that she wasn't.

"Taori so…"

Peter knew what that meant. He jumped from his chair as she dropped the knife, just managing to leap around the table and catch her before she collapsed to the floor.

"It's OK, I've got you," he said, as he once again cradled the girl in his arms, her long hair once again falling to the floor.

***

The Englishman carried her back to the bedroom in his sheltering, protective embrace, just as he had at the cave. And now she knew his name, Peter, like in the Christian bible.

As he lay her down, their faces were so close. For the first time Nene saw his eyes. They were blue, so beautifully blue, the most beautiful she had ever seen.

As she slipped into unconsciousness, she recognized that she had been wrong about him and this place.

This was sanctuary.

She was safe.

***

Peter slid the bedroom door shut and then slumped himself down on the on the sofa.

"Jesus, Walker," he said. "Do you have any idea what the hell you're doing?"

Ten

It was one-seventeen PM.

The girl had been solidly asleep for hours, not stirring at all, not even when he'd crept silently into the bedroom a couple of hours previously to lay the tracksuit on the bed next to her in case she needed to change clothes when she woke up.

It was then that he'd realized how extraordinarily beautiful she was, though in truth it wasn't the first time he'd felt that way. That realization had started when he'd found her in the cave and continued when she'd fainted into his arms that morning. It hadn't been too difficult then to compartmentalize those thoughts, those auto-psychosomatic responses, into the male equivalent of 'I'm-her-knight-in-shining-armour' syndrome - if there was such a thing - and bury them deep behind his need to understand, to evaluate, to decipher and discover.

He'd hadn't felt that way when he was sliding back the door with the tracksuit in his hands, not at all. Shit, Jane would have had a field day with that, and "stop gawping" would have been the politest thing she would have said. Shouted, not said.

What else could he have done? He'd make a hopeless nurse, but couldn't just leave the girl there unattended, uncared for. He had to do something. Even so, he'd felt like an intruder, a voyeur, so had been as quick and unintrusive as he could – a million miles from the brave 'Sir' rescuing the damsel in distress. But when he had glanced down as she slept, her head titled to one side and her hair laying long on the pillow, he'd been struck by her loveliness, her femininity, her softness – and her strength.

He'd left the bedroom as quietly as he had entered and had been since sitting at his desk trying to think things through. He had made scant progress; it was becoming harder to keep those thoughts of her in check.

He needed to knuckle down, to focus, to stop going around in circles. He picked up the remote from the sofa and turned on the TV, setting it to NHK, the volume low. The random background noise usually helped him concentrate, especially when everyone was speaking Japanese; just as long as it wasn't loud enough to wake her up.

He reviewed the event detection log on his Mac for the umpteenth time. Unsure what he was looking for, he hoped whatever it was would jump out at him from the data. The trouble was, there had been so much jumping out at him in the past few hours, he didn't know where to start.

He opened the incident notification:

Event Detected
Time:	01:02:54
Bearing:	-58.09 degrees true
Distance:	74,234 +/-22 m
Duration:	7.03s
Re-calculate:	Y/N?

He could start there. Or re-start there, to be accurate. He erased some space on his whiteboard and copied the details to the top right corner, surrounding it with a red box. That left the oscilloscope-like MP4 recording of the sine wave itself. The multiple lines, each of which were responding to a different frequency slice of the electromagnetic spectrum, were a jumbled, overlapping, inconclusive mess. It was as if someone had hit a flat metal plate of sand with a giant hammer and everything had bounced around–

Shit! The idea struck him like that hammer.

Cymatics! The almost scientific art of covering a metal plate with sand, attaching it to an oscillator, and observing the resulting patterns formed at the regions of maximum and minimum displacement. It was one of his favourite YouTube pastimes, when he wasn't laughing at flat-earthers. He'd have to write some software to convert the time-based frequency data into a geometrically-bound standing wave, which could take a few days. Unless someone had already done it.

He opened Safari and searched for anything relevant. There was a lot more than he had anticipated. He found a paper, *Microscale Assembly Directed by Liquid-Based Template,* by P. Chen and several of his colleagues – or her colleagues, he couldn't tell. Peter read the abstract:

A liquid surface established by standing waves is used as a dynamically reconfigurable template to assemble microscale materials into ordered, symmetric structures in a scalable and parallel manner.

They might have built some tools that would cut short his own program development time.

He downloaded the paper.

***

I am at home, with father. The visitor is there, with us. We eat. All is quiet, peaceful.

An earthquake!

No, it's the tunnel!

It opens next to me, claws at me, drawing me into its light. I hold onto a wooden beam, but the pull is too strong, I cannot hold on any longer. I must let go, I have no choice, cannot resist.

The visitor calls my name.

"Nene!"

I cannot reach his outstretched hand.

I am gone, into the tunnel, my screams lost within the terrifying sound.

The visitor's face is the last thing I see.

His eyes are so blue, so beautifully blue.

***

Peter grabbed the remote and turned down the TV. Was that a scream? No, not a scream, more like cry for help.

He went over and put his ear to the bedroom door. It was quiet now, but if the girl had been having nightmares, well, he wouldn't be surprised. He turned off the TV, just in case.

***

Nene woke with a start from the dream, the first she'd had in the house – though *dream* was not the right word; *akumu,* a nightmare, was more suitable.

There was some kind of pink clothing laid out on the bed next to her. Her chest and stomach were still damp. She'd need to change, or she'd catch a chill. And bathe; she felt so dirty.

Her stomach growled with a hunger she had never known before, not only to eat but to also understand why the Englishman called Peter was in her dreams.

***

The bedroom door slid backwards. It was the girl, dressed in the tracksuit he had bought for her, wearing the tennis socks he had guessed would be the right thing. As for the undergarments, well, he wasn't going to ask – he'd been embarrassed enough paying for them. Apart from her long, long hair she looked so normal, so modern, so present-day.

Peter reckoned he was right; she'd woken from a bad dream. Well, she was safe here, now, with him.

"Hello," he said.

She nodded in reply. Peter stood up. The girl took a step back.

"It's all right," he said. "There's no need to be afraid. You are safe here."

"I am not afraid," she replied.

"Good, that's good," he said, mindful not to stare, to not be sidetracked by her beauty.

Too late for that. He put the thought aside and waited for the next inspiration. Nothing came to mind. Shit, he was already screwing this up.

A thump, thump, thump crashed into the awkward silence. It was a Chinook - Peter instantly recognized the familiar sound - coming over the mountain behind the house. The girl went to the window. She really wasn't afraid.

Peter stood behind her. "It's a Chinook, a helicopter, a flying machine," he said, happy to be able to explain something. "There's a base near here, they fly overhead quite a lot. It gets pretty noisy sometimes. There was one earlier, I thought it might have woken you up."

"I was already awake," she replied.

Where did she learn to speak English? He'd ask her later, along with the million other questions in his head. They watched the helicopter until it disappeared from view.

"I expect you have a lot you want to ask," he said. "But would you like to eat something first? You must be very hungry."

"I am," she said.

"It's over there."

Peter led the way to the kitchen. He'd already laid out the food that he'd bought from the 24-hour superstore earlier. He'd chosen it carefully, too: natto, tofu, rice, fish, miso soup; all on the basis that this would be the kind of thing she was used to.

Peter took hold of two rice bowls. "I'll need to warm these up." He put them in the microwave and set the timer for two minutes. *Wait 'til she sees this!*

"Please, do take a seat."

The girl sat.

"This thing, this machine, is a called a microwave oven. It works by... it heats things up, in a special way."

Hopeless! He was going to have to explain things better than that.

"It won't be long. A couple of minutes. Please start, no need to wait for me."

That was better.

"*Itadakimasu.*"

It wasn't a reply. The girl already had a pair of chopsticks in her hand and was tackling the tofu. God, she must be so hungry, yet she is so elegant, so controlled, so graceful.

Stop staring!

Peter turned around just as the microwave sang its little *'I've finished'* song. He removed the rice bowls and set them down on the table. He hadn't eaten that day yet either, having reasoned it would be best to wait for her and eat together. He was just as hungry as she was.

Perhaps not.

The girl took the natto bowl and scraped the contents onto her rice. Had she even noticed his big moment with the microwave? Apparently not – she was too famished for that. Never mind, he'd come back to it later, along with his idea of how to explain to her where she was, and how she came to be here.

The miso!

He got up and switched on the kettle. "I'm just making the miso soup."

The girl looked up at him but was too entangled with her natto to reply. Another thing to come back to later.

The soup was the dehydrated kind, sold as square clumps in small packets. It was good enough for him, but probably not what she was used to. Either way, it was better than he could make himself. When the kettle boiled, he made two bowls of the stuff and set them down on the table.

"Here you are," he said.

"Thank you," she replied.

***

They ate in silence, not because Peter had nothing to say, but because he wanted to let her eat without interruption.

"I'm sorry. For before, this morning, I'm sorry," the girl said when she finally finished.

"It's OK," Peter replied. "But you did scare the crap out of me a little back there."

The look on her face said she didn't understand. So, she didn't have perfect English, then. Or, rather, not perfect modern English.

"You did scare me, with that knife," he said.

"I am sorry."

"There's no need to be sorry. But, like I said, you're safe here. There's nothing to fear."

"And like I too said, I am no longer afraid."

Would he feel the same if the reverse had happened to him, and he'd ended up in her time? OK, so he still hadn't established that he was right about that, but even so, he'd have been a lot more panicked than she was.

She? "Would you tell me your name?" Peter asked.

"My name is Nene. Shinbori Nene."

"Nene. That's a nice name. And I am Peter. Peter Walker."

"You have already told me your name."

"Yes, that's right, I did, didn't I."

"And you are from *Igirisu*, from England."

"Yes, I am," he said. "How did you know?"

"You are speaking English."

Peter smiled. It was reasonable logic. "Good point," he said. "But I could be from the Americas."

"Then you are still English, are you not?"

Peter thought about that for a few seconds. "Yes, of course, no revolution yet."

"And yet you live in Japan."

"Yes, I do. Actually, quite a lot of us *gaijin* do these days, from all over the world."

The sound of the cat-flap clacking made them both look towards the front door. It was Pebbles. Peter had completely forgotten about her. Where had she been all this time? She skipped across the floor and rubbed her neck on Nene's ankles.

"It's my cat," he said, as if Nene needed the explanation.

Nene picked her up. "Nya-Nya?"

"Her name is Pebbles. She came with the house, and usually doesn't like visitors. She seems to like you, though."

Nene released Pebbles, who headed for her food bowl. "She is so like Nya-Nya, my own cat," she said, watching her eat.

Nene turned to Peter. "I am ready now."

***

The Japanese history book was open at the timeline, the one that stretched across two pages. Nene pointed to the 16th of December 1707.

"Here, this day," she said.

"The last time Fuji-san erupted. Interesting. And I was born here, in March nineteen eighty-five, which is thirty-four years ago."

"Thirty-one, is it not?"

"The book's a few years old," he replied.

Nene had come to know a great deal about Peter-san since she had awoken from her dream. From the way he had cleared their plates and bowls to the rather untidy way he kept his house, she had learned that he cared little for maintaining the order of such things. He lived alone, too; the woman was evidently not his wife. He was also strong, like father, and intelligent, like mother had been. Not so courageous, she sensed, but he was kind.

"So, the question is, how did you find yourself in that cave?" he said. "Was there something like a tunnel, twisting and turning, full of light, something like that?"

Nene recoiled at the memory, but she must explain, she knew it was important.

"I was at home, with my father," she said. "I felt, shaking, like an earthquake. Then a door opened. No, not a door, just, an opening, there, behind me. It pulled me inside, like, how do you say, when water twists, like this," she swirled a finger. "An *uzumaki*."

"A whirlpool?" he said.

"Yes, a whirlpool."

"And that took you to the cave?"

"Yes," Nene answered.

Was he truly the one in her dream? Something within her was saying *'not yet,'* hold back, wait until he was ready, until they both were ready. She would tell him when their connection became clear, not before.

"Can you remember anything else?"

"Only being alone in the cave, so far from home, and so afraid. But then you came and rescued me."

Peter-san flushed. She watched his eyes as he turned to the back of the book, where there was a map of Edo.

"Where is your home?" he asked.

"My home?" Nene pointed to an area near Edo castle, now the Emperor's Palace. "Here."

"That's Akasaka, I think. I go there quite a lot," he said." Well, I used to, not so much these days. There are some good pubs there."

Nene tilted her head, as she tended to do when she didn't understand.

"Drinking places, like an izakaya," he said.

Nene let her fingers glide over the map. It was her world, her life, the places she knew, the things she understood. She suddenly felt so distant, so completely separated from everything she had ever known or loved. She pictured her father, left alone, not understanding where his only child had been taken to. How could he? It was beyond comprehension. She wanted to return home, to be with him, to tell him she was safe, and things would be once again just as they were before she left.

"What has happened to me?" It was almost a whisper.

A tear ran down her cheek. She wiped it away.

"Nene, this might be difficult to understand, or even believe," he said. "But I think you fell through time, three hundred years, from your time, to this. Well, I think you know that already."

She looked across the table at Peter-san. He was so gentle, so kind. He surely was the one in her dream, and she sensed no danger from him, but she was still unsure, still uncertain, and had a thousand questions to ask, a thousand things to know, a thousand mysteries yet to be understood.

But before that, there was something she needed to do.

"I was wondering, is there an *onna yu* nearby, where I may bathe?"

Peter-san smiled. "Actually, these days women's public baths are in-house," he said.

***

Peter hit the light switch and opened the bathroom door.

"OK, it's all automatic, which means, if I push this," he said, pointing to the [ふろ自動] button on the wall by the door frame, "the bath will fill by itself."

Peter hurriedly entered the bathroom and put the plug in before the autofill got going, then set the towel he was carrying on to the rail. Nene was staring up at the three ceiling lights, fascinated. She flicked the light switch for herself, turning them on and off. Good, he thought, she's doing better, and is a quick learner, too.

"I'll explain it all later," he said. "But first, let me show you how this works."

Peter gestured for her to come inside. The bathroom was the all-in-one type that practically every modern Japanese home was equipped with.

"This thing is the shower. Just do this." Water sprayed from the shower head as he turned the faucet. "Red is hot, blue is cold, and here is about right."

He turned off the shower. There were a series of plastic bottles on the shelf. "This one is body soap, and this is shampoo, for your hair. And this is conditioner. This first, then this. It's got Japanese instructions on the back, so you can read what to do there. The bath will stop filling when it's ready, so you don't need to do anything, apart from wait."

Nene ran her fingers through the half-centimeter of warm water that had already flown into the tub. "What is that?" she asked, nodding towards the toilet, which was set behind a frosted glass partition.

"That is, er, when you want to do something that you need to do. If you do, that is." Peter said, awkwardly. He hadn't much appreciated the compromise that the re-form company had taken - he thought they should have built a separate room for the thing - and now he was doubly sure of that. And what was the Edo-period Japanese word for toilet? He had no clue.

Nene tilted her head. "A *kawaya*?"

"Could be," Peter said. He lifted the lid, "You lift this." He depressed the flush lever, "And push this when you're, you know, finished." He pointed to the roll of toilet paper, too embarrassed to say what that was for.

Nene smiled for the first time. "Thank you. I think I understand."

"Well, I'll leave it with you," Peter said. "Shout if you need my help."

"Why should I shout?"

"It's just an expression."

***

Jane had taken the train to central Tokyo right after mister Incredibonk called to say that his Hokkaido trip had been cancelled.

She could have waited for him at his place, she had a key, but she hadn't felt much like sitting in that big house all by herself, so she'd found her favourite spot in the little coffee shop around the corner and sat watching the world go by, alone with her troubled thoughts, ninety-nine percent of which were about Peter.

Just what did that idiot think he was up to?

Whichever way she looked at it, the whole thing was absurd. Women falling through wormholes, and you happening to find one, in cave, in a mountain? Come on, Peter, please. Had his schizophrenia returned? Christ, she didn't want to think about that. No, not true. That's *all* she'd been thinking about, *all* sodding day.

Jane checked her watch; half-three. He'd be here soon enough, and if anyone would know, it was Shohei.

Speaking of the devil.

Mister Incredibonk waved from the back seat of the taxi that had just pulled up outside. Jane waved back, watching him pay the driver, who then helped retrieve his travel bag from the boot. Shohei came in through the main entrance and headed straight for her corner.

She hugged him tightly.

"Is everything all right?" he asked.

It must have been the look on her face.

"If your oldest, bestist friend was doing something completely stupid. What would you do?" She almost blurted it out, but it had been bottled up inside her for hours.

"That rather depends on what they were doing," Shohei replied. "Why don't you tell me all about it."

***

Nene had been in the bath for nearly an hour.

Peter wasn't too concerned, she hadn't shouted, and it had given him more time to think; most of which was spent wondering just what the fuck he thought he was doing. He'd found some space, though, to write the essential issue on his whiteboard: *'Who made the wormhole?'* A few moments later he'd added an *'s.'* There were two wormholes, at least. One in the cave that he had seen, and one in Nene's house.

The one in the cave made some sense; it was evidently the site of the future ERG, the Einstein-Rosen Generator, a name he had made up in the cave but which he rather liked. The other one, however, made little sense. Why would someone have created a wormhole that opened in a house in Akasaka, in the year 1732? The year was an assumption, but Nene had said she was 25 years old. Or was it Jane who said that? It didn't matter; 1732 would do until a better date came along.

The 'how' it was done could wait. It was the 'why' that he was concerned about. What could be important enough about Nene's father's house to call for such an event?

And speaking of events, he'd put the history book back on the shelf, thinking that it was too soon for Nene to discover the horrors of Hiroshima and Nagasaki, and the terror of the *tsunami* that had wiped out thousands of lives in the reborn, post-war Japan. It may even be better for her *not* to know about the history of her country, or the future of it, just in case she did end up returning to Edo. OK, it probably wouldn't matter that much in the great scheme of things, but what if she went back home and penned the definitive '*Prophecy of Japan*' that then created a cult of followers who worshipped each word she had written? The nudges to the timeline that could arise from that were incalculable, and might well be a lot more than just 'nudges,' too.

On the other hand, who did he think he was he to withhold anything from her? If the roles were reversed and he had jumped 300 years into the future, he'd want to know *everything* there was to know about *everything*.

He decided to tell her when the moment arose, when the opportunity presented itself, when she asked to know more. And if she found the book on the shelf once again, well, he'd take that as a sign that she was ready and simply let it be.

He'd also backtracked on the universe-ending paradox theory, ostensibly because the universe hadn't ended. That didn't mean he was dropping the notion completely; it was still worth investigating, but with zero activity coming from his detector the implications were that, whatever had caused the chaos at the ERG, someone had gotten it under control. Even so, his task was clear; he had to figure out how she had gotten there, what had happened to both her in the past and to the ERG of the future. From there, he'd work out a way to warn the builders of that machine that something was going to go very wrong.

It also meant he had been gifted the opening to make a name for himself, like Neil deGrass Tyson, who was on the National Geographic channel right then. But first, he needed incontestably irrefutable evidence, which, apart from Nene herself, wasn't exactly in abundance. Peter watched Neil explaining the mysteries of the universe with that incredibly clear, simple, and engrossing way of his.

If only he knew.

***

Nene lay in the *o-furo*, the *bath* as an Englishman would say, staring at the light in the ceiling. How could people make such a thing? Just push the *sore*, the small white *thing* on the wall, and it came to life. How wonderful! And the warm water that came from the opening by her feet, sometimes coming, sometimes stopping, so it was neither too hot nor too cold. How was it done? And that, what did Peter-san call it, the *shower*? Water came just by turning the, the *sore*. How?

Nene smiled; she couldn't just keep saying *sore* for things whose name she did not know, but there were so many new wonders here, so many discoveries to be made in this amazing new world. She had already made one; there had once been a woman in this house. The hair soap, the *shampoo*, was not made for a man; she could easily tell from the way the Japanese was written on the back of the bottle. She sensed, too, that it was not the foreign woman who had cared for her earlier.

She closed her eyes and lay back as the water flowed around her, bathing her with its warmth, soothing her with its tenderness, calming her mind and spirit. Then she saw her father's face, his eyes filled with sadness.

"I will find my way home, *Chichi-ue*," she said. "I promise."

Eleven

The bathroom door slid open to reveal Nene, bath towel in hand, barefoot, her wet hair falling long across her shoulders and down the back of the pink tracksuit.

Peter stood up. It was more of a reaction to her presence than an expression of politeness – as if he knew how to be a gentleman. That kind of thing was beyond him, he'd always thought. Irrational numbers, wayward protons, entangled particles, and Schwarzschild metrics were his area, his world. Being alone in a Japanese farmhouse with an extraordinarily beautiful woman who just happened to be three hundred years older than him, was something new, something far outside his comfort zone.

Shit, the whole thing was like that.

"How was the bath?" he said, feigning control.

"It was most wonderful," Nene replied, "I'm sorry I took such a long time, but I-"

She stopped in mid-sentence, her mouth slightly open, her head tilted, staring. Peter followed her gaze. The TV was still on. After Neil had finished, he'd set it to a Japanese news channel and turned the volume down to zero. Nene looked at Peter, then back at the TV. She moved closer to the flat forty-two-inch 4K Sony, where a pair of newsreaders, one male, the other female, were saying something inaudible.

Peter took the towel from her and set it on the back of his desk chair. "It's called a TV," he said, enjoying Nene's fascination with the ubiquitous slab of consumer electronics.

Nene knelt and reached out to touch the screen. "May I do this?" she asked.

"Sure," Peter said. "It's quite safe."

"It feels quite hot."

"Yeah, they all are. It's quite normal, don't worry." Peter grabbed the remote from his desk and knelt next to her. He turned up the volume. The newsreader voices were now loud and clear.

"It is wonderful!" Nene gasped.

"Maybe we should stand back a little," Peter said. "It'll be easier to see."

They rose, stepped back and watched as the studio cut to a reporter interviewing an unusually young farmer about the threat of rice imports from the US.

"You can control it with this thing," Peter said, showing the remote to Nene, who was too enthralled to notice. "Just push this, and you can change the channel, the program you're watching."

Nene was still mesmerized. Peter waived the remote around, trying to catch her attention. It worked, she looked at him.

Her eyes. They really were incredible.

Peter collected himself for the second time. "Watch this," he said, and flicked through the next four offerings, stopping at a Premier League replay of Liverpool thrashing Norwich.

"Do you want to try?" he asked.

"Yes."

Peter handed her the remote.

"Push here," he said. "And see what happens."

"This one?"

"Yes, that one. Try it."

Nene pushed the channel change button but kept her finger down so that the TV raced through multiple channels.

"Not too fast."

Peter put his hands on hers, intending to release Nene's finger before she crashed the cable modem. The effect on him was instantaneous, transformative, electric, as if he'd just earthed the entire national grid by touching an overhead high-voltage power line. Oxytocin, he immediately told himself. That's all it was. A flood of chemicals in the brain, nature's way of replicating DNA, of ensuring survival of the species; no more than that.

"Just one push at a time," he said, more awkwardly than he'd wanted to.

"Like this?"

Had she felt it too?

"Yes, one push, then another," he replied.

Nene pushed the plus mark on the button, changing to the first of the movie channels that came with the standard J-COM package. It was the scene from the second Alien film where the space-marine hero was poking his head through the ceiling grating, just in time to see a crowd of xenomorphs scrambling their way through the ventilation system. Suddenly guns blazed and multiple aliens fell through the paneling, exploding in a sea of acidic blood that was set to melt everything in sight.

Peter grabbed the remote and switched off the TV. "Sorry, that was a little too dramatic," he said.

Nene looked at him, wonder in her astonishing eyes. "How can you do this? All these things?"

Peter smiled. This was safe ground, familiar territory, and he was ready.

"Let me show you," he said.

***

The kitchen table was covered in small objects, none of which Nene could name, although she had decided that she wanted to understand, to know, to discover as much as she could – and then find her way home.

Peter placed two cups on the table, then sat opposite her.

"Twinings English Breakfast," he said. "The best afternoon tea in the world."

Nene looked down at the unusual brown drink. Why had he added milk from a cow? Did all Englishmen do that? How strange.

"Let it cool for a while," he said. "Or it'll burn your tongue."

Nene nodded, although she'd made plenty of *O-cha* in her life and knew what it meant to drink too soon.

"OK," Peter said, his eyes on the items on the table. "This is how the modern world works." He picked up a small box and handed it to her. "This is called a battery. Here."

It was a made from a kind of metal and felt cool in her hand. There were two ears - she didn't know what else to call them - coming out from one end.

"What is it?" she asked.

"Ah," he said, his wonderful blue eyes smiling. "It's the secret of everything." He gestured for her to return it to him. "May I?"

Nene handed it back. Peter took two short lengths of hard red thread and touched them to the *battery*, one on each ear.

"This," he said, picking up a small round glass *sore*, "is a light bulb." Peter wound one red thread around the metal part of the *light bulb*, then touched the other to the lower, more pointed end. It lit up, like the ones in the ceiling did. Nene stared at its radiance.

"It is like magic," she said, cautiously touching the light.

Peter picked up a small black box. "And for my next trick."

He pointed the box to the far wall where the TV was. The house was instantly full of music, the singer's voice clear and powerful, the words she sang carrying a deep, heartfelt emotion. Nene looked around. Where was it coming from?

"That's a lady called Eva Casydee," Peter said. "And she's coming from up there." He nodded to a box on high on the wall.

"It's quite beautiful," Nene said.

"Yes. She was."

Peter picked up a small blue box, like a book, with a small eye, which he held facing her. He touched the inside. It made a noise like a child's playful kiss, or that of a knife being sharpened.

Peter gave the book to her and said, "Instant portraits, twenty first century style."

It was her picture, unlike any she had seen before. "It is like the TV," she said.

"It's called a phone, and yes, they're pretty much the same thing. We call this kind of thing a device, everyone has one. Well, almost everyone.

"May I try?"

"Of course you can." Peter reached forward. "Can I have it back for a sec, first?"

Unsure what a *sec* was, Nene handed it back to Peter. He ran his fingers over the flat glass, then passed it back to her, his fingers touching hers as she received it. Nene felt the same instant connection as she had when they were at the TV. She was sure now; he was the one in her dream. She would tell him, but not yet, not until she understood, not until the time was right.

"Hold it like this," he said. "So you can see what you're going to photograph, and then push this button thing here."

"Like this?

"That's it. And then push the round circle, there."

Nene pushed the circle. The box, the *phone,* made the sound again. The glass showed a picture of Peter.

"It is... amazing me." It was all she could say.

"It's amazing me too," Peter replied.

Twelve

Nene, Peter realized, had an astonishing mind. She really understood things. Not at a fundamental level, of course, but she was surely capable of that, given time.

They were sitting at the kitchen table, on their third cup of Twinings, which for Nene had been love at first sip, or maybe that was first dip of the digestive biscuits that he had remembered were still in the cupboard. His coffee-table book of the universe was open at a Hubble photo of Andromeda, while his Mac was open at his wormhole simulation software and the TV, acting as an extended monitor, was showing a Google Earth view of Tokyo. He'd also unhooked the whiteboard from the wall, lain it flat on the table and covered it with wormhole sketches and timelines.

He'd already shown her every device in the house, plus the boiler outside the back door. Nene had insisted on knowing how the bath worked, how it kept the water warm, and where all the water went after Peter had remembered to pull the plug out. What she made of the two giant antennae was less clear, but he'd done his best to explain a standing, bi-synchronous, bi-oscillating radio-wave. Even he didn't really know how it worked, he just knew that it did. The fact that it had all come to him years before, during one of his 'episodes,' was his little secret.

The multifunction HP fax/printer had taken some explaining - Nene had a hard time understanding how pictures could travel down a wire - but they'd gotten there, near enough. And once she'd understood how the kitchen tap worked, well, she wouldn't be in danger of walking around soaking wet again.

But of all the every-day marvels of the twenty-first century that he'd shown her, it was the rather mundane aircon that Nene had liked the most. In late October they weren't usually necessary, but the one keeping his contraption cool was, and the combination of that crisp breath of air and the mysterious lights from the valves was more than enough to peak both her curiosity and appreciation.

"I would want one in my own home!" she had exclaimed.

And how many languages could she speak? Japanese, of course, and English, fluently. Plus quite good Portuguese, a smattering of French, and a lot of Chinese, which she thought of as her third language. She didn't speak Dutch, although it seemed Sakae-Sensei, her teacher, did. It was he who looked after the delegation from the Netherlands and did the interpretations for their meetings with the Shogun. Peter knew that they'd had an island, or an allotment, or a port somewhere down near Nagasaki, and for years were the only westerners allowed in the country.

She'd told him about her mother, who had died giving birth to her stillborn brother when Nene was young. She was Chinese, which explained Nene's ability with that language. Her samurai father was a special advisor to the Shogun on foreign affairs, and as such was in a special, privileged position. Which was why Nene was so gifted, so remarkably intelligent; she had read hundreds of imported publications from Europe, one of the few people in the country who had the opportunity to do so.

And if Nene was physically tired, which she must have been, it didn't show, which was just as well, given the subject at hand.

"Is all this hard to understand?" he asked.

"A little," Nene answered, "But it is all so, so wonderful."

"The important thing is that you came in here," Peter pointed to '1732' on the whiteboard, the starting point of his badly drawn wormhole.

"And came out here." Nene pointed to 2019, the end point.

"See, you do understand," he said.

"Not like you do."

But you are capable of understanding, that's the point.

"Tell me more about the tunnel. What was it like inside?" He'd already asked her but hoped one more time might jog her memory.

"I told you, it was full of light, and a sound so loud, like thunder."

"But you can't remember much else, apart from that, right?"

Nene shook her head.

Peter's plan to figure everything out had hit a snag. If the journey had created temporary amnesia, then Nene couldn't be a reliable witness. Shit, he was doing it again, being a fake lawyer. He'd need to better than that.

"Was there anyone else there, besides you?" he said. "Maybe some serious faced men in long white coats, with big foreheads and inch-thick glasses."

Nene shook her head. "There was only myself. Where is the tunnel, Peter-san? Can we not go there, so I may return home?"

Go home? That was the last thing he wanted. It was academic anyway, considering he had no idea how to make that happen. He wasn't even sure it *could* happen, bearing in mind the chaos he had seen at the ERG.

"I don't know, Nene," Peter said. "But I think there's a machine in the future that created a tunnel to the past, which brought you here to the present. And I think the tunnel is closed right now."

"So, I am trapped here. I am your prisoner."

Peter couldn't tell if she was joking. "Not at all. You're my guest," he said.

"And yet I cannot leave."

Not until I've understood it all. "Let's just take things one step at a time," he said, "and see where we get."

A bright light suddenly filled the kitchen, startling Nene. It came from outside. Peter at once knew the source - headlights - and given that the farmhouse was at the end of a no-through road it could only mean visitors. He glanced at the kitchen clock, it was six-forty-two and dark outside. He'd lost track of time, and he had a suspicion his visitor had timed her arrival then because she knew he'd be there. Correction, they'd both be there.

He stood up to look out through the window. It wasn't the taxi from the station that he'd been expecting. It was her, though, clearly visible in the passenger seat. But who was that driving?

"What was that light?"

"It's my friend Jane," said Peter. "The one who looked after you, when you got here, shit, just this morning."

A lot can happen in a just a few hours. The big question was, what was going to happen next?

"What does 'shit' mean?" Nene asked.

"I'll tell you later," Peter replied, suppressing a smile, though he didn't feel much like laughing.

The doorbell rang.

"I'd better get that." Peter went to the door. He opened it to find Jane and someone, and he had a pretty good idea who that someone was.

"Jane," he said. He declined to add a sarcastic, *'What took you so long?'*

"Hello Peter. This is Shohei," said Jane, gesturing to her companion, who looked solid, dependable, well-balanced, and about ten years older than Jane. And not poor, either. That was a BMW 7-Series they'd turned up in.

Shohei extended a hand. "It is a pleasure to meet you, Peter-san. Jane has told me so much about you."

They shook hands.

"And me about you." Peter said.

"May we come in, Pete?"

"It's not particularly convenient, Jane."

"Well, that's why we're here. Shohei wants to talk to her, that's all."

"What's he got to do with this? Sorry, no offence meant."

Shohei smiled. "None was taken," he said.

"Shohei's professor of psychiatry at Tokyo Medical University."

"Is that so?"

"Peter, look, it's either us or a bloke with a badge. What's it to be?"

"Well, if you put it like that."

Peter stepped back and gestured for them to come in, glaring at Jane when he thought Shohei couldn't see. Jane glared back as she slipped past.

Nene was standing by the kitchen table.

"Hello, luv. Do you remember me?" Jane said.

Nene nodded.

"Are you feeling OK now?"

"Yes, much better, thank you."

"That's good. I'm Jane, by the way, and this is Shohei."

Shohei stepped forward, bowed, and spoke in Japanese. *"I am Taniguchi. It is a pleasure to meet you."*

Nene returned the bow. *"I am Shinbori. It is a pleasure to meet you."*

"Well," Jane said, "now that we all know each other. How about some tea?"

"You came all this way for tea?" Peter retorted.

"And a room where Shohei can talk privately to, er..."

"Nene. Her name is Nene."

***

"That's mister Incredibonk, I take it."

They sat at the kitchen table, teacups in front of them for the second time that day, the muffled voices of Shohei and Nene coming from behind the closed door of Peter's study.

"He has hidden talents," Jane said.

Peter had decided to stop being angry with Jane, although that didn't mean he was feeling helpful, either. He knew she meant well, but there was far too much at stake, including the outside chance of a universe-ending paradox, about which he was still in at least two-minds, if not four.

"And what's he doing?" Peter said. "Testing whether she's a lunatic or not, I suppose."

"He has a few tricks up his sleeve."

"I bet he does. And am I next?"

"It's not like that, Pete."

He leant forward. "Then what is this all about, Jane?"

"It's about Nene, you wally. You can't just keep her cooped up here like that, can you. What do you think's going to happen when she remembers who she really is, and you get accused of all sorts of things?"

"Like what?"

"Kidnapping. Confinement, holding her against her will. All she has to do is cry rape and you're done for. It would be your word against her's, and the 'I'm sorry, me lord, I thought she stepped through a wormhole' defence probably won't go down that well."

"Very funny. So, you still think I was hallucinating?"

"It was pitch black in that cave. You never know what kind of effect that can have on a person's mind."

"I told you, Jane, that's ancient history."

It was Jane's turn to lean forward. "Then how come she speaks such perfect English, then? Explain that, Einstein."

"Her father's an advisor to the Shogun, he brings in all sorts of foreign books, especially from England. And there was some Japanese guy who taught her, too."

"Really? And he attended the Edo school of modern languages, I suppose."

"She also speaks Chinese and Portuguese and a bit of French, amongst other languages. She's a natural linguist, unlike someone I know."

Jane sat back. "Natural linguist, is she? I see."

Peter detected a hint of something in Jane's voice. "Yes," he said, cautiously. "I think she is, anyway."

"And she's feeling much better than yesterday, right?"

"This morning. And, yes, she said so herself."

"She did, she did indeed, she did. I asked her if she was OK, and she said, 'much better, thank you.'"

Why do I get the feeling I'm walking right into something?

"She did, Jane. You're right about that. Fantastic powers of recall."

Jane pulled her phone from her handbag. "Right, clever clogs, then figure this one out." She tapped the screen. "From

Wikipedia, what his lordship over there spends far too much reading," she nodded towards Peter's study. "And I quote: '*Allen Walker Read identifies the earliest known use of OK in print as eighteen thirty-nine, in the twenty-third of March edition of the Boston Morning Post.*' And then there's this other one: '*How the word OK was invented a hundred and seventy-five years ago. OK is one of the most common words in the English language, but linguistically it's a relative newbie. It's just a hundred and fifty years old, and-*'"

"OK! I get it!" Peter said.

"Well, I'm glad you do, because I don't. I mean, how could a three-hundred-year-old Japanese woman possibly know the meaning of one of the most commonly used words in the English language, when it hadn't even been invented yet?"

Peter didn't want to admit that Jane had, in fact, come up with something. On the other hand, it wasn't definitive proof of anything, either.

"Maybe she heard me say it before," he said, "and figured it out for herself. You yourself said 'are you OK' when you came in, so she could have figured it out from there. She's pretty smart, Jane, actually."

"Glad to hear it. But it still needs an explanation, and yours isn't particularly convincing, despite what you think."

Peter sat back and crossed his arms, which he hoped was a clear message to Jane that this was turning into 'he-said-she-said.'

"I bet you spent half the drive here laying that little trap," he said.

"It's not a trap, for God's sake! We have to do the right thing here. For Nene, and for you too, twerp that you are."

"I am doing the right thing."

"No, you're not, actually, Peter."

***

"And when you woke up, it was completely dark?"

Nene was intrigued by Taniguchi-Sensei. He reminded her of one of her father's closest allies, who lived a short distance from their own house. He was from an old samurai family of the same name who had transformed into merchants, trading in silk and textiles, and had recently become one of the most important money lenders in Edo. Their daughter, Hana-chan, was a good friend, and like Nene her mother had died when she was young, although her father had since remarried. Was it the same family? Three hundred years was a long time, but the resemblance was so close, so uncanny, so mysterious.

"Yes," Nene answered him, glad to be speaking Japanese, though his manner and way were different. Were all Japanese people like this, in this new world?

"And there was nobody else there with you in the cave?"

"No."

"You did not hear any voices, or feel any presence?"

What kind of doctor was he? His questions were not what she had been expecting.

"There was just myself," she said.

"I see. Am I making you uncomfortable?" he asked.

Peter-san's special room was small, and that strange thing he called his *contraption* was full of lights, but the *aircon* machine on the wall was blowing cool air. Perhaps Taniguchi-san was talking about the small chairs they were sitting on.

"I am fine, thank you," Nene replied.

"That's good. Now, I'm like to show you something, if you don't mind."

Taniguchi-Sensei reached into his leather bag and pulled out a *futo* – an envelope. He opened it and removed some sheets of flat paper, like the ones in the machine on Peter-san's table. He held one towards her. It was a strange picture, as if someone had spilled ink on the page and then folded it in half to make it look like a bat, or the *ryukyu*, the fox that could fly. She had seen one once, brought to her father's house by a merchant returning from a foreign land. This was different, almost sinister.

"Tell me, what do you see?"

Nene understood his purpose now. He was testing her, just as Jane-san was no-doubt testing Peter. She could see it clearly; if people of this time did not believe Peter, why would anyone believe her? She felt like an intruder, an unwanted visitor who didn't belong in their world.

"I see someone who does not believe me, who thinks this is just my dream," she said.

Taniguchi-san put down the strange picture. "I am simply trying to understand what has happened to you," he said.

"I know the Taniguchi family," she said. "I was an honoured guest at their house many times."

"Is that so?"

***

"Do you actually know what a causality paradox is, Jane?"

"I'm looking at one," she replied.

Peter ignored the quip. "Fred goes back in time and shoots his grandad," he said. "The problem is, if grandpa dies before Fred's mother was even conceived, how was Fred ever born in the first place? And that's the paradox. If you read my paper, you'd understand."

"I do know what a paradox is, Pete. But no one's shooting anyone here, are they?"

His whiteboard was on the kitchen table, just as it had been since they'd sat down. Why couldn't she understand that he wasn't making this all up?

He picked up a marker. "When the future happens before the past, spacetime gets twisted into a loop, circling back on itself again and again, like this."

His ∞ sketch resembled something between an infinity symbol and a mobius strip.

"The past becomes the future, the future becomes the past, and space just spins around and around on itself, at the speed of light, trying to correct the imbalance. But it can't cope, it can't fix it. So, what does it do?"

"Can't wait to find out."

"It creates a singularity, a black hole, right here, on planet earth, stretching back three hundred years and two thousand billion kilometers across."

"What?"

"The entire solar system is moving at two hundred kilometers per second around the Milky Way. Multiply that by three centuries, and you get a bloody great big black hole."

"I'll take your word for it," Jane said.

"And when that happens, the present no longer exists. Nothing does."

He was exaggerating, going for effect rather than demonstrable science and exact mathematics, but he needed her to get it, to realize he wasn't playing games, that if he was even vaguely right then they'd all be in a heap of shit.

Jane made an obvious show of looking around the house and through the window. "Everything's still here, as far as I can see."

"Jane, for God's sake," Peter said, his exasperation levels rising. "Don't you get it? Someone, somewhere, and some-when, created that wormhole. And things didn't go as planned. Who knows what the hell could happen as a result."

"Well, if you're so worried about it, why don't you tell someone?"

At last, a gap in Jane's three-inch thick Tiger-Tank armour. It was the first time she had acknowledged that he might be telling the truth, that he might even be right.

"I will," he said. "Just as soon as I have some incontestably irrefutable evidence. Otherwise everyone will think I'm some kind of nut."

Jane gave him a look; her armour was back on.

The door to Peter's study opened. Shohei, being the gentleman he was, allowed Nene to exit first.

"You all done?" Jane said.

Shohei smiled. "I believe so." He turned to Nene and said, "Thank you for your time. I am so sorry to have disturbed you."

"Not at all," Nene replied.

Shohei looked across to Jane. "Shall we go, Jane? It is getting quite late."

Peter glanced at the clock. It was approaching eight, and they hadn't eaten yet. "I'll see you to the door," he said.

"Goodbye, luv," Jane said to Nene. "I hope we'll see each other again soon."

"Goodbye, Jane-san," Nene replied.

Peter led Jane and Shohei to the front door. "So, did you get what you came for?" he asked softly as he held it open.

"I need some time to further consider what she told me," Shohei said.

"And what's next? Bring in NASA, have them confiscate everything and cart us all over to area fifty-one?"

"I told you, it's not like that," Jane said. "What do you take me for anyway?" She turned to Shohei. "Come on you, let's go."

"I am sorry for disturbing you," Shohei said, offering his hand. "Thank you for your kind understanding."

They shook hands.

"Hopefully your next visit will be a little more relaxed," Peter said.

"I hope so, too."

Jane gave Peter a soft kiss on the cheek. "Bye chuck. Be good. I'll call you, OK?"

***

Jane fastened her seat belt while Shohei carefully placed his briefcase behind the driver's seat.

"Well?" she asked, impatiently as Shohei fastened his own seat belt and started the car.

"I am not sure," he replied.

"You did that Rorschach test whatsit, didn't you?"

"Yes, but that's not definitive, Jane. And, as it turned out, it wasn't even relevant."

"Meaning what, exactly?"

Shohei sighed, deeply, a sure sign he was about to say something Jane didn't want to hear.

"She knows things about my family history that only I know. Things I did not even tell you. She also knows things I myself don't know, so I need to do some research when we get home."

"She could have read about that somewhere, I suppose. Your family is quite well known."

"We did not publish those stories. And she knows the family home in Azabu-Juban. She described it in perfect detail."

"Ah, but that was built thirty years ago, now, wasn't it," Jane countered.

"Demolished and rebuilt thirty years ago, Jane. But she described the old house as it was, perfectly."

"So, she saw some photographs. Or read about it in a book. It's all explainable."

Shohei slipped the car into drive and headed down the narrow road.

"Not that house, Jane. The old house, the one that burned down in seventeen thirty-two."

"What?"

"The original plans are in the family safe. They're like our family treasure, and they never come out. As the head of the family, I'm the only one with access. She could not have seen them, ever. I know that for a fact. Some of the things she described, the design, the layout of the gardens… I can't be completely sure. I need to check when we get back."

"So, what are you saying, Shugs?"

He looked across at her. "We may need to consider the possibility that Nene-san is telling the truth."

"Oh God, not you as well?" Jane stared out of the passenger side window. "So now what do we do?"

"We go home and open the safe."

"And then what?"

"That, my dear, depends on what's in the safe."

***

Peter watched the BMW drive away into the night.

That could have been a hell of a lot worse, he thought as he shut the door, and at least Jane had left on speaking terms. Good, that was a step in the right direction. He'd call her tomorrow, or the next day, and try explaining things again. It would be good practice for when he broke the news to Tom, which was going to be a fun challenge. Peter turned towards Nene. She must be hungry by now. He certainly was.

She was standing by the kitchen table, tears falling down her cheeks, dinner far from her mind. He went straight to her.

"Nene, are you all right?"

"I do not belong here in this world, Peter-san. This is not my place. People will say, look at her, the girl who fell through time. How different and strange she is."

"It doesn't have to be like that. You are safe here. I won't let anything happen to you."

"And my father. I keep seeing his face, living his life without knowing what has become of me. I cannot bear this sadness. How may I return home?"

"We'll find a way, Nene, I promise," Peter said, knowing it was a lie.

"I truly wish I could believe you."

Nene turned and went into the bedroom, leaving Peter standing as she slid the door shut.

Thirteen

Peter woke with the dawn and sat up. He hadn't slept on the sofa this much since the big fight with Mariko, and his neck ached now just as it had then. He rubbed his shoulders, then pushed hard with his thumbs on the *tsubo* points in his lower back, reaching as high towards his shoulder blades as he could.

In fact, he hadn't slept much at all.

He'd thought about it half the night; he'd misled and deceived Nene, Jane – and himself. And Nene had only been there a day; he really had been off to a flying start. Jane was right; Nene wasn't a science experiment, and he had no business keeping her there.

More than that, if he was even half right then he had a duty, a responsibility, an obligation to tell the scientific world. The greatest minds on the planet would need to know, to analyze, to figure out if there truly was a causality paradox forming, one that couldn't be reversed, one that could destroy everything locally, if not the entire galaxy, and beyond. By keeping Nene in the house he could be inadvertently sealing the fate of everything that ever was, or ever will be. And if he was wrong about that, which wouldn't be a bad thing, then he'd still be the one who'd made the initial discovery.

Just a few more days, he told himself. He'd run the detector until Wednesday, and whatever was there, or not there, he'd share it all with Tom. Tom wouldn't believe him, not at first, but he was a good friend with a sharp mind, and the fact that Peter had a 300-year-old daughter of a Japanese samurai in his house might win Tom over. There might even be a DNA test that could be done to prove her age, or at least the era she was born in, although he didn't much like the thought of Nene becoming someone else's scientific experiment, but he couldn't see any other way. What could her offer her anyway?

A shower first, and then, well, as he said to Nene, he'd have to take things one step at a time.

***

Nene slid back the bedroom door to find Pebbles waiting patiently. She bent down and picked her up.

"You are Nya-Nya, aren't you," she said. "Did you follow me here?"

Nene put the cat down again and looked around for Peter-san. He wasn't there, which worried her for an instant, but then she heard water flowing. She went to the bathroom door; it was the shower. He was still with her. Of course he was. Why would he abandon her?

Nene turned around. The *chanoma,* the living room, was untidy. No, worse than that, it was a mess. Peter-san's desk was littered with papers and items of clothing adorned the back of every chair. The *daidokoro,* the kitchen, was still dirty, with unwashed plates and other utensils in the *araiba,* the sink. How could he live this way? She had seen it the day before, but then she had been concerned with other matters.

Her stomach growled. Yesterday, Peter-san had shown her how to use all the cooking machines, as if that were his expectation of what a woman should know. Despite being fascinated by how much easier life had become, she was more than just someone who would cook and clean. Father had always impressed upon her that she was born to discover, to learn, to understand. What would he think of his daughter now?

"Proud, he would be so proud," Nene said to herself.

He would want her to be brave, though. If she could not go home to him, as she was beginning to realize might be her fate, then she would have to find her place in this world.

Mother had come to her during the night, within her dreams as she sometimes did. *'Do not be afraid, my child,'* she had said. Nene had reached out for her, but *ka-chan* had slipped beyond her grasp. Nene had found comfort, though, in her presence, and reassurance in her words.

Yes, today was a new day, and Nene knew what she must do.

***

It wasn't Peter's record for his longest ever shower, but it was pretty close. That was when he was fifteen and had spent an entire day following both his nose and his compass orienteering across the South Downs in the English summer rain. If you counted that and the proper shower in the locker rooms afterwards, well, it was a record that would never be broken.

His record for being an ignorant dumbass, on the other hand, was under constant threat. Yes, he had a duty to tell the world about Nene and the ERG, even if no-one would believe him. That was his clear, unarguable, incontestable scientific obligation. But what was he going to say about the similarities of the ERG he had observed in the cave and the 'thought-experiment' design he had put in his paper? People would think he was just shamelessly promoting himself, drawing attention to his ideas and his work, to get noticed.

The answer to that conundrum was obvious: *Don't say anything about it.*

That was the easy part. The hard part was going to be figuring out the connection. What if the ERG of the future *was* based on his ideas? That really would be something extraordinary. But the chances of Peter being at the center of this intersection of all these improbable coincidences was, as Spock might say, *'Approaching zero percent probability, Captain.'*

Peter sighed, deeply. He'd been going around in mental circles for far too long. It was time to make some breakfast and do his best to look after Nene while scouring the universe for echoes of traversable wormholes.

He finished dressing and opened the bathroom door. "Oh," he said.

The single-guy disaster that made for a home had been transformed; discarded clothing placed neatly on the sofa, the papers on his desk stacked in an orderly pile, the mess in the sink gone. Nene had cooked, too. Breakfast was ready on the kitchen table, and it looked a lot more appetizing than the meal he had prepared the previous day. She'd even grilled the fish.

"A clean home will help calm your mind," said Nene.

"And bring you joy," Peter replied.

"Of course. Now, shall we eat?"

Peter went over to the kitchen table. "Real Edo cooking," he said. "It looks delicious. And you figured out how to use the grill." He pointed, just to make sure Nene knew what he was referring to.

"You showed me yesterday, do you not remember?"

"I do, yes, but, you know, it's a modern thing, quite new for you, I thought–"

"You are surprised that a three-hundred-year girl can learn about your world so quickly?"

Nene said it with a smile, but even so it took Peter a few seconds to realize that she was teasing him.

"I think you can do anything you put your mind to," he said. He meant it too, even if Nene didn't quite catch his meaning.

"*Dozo,*" she said, gesturing for them both to sit.

Peter sat, picked up his chopsticks. "*Itadakimasu.*"

"*Itadakimasu,*" Nene echoed.

Peter felt Nene's disapproving gaze as he dug into his rice bowl.

"In my world, this is how we eat rice," she said, holding her bowl in her left hand.

Peter knew that; he just preferred to leave the bowl on the table. "Sorry," he said, picking it up in the correct manner.

"I thought all Englishmen were gentlemen," Nene said, teasing him again.

"Once, perhaps. A few hundred years ago."

"And from now, too."

"I'll do my best," Peter replied, gently teasing her back.

Nene smiled.

Ye Gods, he had never seen anything like it, like her. The way her eyes looked straight into the depths of his being, the soul of his existence, the inner realms of his consciousness.

Stay focused, he urged himself.

"I am sorry for the way I was last night," Nene said.

"It's OK, Nene," he replied. "All of this must be very difficult for you."

"Yes, it is. But I wanted to ask, is it far from here to go Edo, I mean, to Tokyo, in your... what is that?" She pointed to the roof of his Mini, just visible through a side window.

"My car. *Kuruma* in Japanese. And no, it's not so far."

"I should like to see where I live. Where I once lived. I thought it might help me to remember."

"Good idea," Peter said, wondering why he hadn't thought of it himself.

"But first, I should like to see the mountain where you found me."

"You mean Mount Nyukasa?" he said, suddenly realizing he'd forgotten to pick up the fucking enormous bolt-cutters.

"Yes, Nyukasa-san. Is it far from here?"

Peter accessed his mental map.

"Well, it's about two hours that way," he said, pointing northwest. "Then two and a half that way to Tokyo," he pointed east. "Then, about an hour and a half back here."

"So quick!"

"It is?"

***

The sky was one of those late October cloudless seas of blue that Peter loved. Warm, sunny, and beautiful, he'd always considered Japan to have the best autumn anywhere in the world, at least when there were no late season typhoons around. It was the reason he'd agreed to buy the convertible in the first place.

"It's a beautiful day," he said. "Shall we take the roof down?"

Nene tilted her head. Peter liked the way she did that when she didn't understand.

"Watch this." He lifted the small rocker switch that moved the sunroof back, then lifted it a second time to lower the assembly itself into the space behind the back seats. Nene watched the entire operation unfold. Or fold, if you were going to be accurate.

"Fully automatic," he said.

Nene smiled that smile of hers.

"We need to put on our seat-belts." Peter reached back across his shoulder and demonstrated. "Pull here, and then put this bit in here." He clicked the buckle into place. "Like that."

"Like this?" Nene pulled too hard, inadvertently activating the inertia-reel mechanism and jamming the seat belt.

"Here, let me help you with that."

Peter leant across and released the lock by pushing Nene's wrist back a few centimeters. He felt the same electric pulse from her soft skin as he had before, this time compounded by the proximity of their bodies and the brush of her hair on his arm.

"There you go," he said as fixed her buckle. He quickly sat back. "And you'll need these." He reached into the glove box. There were two pairs of sunglasses, his and Mariko's old ones. He put his on and handed the other pair to Nene.

"Sunglasses. To protect your eyes," he said.

Nene fumbled them on. Peter pulled the passenger-side sun visor down and opened the slider to reveal the small vanity mirror.

"There you go," said, trying to hide his all-too obvious amazement at how quickly Nene could be transformed into a twentieth century woman.

Nene repositioning the sunglasses until she was satisfied with her look. Definitely a modern girl, Peter thought. He hit the starter button and reversed out from under the car porch.

"OK," he said. "Let's go."

***

In all of her life, Nene had never known such wonder, such amazement, such joy – and such speed!

The world rushed past so fast she had to wrap her long hair around herself to stop the wind from blowing it everywhere. She didn't mind and did not care; not even riding the fastest horse could have been so exhilarating.

Peter pushed a 'switch,' as he called it, and the glass window beside her rose up by itself.

"Is that better?" he said.

"A little," she replied, though in truth she preferred the rush of air on her face. But at least this way she could hear his voice.

"Let's have some sounds," he said.

Peter pushed another switch. No, not a *switch*, that one was a *button*. Music filled the car.

"Bon jourvee," he said. Nene recognized the French word, although his pronunciation was incorrect.

"It is very loud," Nene said.

"Sorry. Shall I turn it down, make it quieter?"

"No, I don't mind. I like it." She did too, although it was hard to make out the words that the singer was singing; something about a prayer.

***

There were many other cars like theirs on the roads, of all sorts of shapes, sizes and colours, but they all kept their roofs on, despite the most beautiful sunshine. They drove past a big, noisy one with huge wheels. The man inside looked down at her and nodded. Nene smiled back at him.

"That's called a truck," Peter said. "And that thing over there is a train," Peter pointed to a long orange snake on a metal road in the valley. "It goes all the way to Tokyo. Eventually."

A man on a two wheeled machine roared past them. "And that's a motorcycle," Peter said, "going way too bloody fast."

"How does it not fall down?"

"Well," he said, "in the case of a bicycle, which is one of those things without an engine, people used to think it was gyroscopic precession of the front wheel, but I read a paper a few weeks ago where that view was being challenged by..." Peter stopped. "Too complicated?"

Nene laughed. "You often use words that I do not know."

"Sorry. I'll show you when we get back home." He pointed ahead. "There's a tunnel coming. It'll get pretty noisy, so don't worry."

"OK," she said.

He was right; it was noisy inside the tunnel, and dark, too. She copied Peter and took off her *sunglasses.*

"The air smells so bad in here." Nene had to shout to make herself heard.

"Yeah, I know. That's one of the problems of modern times. It's called pollution."

Nene could barely make out his words, but she could see the end of the tunnel and would ask him later. Until then she would listen to the music, but the singer was even harder to understand than before.

They exited the tunnel into bright sunlight. Peter had his sunglasses ready and put them on. Nene did the same. When it came to the next tunnel, she'd be ready, too.

***

The green signs above the road said they had arrived at Otsuki JCT on the Chuo Expressway and were about to head west towards Nagoya and Nagano. The east road, on the other hand, would take them to Tokyo.

"It means junction," Peter replied when she asked him the meaning of JCT.

"You can follow where we are on this. It's called a GPS, but it's basically just a map. If you turn this controller thing, you can zoom in and out."

Peter turned the *controller thing* – the map changed. "That little triangle is us. Why don't you have a go yourself?"

"It's quite wonderful!" Nene said, as the map changed under her fingertips – so different compared to the ones that adorned the walls in her father's library.

Peter turned another controller. "This one does the music," he said. "You can turn it down if it's too loud."

Nene turn the controller to the right. The music became louder. "I like it!" she said.

"Yeah, me too."

Nene rather liked the way Peter smiled when he said that.

***

The drive to Nyukasa-san took an hour and forty-eight minutes, during which time Nene discovered she liked the music of Bonne Journee very much, less so Aceey Deecy, but her favourite was Eva Casydee, whose words continued to touch her heart.

The journey had taken them past towns and villages, the names of most of which she did not know, save for Kofu-Shi and Suwa-ko, near Matsumoto – although they turned off towards the mountain fifteen *kilometers* before that famous lake.

There were several *factories* along the way that made smoke, the pollution that Peter spoke of. Didn't the people of this day care about their world? And some parts, especially Kofu city, seemed so crowded, the houses stretching for miles. The landscape on other parts of the journey, though, was wonderful.

Yes, Nene concluded, a car is a marvellous way to see the splendour of Japan, especially when it could bring you to the top of a mountain in no time at all, from where the view down the valley towards Fuji-san was astonishingly beautiful.

"It is my first time to be this high," she said as they stood at the edge of the '*Yatsugatake View-Point*' a hundred meters below the summit. Or as Peter had estimated, about a hundred and fifty times the length of her arm.

"Second," he said.

"Second?"

"You were here a couple of days ago, remember?"

"A little. But that is why we came here, is it not, to help me remember?"

"And do you?"

Nene pointed to the cave. "It was night, and you carried me out through there, to your car, which was here, just as it is now."

"What about before that?"

"You found me in the cave," she said.

"No, I mean, before then. Can you remember anything else?"

Nene shut her eyes. The mountain breeze caressed her hair and cooled her face. She searched her mind, letting images come and go as they wished, neither stopping them nor questioning them. But no memories came beyond those she had already shared with Peter. It had not worked, coming to this place.

"I cannot," she said. "I'm sorry, to have made you bring me here for nothing."

"It's not nothing," he said. "Every little thing is important. And later, in Tokyo, well, there might be something there that will help you remember."

Peter wandered into the middle of the road. He was quiet for a while, staring at the cave entrance, as if searching for something.

"You know," he said, turning to face her. "When I parked the car that day, right there where it is now, I still don't know why I did it. I mean, I just had this feeling that I should. And then I went in, and it was so dark. And you were in there, trapped inside, right in the middle of the mountain. It was like, I don't know, like I was supposed to find you, as if-"

Nene recognized the sound from the journey on the expressway and immediately sensed the danger. She leaped towards Peter and threw herself upon him before he even knew what was happening. As they fell, she twisted herself beneath him to protect his head from the hardness of the road.

Together, they slammed to the ground as the sound rushed past, no more than half the length of her arm away. With a loud screech, like an owl at night, the motorcycle slid to a stop.

"Bakayaro!" the rider shouted, then sped away.

Peter rolled to one side, got to his feet, and pulled Nene up by her hand so firmly their bodies slammed together.

Embarrassed, they both took a step back.

"Are you all right?"

"I am fine, thank you," she answered.

"Thank you," he said. "That could have been a bit bloody nasty."

"You must not lose your awareness, Peter-san," she said. "It is very important."

"Yeah, I can see that." He started dusting the dirt from her back. "You're covered in crap," he said.

Nene let his hands touch her.

"It's everywhere," he said.

Her breath quickened as his fingers ran through her hair. "I can do it myself," Nene said, stepping away from his reach before clearing away the remainder herself.

"Is it all gone?" she asked.

"All gone."

"Then, may we now go to Tokyo?"

"Yes, of course we can," he said.

Nene got back into Peter's car and fastened her seat belt. Later she would ask him about the words he had used, but she sensed they were not the kind of polite language she should study.

And later, much later, when they were back home and she could quieten her mind, she would try to understand how this blue-eyed Englishman from the future could be having such an effect upon her.

***

The memory of Nene's hair lingered long in the tips of Peter's fingers as they headed down the mountain road.

She'd risked herself to pull him out of the way with that Jiu-Jitsu throw-thing she'd used. The bike had been going way too fast, but it had been his own dumb fault for standing in the middle of a blind curve wondering where the fucking enormous bolt cutters had gotten to, and for being too unaware to have heard the approaching machine. Either way, Nene may have just saved his life, at Mount Nyukasa, where he had saved hers.

The irony of it all.

The GPS showed almost three hours to the center of Tokyo. It was going to be a long day, but there was plenty of time for him to figure out just what the hell he was going to do next.

Fourteen

The journey to Tokyo was long, but Nene had been able to sleep due to the *reclining* seat button by her left thigh. Peter had told her where it was, rather than leaning across to show her.

Something is happening between us. He feels it too.

She must prepare herself, so that she would be able to step back, to walk away when the time came to return to her father. Yes, she would need to be ready for that day.

Nene wasn't ready for Tokyo, though. Nothing could have prepared her for that. The modern-day Edo City was the most extraordinary thing she had ever seen. It started from when Peter had woken her just before the sign that said the city was fifteen kilometers away, less than a day's walk. In the distance she had seen enormous buildings that seemed to touch the sky. Giant metal structures, like those in Peter's garden, carried long lines for hundreds, possibly even thousands of *Cho. Power lines,* Peter called them. Nene quickly calculated that there must be about ten *Cho* in one *kilometer*, and four kilometers in one *Ri*. She was beginning to adapt to her new life.

No, my life is at home, with my father.

***

The *traffic* was *heavy*, which was why they were moving so slowly. It gave Nene the time to look around at everything there was to see. And there was so much! So many buildings, cars, trucks, lights and people on the streets below, and so many giant TVs on the sides of buildings.

They were at Shinjuku, Peter said, but it was so different, so changed from the *Naitō-Shinjuku* of her world that she recognized nothing about it. It was gone, lost to the past, replaced by those huge, huge buildings. She was about to ask Peter how tall they were when a loud roar pulled her eyes skyward. A giant bird was flying above the buildings. No, not a bird, it was a machine. She looked at Peter.

"It's an airplane," he said. "A bit like that helicopter yesterday. People fly all over the world in those things. One of them brought me here to Japan."

Nene watched it fly away.

"Where is it going?"

"To an airport, Haneda, over there." Peter pointed towards the afternoon sun. "That's where they land, people get on and off, that kind of thing."

"You came from *igirisu*, from England, in one like that?"

"Yep. Took thirteen hours, too."

"Only half a day? From England?" Nene's eyes were open in child-like amazement. "So fast."

"Oh yes. Pretty quick. Unlike this bloody traffic." They were next to a slope that led down to the streets below. "Let's get off here, shall we?" Peter said.

He drove the car down the slope, through a gate that said 'ETC' and on to the streets of Tokyo. The expressway carried on above their head, supported by huge columns of metal and stone; *concrete*, as Peter called it.

He took Nene on a tour, a guided journey around her unrecognizable youth; Akasaka, Shibuya, Tokyo, Marunouchi, Ginza. Nothing was as she had known it. She didn't even know the place names of this new city, except for Tameike-sanno, which she had known as separate areas. The waterways and rivers were gone, covered by roads or moved underground, according to Peter, as part of the changes after the big war seventy years before. She would read about that later in the history book, she decided, when they returned to his house.

Some parts of the city she liked, such as the tall buildings, the *skyscrapers* that reached the clouds, and the way green and red lights told the cars when to stop, and when to go. Other parts seemed dirty, crowded, filled with grey buildings that had no beauty and blocked the view of the mountains, even of Fuji-san. Nonetheless, it was fascinating and at times enchanting, despite the pollution and the absence of trees. There was something magical about this city. If she had to stay, if there was no way back home, then perhaps she could learn to live this in new world.

Father, please do not worry about me. I am safe here, but I long to see your face again.

"What is that?" Nene asked, as the tallest of all the buildings came back into view, much closer now than it had been before.

"It's called Tokyo Skytree, and it's the tallest structure in all Japan." Peter pointed to the top of the tower. "Do you want to go up, and get a bird's eye view of Tokyo?"

"We can go up there?"

"Yes. And eat something, you must be starving. I know I am."

"I should like that very much."

***

They sat at a small table next to a window that sloped downwards at such an angle that all of Tokyo was visible.

"The view is better at night," Peter said. "You can see all the building lights. It's pretty good, then, actually."

"It is quite wonderful," Nene said. "I cannot believe that people can build such things. How high are we now?"

"The secret's in the name."

Nene tilted her head.

"I mean, it's in the name of this café."

Nene looked towards the central *hashira,* the huge pillar that ran through the middle of the restaurant.

"Skytree café three four oh," she said. "Does that mean we are three hundred and forty meters high?"

"We are indeed. And how's your high-altitude vegetable curry?"

Nene glanced down at her plate. "It is quite delicious."

She'd lied, but it wasn't a bad lie, and she had no desire to hurt Peter's feelings. For their next meal she would ask to go somewhere more akin to her tastes. Or, better than that, she would cook for him once again. But Nene didn't mind the food, not when the view was so wondrous, so magnificent. It was as if she were on top of the world.

"Do you recognize anywhere?" Peter asked.

"Not one thing."

"That's Shinjuku, that's Shibuya," Peter pointed as he spoke. "That's Roppongi, and that tall building is Mori Tower, which used to be the tallest in Japan. Over there is Ueno, that's the zoo, and that's Tokyo station, and if you follow the road down you get to Ginza, then Shinagawa. And if you keep going you get to Yokohama, over there. And that red thing there is Tokyo Tower, which about fifty years ago was the tallest structure in Japan. It's down near Zojoji Temple, I think it's called. Do you know it?"

"Of course."

Nene, as she had sometimes seen *ka-chan* do with her father, set her elbows on the table and rested her chin on her interlocking fingers, causing her to naturally lean closer to Peter. She knew she was crossing that invisible barrier that separated people from each other, but the pull from his smile and his blue eyes was so strong.

"It's like a dream," she said. "To be here, in this world, like this, with you, Peter-san."

What was she saying?

"I mean," she continued, "to be here, three hundred years in my future. It seems I should wake up at any time and find myself back home, on my futon, alone in my room. How could that be?"

Peter looked away towards Fuji-san. She'd embarrassed him, and herself a little, too.

"I don't know what happened, Nene. Not yet," he said, turning his eyes back to her. "But it's not a dream, definitely not a dream. Unless it's mine."

Nene kept her eyes upon his.

"OK," Peter said, clearly trying to conceal his awkwardness. "Let's finish lunch and get moving, shall we? Lots more to see and do."

***

"Here we are." Peter stopped the car at red lights. "Recognize it?" he asked, pointing.

Nene hadn't at first, but when she saw the *kanji* on the high stone wall, she knew where she was.

"Hie Jinja," she said.

They left the car in an underground area and headed towards the shrine. Nene stopped at the *torii*, the gate that heralded the main entrance. In her time it had been made of wood from giant *hinoki* trees, but this one was made of concrete.

"My father's house was just there," she said. "Just a short walk down that hill. When I was a child I played in these streets. They are so different now." She turned to Peter. "How did you know to bring me here?" she asked.

"It's one of the oldest shrines in Tokyo," he said. "And it's in Akasaka, where you once lived. It was quite obvious, really."

Nene smiled. He was so kind, thinking of her like that, she wanted to tell him, but first there was…

She felt dizzy. Not as if she would fall, but a lightheadedness that caught her off guard. She placed a hand on the *torii* to steady herself.

"Nene, are you OK?"

Peter was talking, she could hear his words, but they were unclear, as if through water. Then, without warning, the mechanical, machine-like sounds of Tokyo were gone, replaced by the gentle noises of people talking, moving. The *torii* faded from grey to brown, from concrete to wood. The buildings surrounding them shrank, the glass disappeared. Where there was once form, there was now void. No, not nothing, not emptiness; trees, familiar streets and houses.

She was back home, back in Edo City.

Joyous laughter followed small children as they ran in circles around a tall, fair-skinned man, dressed in the strangest clothes; a white top, with unusual blue *hakama* leading down to the oddest red and white shoes.

He turned around and smiled at her.

It was Peter.

"Nene!"

He was calling out to her.

"Nene!"

The touch of his hand on her shoulder.

"Nene?"

She was back in Tokyo city.

"Are you all right?"

"Yes," she said. "I am fine."

"You sort of went somewhere for a moment there."

"I was remembering," she said, truthfully, now certain that it had been Peter in her dreams. There could be no doubt; and it wasn't just a dream.

He had been there!

She must tell him, but first she needed time to understand. Nene looked up towards the *jinja,* the shrine, at the top of the stone steps. It was calling out to her; she knew she must go inside.

"May we go in?" she asked, although it wasn't a request.

Peter followed her gaze. "Sure."

***

The shrine forecourt was unchanged, just as it had been since her childhood, but this day it was so much quieter; there were only a few people there. Nene bade Peter to clean his hands at the *temizuya,* the small water pavilion near the entrance. It seemed he had done this before and needed no guidance from her.

"Come," she said, and led the way to the *haiden* at the hall entrance.

"Do you have a coin?" she asked as they arrived at the *saisen-bako,* the box where those who wished to pray should first offer a small amount of money. Peter smiled. He had two coins ready. He offered one to her.

Nene checked the inscription. "Go-en, five yen," she said.

"Because it sounds like *go-en*, the word for good luck," he replied.

"You know these things well, Peter-san."

"I have my moments," he said.

Nene wasn't sure what he meant by that, but thought that, yes, perhaps he did. She gently dropped her five-yen coin into the box and pulled the rope to ring the bell that would summon the shrine deity. She bowed twice, clapped her hands twice, then silently prayed for *Kami-sama* to kindly tell her father that she was well, that she was unhurt, that she was living in an incredible world 300 years in the future, that she was being cared for by a blue-eyed man from *igirisu,* whom father would like, and not to worry about her – and that one day, she did not know when, she would see him again. And mother, too.

Nene bowed again and glanced to her left. Peter had prayed too, though it may have been from a sense of politeness, rather than…

The old tree!

The thought hit her with an almost physical intensity. Nene turned to her right. It should be behind the main building, in the far corner next to the *Sanno-inari* shrine. Was it still there? She headed through a short passageway towards where it had stood since before she was born. Peter followed.

There it was, almost unchanged, looking the same as it always had, except taller. She placed a palm on the trunk to feel its message.

"Nene?" Peter asked.

"This tree," she replied. "It was calling out to me. To come to it."

"Why?"

Nene stepped back. "I do not know."

"Perhaps it just a memory, a connection with your time, before you came here."

"Perhaps," Nene said, although the pull was stronger than that. There was something important here, but like the ephemeral sigh of a fragile thought she could not hear its voice, could not grasp its meaning.

She turned to face Peter. Two well-dressed young women were walking past. One of them said something to the other, and they dipped their heads to conceal their childish amusement. Nene knew what it was. She looked down at her pink clothing, the *tracksuit* that Peter had bought for her. It was so different, so plain, so ordinary, so unlike the clothing that women of this time were wearing.

Peter noticed. "I have an idea," he said.

***

It didn't take Peter long to figure out that his brilliant idea was going to put a big dent in his less-than-brilliant credit card.

He'd brought Nene to the Lumine department store in the Shinjuku station complex, which had seemed like the right place to be, except that Nene had insisted on trying on just about everything in each and every one of the small boutiques on the ladies' fashion floor. The problem was, there were so many of the things they'd be there for hours at this rate.

He couldn't blame her. For Nene it was a fantastic new world of modern styles and colours; a shopper's paradise in any era – enhanced by her fascination with the doors that opened just by standing in front of them, and the stairs that moved by themselves. Motion sensors and escalators, he'd explained. In fact, he rather liked accompanying her, and whenever she was in a changing room it gave him the opportunity to use his iPhone to check his OneDrive, where he'd set up a live feed of the log from his detector. Not strictly live, to be accurate, the file was updated every three minutes, and then only if there had been any activity. Needless to say, there was nothing.

"How is my look?"

Peter glanced up from the bench where he'd been patiently waiting, surrounded by bags of newly acquired shoes and clothing. Nene had just emerged from behind the curtains in jeans, white T-shirt, fake red leather jacket and white Reeboks. Of all the items they had bought, those Nene was wearing now suited her best. A fellow foreigner shopping with his partner was staring, trying not to make it obvious.

I know that feeling.

"How do *I* look."

"How do I look?" Nene repeated.

"It suits you," Peter said, completely failing to say what he really wanted to say. He placed another dent in his plastic, and they exited the boutique.

"There is one more thing I would like to do," Nene said.

"Sure. And what would that be?" Peter replied, relieved to be nearing the end of today's particular trial of strength.

"I saw it earlier. At the end of this floor, over there."

Peter knew what she meant. "Ah, yes. There. But do you know what to do? It may be different from your time."

"I am still a woman, am I not?"

"Of course you are," he said.

***

The lady at the Lancôme booth was only too willing to help Nene decide on an entire portfolio, or collection, or set, or whatever it was that women called their makeup.

Peter sat and waited once again, as he had been doing for the past several hours, while the Lancôme lady applied the undercoat and the various topcoats that went with it. Nene had her back to Peter and was too far away for him to hear what they were talking about. He wasn't too concerned. In the car he'd advised her to pretend that she was studying the history of the Edo period. That way she could talk about her 'speciality' without raising too many suspicions.

The Lancôme lady was captivated by Nene's hair, though, that much he could see. The fact that it reached down to her knees might have been the reason. The lady was figuring out how to tie it half-way using some sort of tie-thing, whatever it was. He really had no vocabulary to describe what was going on in the Lancôme booth.

Stick to what you know, he told himself.

So, what *did* he know? Not much beyond a couple of wormholes, most likely created by a destroyed ERG wormhole maker somewhen in the future, plus a girl from the past whom he'd found in a cave and then decided to take shopping. *Shit,* the single greatest discovery of his life was sitting on a stool choosing makeup. No, Nene wasn't a 'discovery,' he'd already decided that, but he needed answers to all those hard questions that plagued him, answers that weren't going to be found on the fifth floor of a department store in Shinjuku.

Maybe he wasn't even asking the right questions. In which case, what were the right questions? Who made the ERG? Sure, that was one of them. Was there a paradox forming? That was another. Was the ERG based on the design outline he'd included in his paper? That was a good question. What was Jane going to do about Nene? That was a very good question. Did he have the slightest bloody idea what he'd gotten himself into? An even better question, that one. Was he going to solve this little mystery before his self-imposed Wednesday deadline?

"That, Peter Walker, is *the* question." He said it out loud, but no one was close enough to hear.

The Lancôme lady gave him a polite wave; they'd finished. Nene stood up and turned around and took his breath away; completely, utterly, totally.

"How do I look?" she asked.

"Very… nice." What he meant to say was, *'You are the most beautiful woman I have ever seen in my life.'*

"Thank you," Nene replied.

There was a moment of stillness, a recognition of something growing but not yet understood.

Nene broke the silence. "What shall we do next?"

Peter recovered his composure. He'd had the idea earlier when he was scouring Google Maps. "First, I'll settle-up here, and then I was thinking, there's a place not far from here I think you might know. Why don't we go there?"

"I would like that very much," Nene said, even though Peter hadn't yet told her where it was.

***

The Koishikawa Kuraken Garden was started by Mito Yorifusa in 1629 and completed by his son Mito Mitsukuni, with advice from the Chinese scholar Zhu Zhiyu, incorporating elements of both Chinese and Japanese taste. Or so it said on the tourist board at the main entrance.

The gardens themselves were an oasis in the center of Tokyo. Peter had never been there before, the nearest was when he'd been to a U2 concert at the Tokyo Dome next door, the home of the Tokyo Giants baseball team. He'd thought it might be redundant bringing Nene here, having already taken her to the Hie Shrine, but it was his way of trying to get Nene to re-connect with her past, as if doing so might trigger a few synapses and help her to remember what had happened in the moments leading up to the wormhole opening in her house.

A wormhole in Nene's home? The notion was still bizarre, but there had to be a reason for it, and he needed to know. At least, that had been his original plan. Since the Lancôme event, however, he was becoming increasingly distracted.

"When I was just a child I came here with my mother," Nene said, interrupting his thoughts. "Then, after she died, I did not come again. It is as if nothing has changed. And yet, everything has changed."

"Do you remember her? Your mother, I mean?"

"Her face is fading from my memory now. I remember her by this."

Nene raised her wrist to show her bracelet, which was no more than a leather strap decorated with Kanji. Peter had been meaning to ask her about the inscription.

"What does it say?" he asked.

"The winds of the heavens shift suddenly, as does human fate."

"That's true. Is it Japanese?"

"Chinese, of course."

"Of course."

They walked on, arriving at one of the small wooden bridges that spanned the gap between small bodies of water.

"And what of you, Peter-san? How is it that you came to be in my country?"

Good point. He'd been so focused on Nene that he hadn't said much about himself.

"Well, I was basically trying to show that quantum entanglement of separated particles is contingent on space-time harmonics that…. Sorry, that might be a little difficult to…What I mean is, at a fundamental level, I was trying to show that everything in the universe is connected. The planets, the Sun, the stars, that tree, that bird, those Coy. Everything you see, and everything you don't see, it's all connected. Since the beginning of the universe. Or before then, even."

They stopped in the middle of the bridge.

"Of course." Nene said. "We are all connected. Each one to each one another."

"Exactly. And Japan was the only place where I could find that kind of role. Everywhere else I tried was closed. Well, for me it was. But, anyway, that's all finished and now I'm trying to find something in Switzerland, in Europe, but it seems that's not going to happen. At least I still have my private research, you know, tunnels through time, that sort of thing."

"I envy the people of this time. You can go anywhere you want in the world."

"Not anywhere, but most places, yes."

They stared at the water surface for a while, the modern Tokyo landscape reflected in its gentle undulations.

"Your friend Jane. Is she a doctor?" Nene asked.

"Yes, she is. A good one, too."

"In my time, women cannot be doctors."

"Well, things have changed a bit since then."

"Why is she in Japan? Did she follow you here?"

"Well, she was in Africa, helping to stop the return of a virus, a thing called Ebola. She got ill herself, recovered, but it affected her, and after that she just wanted time away. So she came here and stayed. I think because she met that bloke who came with her. That man, I mean."

"You mean Taniguchi-san?"

Peter nodded.

"I know his family," Nene said. "I attended schooling with his great grandmother. Hana-chan. She is, she was, my good friend,"

"Really? Now that is a coincidence. But that's probably his great, great, great, great, grandmother. Maybe a couple more greats somewhere in there, too. But wouldn't she be his great aunt? I mean, she would have married, and then taken her husband's family name, wouldn't she?"

"Her husband took the Taniguchi family name."

"I see."

"There were no sons. Only daughters were born in that family."

"Someone to carry on the family name. That makes sense."

A pair of ducks landed on the pond. Peter spotted three turtles on a rock, basking in the sunlight. Or were they tortoises? He was never sure which was which.

"There was someone in your life, for a while, since you have been here," Nene said, making it a statement rather than a question.

"For a while, yes, but that's over now. How did you know?"

"It is not difficult to see such things. Did she not break your heart?"

This was an interesting line of questioning. "Er, no, not really. We had drifted apart. I mean, well maybe a little. But I had my work and... I don't know, Nene, I've never really had much good fortune in that area. What about you? With male admirers, that is. I'm sure there must have been many."

"You mean, did I have a lover?"

That wasn't what he meant, not at all. Actually, yes it was. "Well, that's not exactly the kind of question an English gentleman would ask," he replied.

"My father arranged for many introductions, but he could not find anybody suitable, so I stayed at home to help with his work. I was happy to do that. Even so, I began to think it was to be my fate to live my life on my own."

Good, they were back on safer, more familiar ground. "Do you believe in fate, Nene?"

"When mother died, grandmother said we must accept our fate, accept that what is to be for us, will be. And now my fate has brought me here, with you."

"Actually, I think it was a traversable wormhole. A light tunnel."

"Then it was my fate to be brought here, by the trav- reversable wormhole."

"Traversable."

"Traversable. And your fate has brought you here, too, Peter-san."

Peter pointed to a Jumbo jet overhead, on its way to Haneda.

"Well, like I said earlier, it was one of those things. But do you really think you have to accept your fate? Maybe the truth is that we just choose our own path, rather than it being decided for us."

"I would choose to go home to be with my father if I could. Is there a way for me to do that?"

"I don't think so, Nene. Not until the machine is built, whenever that will be. Unless someone comes looking for you, and no one has done that yet."

"And yet you say this is choice." Nene turned her gaze away. "I stood here many times, in this same place, holding my mother's hand. If I look this way, I see my world. If I look this way," she turned to face him, "I see yours."

For the second time that day Nene's eyes glazed over, as if she were looking through infinity at the entirety of the universe beyond. She was remembering something, again. Should he push her, to try and encourage those memories to show themselves, or wait for it to happen naturally? No, if the episodes of his youth had taught him one thing, it was better to wait. He'd hated it when the psychotherapists had pushed him back then, and he didn't want to do that to Nene now.

Let it be. Let it all be. All of it.

"Nene, are sure you're OK?" he said.

She returned from wherever she had been.

"It is nothing," she said.

Peter knew it wasn't nothing. He took a step forward, breaking through that unseen barrier that was between them. He placed a hand on her arm.

"Don't worry," he said. "I'll look after you."

She nodded in silent reply. He moved closer until they were inches apart, her incredible eyes staring into his own. He gently brushed her hair away from her face and rested his fingertips on the back of her neck.

A police siren split the air. Nene, surprised at the sound, stepped backward.

"It's just a police car. Nothing to worry about." Peter said, realizing the moment had been lost.

"May we go back now?" Nene said. "I am so very tired."

"Yes, of course," Peter replied.

I shouldn't have done that, he thought, as he led the way to the garden exit.

Fifteen

Nene spent the entire journey sleeping on the back seat. Peter wasn't even sure if she was really asleep, or just pretending to be to avoid having to say anything.

Shit. He had been such an idiot; a complete, brainless, stupid, idiotic idiot. What had he been thinking? What was he thinking now? Who the hell did he think he was, anyway? The same dumb questions whirled around inside his dumb head for the whole two hours it took them to plod through the traffic and arrive back home. It was approaching eight-fifteen by the time he opened the front door.

Without saying a word, Nene went into the bathroom to change.

You've really messed the whole thing up, you moron.

He went into the bedroom and put the shopping at the foot of her bed, then removed the guest futon from the wardrobe and spread it out on the lounge floor.

"Good night, Peter-san," Nene said, when she emerged from the bathroom.

"Good night, Nene," he replied as Nene closed the bedroom door, leaving him alone with his whiteboard and its useless spacetime equations.

None of that lot is going to help one iota.

Peter went out through the side door into the garden. The night was cloudless, the milky way stretched across the entire sky.

He stared at the universe, as if the answers were out there.

***

Nene watched Peter through the gap in the curtains, stepping back into the shadows when he turned towards her.

She could still feel the whispering touch of his hand on her neck, could still feel the intensity of his blue eyes looking straight through to the depths of her soul. If she had not seen her father by the pond in the gardens, if she had not felt his sadness, the loneliness of a life spent not knowing his only daughter's fate, if that strange sound had not come between them just then…

"Let your first be your only." Grandmother had once told her.

"But grandmother, how will I know?" Nene had asked.

"Your heart will tell you, Nene," Grandmother had said.

Nene sat on the bed and listened to her heart.

***

Peter stared at Jupiter, which was exceptionally bright in the night sky, even for the time of year.

"Shut up, Walker," he said.

Did he really think he could put everything out of his mind by indulging himself in a bit of backyard astronomy? Of course not. So why do it? Why not just go straight back inside, knock on the bedroom door and…

"Shut up." He said it again.

A distant flash of lightning flickered across the night sky. Peter counted the seconds, waiting for the thunderclap to arrive. When it did not only had he lost count, but the boom itself was almost inaudible. It must have been fifty kilometers away, if not more. He checked the weather app on his iPhone. Nothing was showing, which meant the storm had just started; the rain radar was typically ten minutes behind the actual status.

More lightning, still a long, long way away.

Well, he wasn't going to hang around to see what was going to happen. He crouched down where the antennae cables went through the study wall, pulled the quick disconnection lever, then plugged the now free assembly into the earthing point he'd prepared for this kind of unhelpful weather. Even though the chances of the storm heading his way were fairly low, and with it the associated chance of a lightning strike on an antenna, it was better not to risk 1.21 gigawatts blasting the crap out of his contraption.

Another flash of lightning, still distant, now strangely blue, like the LEDs on the detector controller unit.

"Now that is odd."

But then again, it had been that way since the instant he'd detected that bloody wormhole.

***

Blow, winds, and crack your cheeks! rage! blow! You cataracts and hurricanoes, spout, Till you have drench'd our steeples, drown'd the cocks!

He'd memorized every syllable of King Lear as a bet when he was seventeen, or was it eighteen? Either way, showing off his powers of recall wasn't nearly as satisfying as being the top physicist in the school. The top in the whole of the South of England for that year, in fact, which would have made him eighteen and old enough to legally drink, although still months away from the need to shave.

All of which wasn't helping him much. The storm was, as the Bard so aptly put, cracking its cheeks. 'Rage' was insufficient; 'barbaric' would be far more appropriate, but that wouldn't fit the stanza for this particular monster.

The farmhouse was a hundred years old and solidly built, but even those thick walls were creaking with the strain. At times it was as if they were in the middle of a string of earthquakes. And that LED-blue lighting – he'd never seen the like of it before. Which part of the spectrum was that? It must be near the ultraviolet, around 400 nanometers.

Ultra-violent.

Yep, that was the right word.

CRACK! BOOM!

Shit! That one was right above the house, the flash strobing the swaying bamboo outside into a medieval mural of hell. Pebbles was already in her hiding place under the table by the wall. If things carried on like this much longer he'd be slipping off from the futon to join her.

Maybe he should check to see if Nene was all right, she must be just as half-scared shitless as he was. But if he did that, then what? Invite himself in? Was that what she would want him to do, what a woman from Edo would want him to do? It was what he wanted to do, of course, but after Nene had said nothing at all following the incident in the gardens, he couldn't be sure if-

"Peter-san."

Nene was standing next to him – he hadn't heard her approach.

"Hello," he said.

"Chotto, kowai desu."

"Yes, very scary."

Peter rolled back the duvet. Nene took the invitation without hesitation, and lay next to him, pressing herself close, an arm across his chest, her head on his shoulder.

CRACK! BOOM!

"Shit, that was close!" Peter exclaimed.

Nene pulled herself tighter.

"I do not think I wish to know the meaning of that word," she said.

"It means *kuso* in Japanese."

"Oh," she said.

KABOOMB!

The loudest, brightest, most intense thunderbolt of the night smashed into the earth meters from the window. The house filled with an intense pulse of light, the walls heaved with the shockwave and the flooring shook as if struck by Thor's hammer.

"Shit!" Nene exclaimed.

Peter laughed. What else was there to do in the middle of a storm when you're lying next to the most beautiful woman in the world? He was just thankful the strike hadn't been any closer, or they may well have been truly blinded by the power of the flash.

Then, without warning it abruptly went quiet, as if someone had hit the off-switch. They waited in silent anticipation as the clouds cleared, revealing the full moon in the night sky.

"Is it over?" Nene asked.

"I think so," Peter answered, wondering just what kind of freak storm that had been. He'd do some meteorological research in the morning. Right now he had other things to think about.

He ran his fingers through Nene's long, silky soft hair.

Don't rush. Let Nene decide.

Nene pressed herself closer. They lay together saying nothing, their hearts connecting, their minds entwining, the space between them no longer existing.

Nene broke the silence.

"When I came here, to this world, I was so scared, so confused, so alone in the dark. But I knew that if I should wait, then someone would come. And it was you, Peter. You. It was always you."

She had decided.

***

I float in the world between worlds.

My head is so light, unbound to the Earth. Each touch sends chills through my spine, as if cool air flows over my body, around me, through me. I shiver with each kiss, my back arches when…there, I never knew I could feel…

He is inside me. I wrap my legs around his back and pull him deeper. I am lost. I cannot control myself. I don't want to.

I never knew it would be like this.

Don't stop, don't ever stop.

My one, my only.

***

"What are you thinking?" Nene asked.

"I was thinking, what is Nene thinking?"

His voice flowed over her, through her, calming with its softness, soothing with its gentleness, guarding with its strength. Tomorrow she would tell him about her dreams, her visions of him in Edo. Peter would understand, he would know, he would find a way to explain. But tonight, this night, was about something else.

"Nene is wondering what her grandmother would say, if she could see us together like this."

"She would probably say it was our fate taking its course."

"And what would Peter say?"

Peter studied the snapshot of the night sky bounded by the living room window. *There are more things in heaven and earth, Horatio, than are dreamt of in your philosophy.* More of the Bard, but no one had ever said it better.

"Peter would argue," he said, "very scientifically, of course, with a bunch of sub-quantum calculations, mixed up with a touch of general relativity and a sniff of uncertainty principle, that the chances of him detecting a wormhole, then finding Nene inside a mountain cave, and then seeing a wormhole appear right in front of him, then bringing her home only to find that she knows the ancestors of his best friend's mister Incredibonk – all those convolutions, these unlikely coincidences, the probability all this could happen as it did, that I would find you like that. It just doesn't add up."

Nene raised her head from Peter's chest.

"I could not understand anything," she said. "Not one word."

"I'm beginning to wonder if maybe your grandmother was right."

"Of course she was. We were born in two different worlds, three hundred years apart, how else could we have found each other?"

Part Two:

Past & Future

Sixteen

Despite the rage of the storm there hadn't been any damage to Peter's antennae, nor to the garden itself, save for a couple of small branches that had snapped on the cherry tree in the far corner by the road.

Peter tugged hard at the bigger of the two, managing to pull it free, and set it on the grass. The small one was too high for him to reach without his stepladder. He'd get to that later. In the meantime, the first order of the day was to reconnect the antennae cable, which he should have done already but got distracted looking for evidence of the lighting strike, of which he found none, save for the broken branches, which had been due to the wind anyway. The absence of scorch-marks, either on the earthing point or the earth itself, troubled him. Just what kind of storm was that?

He reconnected the cable assembly, then peered through the study window. His detector was on and functioning properly. At least it looked that way from where he was standing.

His iPhone buzzed. He pulled the device from his jean pocket:

Stop ignoring me!

It was Jane's sixth message since yesterday. He'd let her stew a few more hours, then call. He wondered how she'd react to his latest story. Shit, he was still trying to figure out his own reaction. He put the phone back into his pocket.

He retrieved the stepladder from the storage box under the car porch and headed back to the cherry tree.

***

Nene watched Peter climb the steps to reach the upper of the two broken branches of the *sakura*.

She was wearing the pink tracksuit and had just finished making their morning tea, the one from Twinings of London, and would take it to him so they could sit in the garden with the morning sun. It was a beautiful day, the most beautiful she had ever known.

Because of what happened in the night.

She smiled. She knew she would never be the same again. There was so much to say; about her dreams of him, how she will stay here, with him, forever. She knew now that was her fate, to be here, in this time, in this place, with Peter.

She picked up the two cups, slipped on her new shoes and went out through the garden door with Nya-Nya at her heels. Peter was pulling hard at the branch. It wouldn't come free; it was almost comical.

My one, my only.

Nene stopped and stared in sudden realization. Those clothes he was wearing – that white shirt, those blue trousers, like the *jeans* he had bought for her yesterday. And those red and white shoes, like the Reebok ones she liked so much.

He was dressed the same way he had been in her visions of Edo.

***

The pulsating, piercing shrill from Peter's Mac was loud enough to be heard throughout the entire area. He had set it that way, channeled through his hi-fi, to ensure he'd catch an event wherever he was, indoors or outside.

Nene, alarmed by the sound, turned around. What she saw took her breath away. No more than ten steps away the air shimmered in a circle, like water rippling on the surface of a pond. And within the circle, dressed in a kimono, staring back at her, was the image of a man she knew beyond all others.

She dropped the cups.

"Chichi-ue," she gasped. Nene turned towards Peter. "It's my father!" she said.

"Nene!" Peter shouted as he jumped down from the stepladder. "Don't move!"

He rushed towards her, towards the wormhole, fifteen meters away. The opening shuddered, like a gong struck by an enormous mallet.

It was destabilizing!

"Nene!" he shouted again.

The collapse started before Peter was even halfway. The wormhole, unstable at its ERG core, lost both form and structure as vast amounts of negative energy clashed with quantum-level fluctuations in the exotic matter feed from the matter-antimatter reactor, producing a gravitational field of enough magnitude to create a local, short-field distortion of space-time and pull in any and all loose material within range.

Ten meters.

Pebbles was sucked in first.

Five meters.

Nene clawed at the air, but there was nothing for her to hold on to. Her fear-filled eyes found his. "Peter!"

Three meters.

She was gone.

"Nene!"

One meter.

The wormhole was closing. Peter dived in through the shrinking, swirling portal after her.

***

Everything was a twisting, turning, thundering cacophony of sound and intense, disorienting vibration.

"Peter!"

He heard Nene's voice but couldn't see her. He could hardly see anything as the vortex spun him around like a deranged thrill ride at a carnival for the insane. It was just as Nene had described it – a tunnel of pulsating, seemingly living tube of pure energy.

He called out to her. "Nene!"

"Peter!"

There she was!

Peter reached out a hand, too late – the vortex separated, sweeping Nene beyond his reach.

"Nene!"

She was gone.

***

He tumbled and churned, bouncing off the semi-solid, membrane-like walls like a rag doll in a tumble dryer, barely able to even hear his own thoughts screaming at him: *Ye gods, I'm inside a wormhole!*

The constant pulverizing knocked the wind out of him, and it was all he could do to curl into the fetal position and keep his hands covering his head. Any more of this onslaught and he'd lose consciousness.

Then, just when he thought he couldn't hold on any longer, the flow stabilized and his tumbling ceased. He was floating, yet moving fast, carried onwards by a force that he could not identify. At least he could see, think, evaluate, discover. The tunnel was four or five meters in diameter, with no discernible start nor end. Other wormholes were visible through the translucent wall, connected to a central, dark, turbulent sphere, all moving around like long grass in the wind. Beyond that there was nothing, only darkness.

He was in a different dimension, a hyperspace.

There was air inside the wormhole; it must have been sucked in at the portal opening.

The wormhole, in his garden, the storm, the cave, they were all connected.

The sphere passed behind him, beyond his sight. The turbulence increased, he was spinning again, like a tumbleweed in a desert gale. He crashed into the tunnel walls, ricocheting from one side to the other: a human ping-pong ball in a maniacal game of table tennis. He tried to grab hold of something, anything, but the soft walls were too smooth, too pure, too perfect for any handhold.

He was fighting for his life. Losing.

All was lost anyway.

He'd failed to protect Nene, and now they were separated. Gone forever.

Lost in time.

The air was thinning.

I can't breathe.

This was it; the end of everything that ever was, or ever will be.

A light, ahead! Everything was light in here, but this was different.

A portal opening!

The outlines of two figures, two shadow beings stared at him.

The flow stabilized; his velocity reduced.

He was through.

Peter crumpled to the solid, wooden floor. He looked up, his consciousness slipping away. As darkness covered him, he saw her.

"Nene?" he gasped.

Then everything went black.

Seventeen

Nene wretched uncontrollably, although her empty stomach had nothing to offer other than a foul-tasting pale green liquid.

She struggled to her feet and threw up once more, bending low to the long grass. It had been like this at the cave, and Nene knew it would soon pass. Nya-Nya was there too, sniffing at her ankles, seemingly less affected by their journey together.

Nene waited for her breathing to settle, then stood tall and wiped the spittle away from her mouth. She looked around. She was back in the garden, right where she had been pulled into the light tunnel. It was different, though; the grass was overgrown and uncared for, the *sakura* was taller, fuller - its two broken branches still broken - tall purple flowers lined the beds of the inner walls and the tall metal structures, Peter's 'antennas,' were gone.

"Peter!"

There was no reply. How could there be? The light tunnel had taken him away from her.

It was early morning, and the shutters on the farmhouse windows were closed. She stumbled towards the back door. It was locked. She hammered on the frame with the side of her fist.

"Dare ka! Tasukete!!"

Nobody was there.

Feeling stronger, she hurried through the empty covered area where Peter had kept his car. The front door was locked. She searched around and picked up a large stone from the side of the road that ran past the house, then rushed to the bathroom window, which had no shutters. As Nene went back through the covered area, she had a sudden, intense realization.

"I remember!" she exclaimed. "Everything!"

***

He lay on a futon in an unlit room that smelled of tatami matting. The ceiling was wooden with no electric light, and the walls were that indeterminate grey-green that spoke of both traditional Japanese homes and their contemporary counterparts. He already knew, though, that this house was anything but modern.

Peter turned to one side and threw up yet again time into the small vessel that Nene had positioned by his head, then collapsed back to the futon. She was still there, kneeling in the corner, just as she had been since he awoke. She came closer, warily, and replaced the bowl before shuffling backwards.

She was so brave – a true samurai's daughter. He wondered how he would have reacted if a portal had opened up in his living room and deposited a stranger from another world right in front of him. OK, so maybe he did know. But even so, she was remarkably composed.

The wormhole had affected him badly, but not badly enough to totally jumble up his deductive reasoning. He hadn't needed to indulge that part of his mind too deeply anyway; it was clear enough what had happened, where he was, and more significantly, when he was. The question was, how had it happened? That would take time to figure out.

He almost laughed out loud at the irony of it all. Time was the one thing he had an abundance of, and the one thing that would soon disappear completely.

"Thank you," he said to Nene.

She stared at him, saying nothing. Then stood up and left the room. He heard the sound of something being pressed against the door, presumably to keep it jammed shut with him inside.

***

Takeshi Shinbori had no idea what he held in his hands.

The front opened like a book, and when it did the glass inside briefly showed a picture of Fuji-san unlike any he had ever seen before. There were small bumps on the sides. He pushed the large one. The picture came back, then soon disappeared once again. He may not have understood what it was, but he knew what he must do.

The door to the *chanoma* slid open. Takeshi quickly hid the book in his kimono sleeve. Nene entered the room and knelt at the small table where he was sitting.

"He seems to be recovering," she said.

Takeshi grunted. There was much that his daughter did not yet know. But he could not tell her, not yet.

"Father, what is happening? Who is this man? And how did he just appear like that in front of us?"

She was scared. Good, it would keep her on her toes, keep her alert while he was gone, though he doubted she would need to be.

"I must go out for a time," he said.

"Go out? Now? Please, father. Do not leave me alone."

"You have nothing to fear from him. Our visitor will bring you no harm." Takeshi declined to add that if he thought otherwise, he'd have killed him already.

"How can you say that?"

He ignored her question. "I will not be long. You must wait until I get back. Keep the door to the room under lock if you are worried."

Father!" Please," Nene begged. "I do not understand this. I am so scared."

Takeshi stood, as did Nene. He knew a day like this would come and had done his best to prepare her for it. But there was too much he did not yet understand, too many unknowns.

"You know of this, father. Why will you not tell me?"

"Wait here until I return," he said.

"Father!"

Takeshi stepped forward. "Wait, until I return," he repeated, gently. "All will be well. Do not be afraid."

***

The inside of Peter's house was dark, dank and unlived in. What looked like bed sheets covered the chairs and other items of furniture. Nene tried the light switch. Nothing happened.

She looked around. The TV was gone, as were the other things that Peter kept on his desk, which was bare, except for the envelope that lay on top. Well-formed handwriting on the front said:

To Nene and Peter - if you should return

She picked it up and tore it open. Inside was a letter and a small square-shaped piece of hard paper marked 'Pay-All.'

***

Nene's father arrived at Sakae's residence and slid back the door – he knew he needed no invitation.

"Oi!" he said loudly, taking off his shoes.

Sakae's home only had two rooms, and he was already swivelling his head to see who the visitor was.

"Oh, Shinbori-san!" he said, happy to see his good friend. "Do come in!"

Takeshi was already in. "Something has happened," he said, passing across the strange book he had found in the visitor's clothing.

Sakae took it from him.

"Where did you get this?"

He was so shocked he could only whisper it.

***

Nene got dressed in the clothes that Peter had bought for her; they were still in the bedroom cupboard, as was Peter's own clothing.

If you should return. He was not here, but she knew what she must do to find him. She opened the front door.

"I'll be back soon, I promise."

Nene hated to have to leave Nya-Nya on her own, but she was a resourceful cat and could fend for herself, even if Nene wouldn't be able to keep that promise. She swung the bag, one of Peter's left in the house, on to her shoulder and started down the road.

There were two letters in the envelope, written on one sheet of paper. The first was in English, for Peter. The second, on the reverse side, was in Japanese, for her. Nene had read both, but it was the one for her that made most sense. She held it in her hand now. The instructions were clear; find the train line that ran next to the river, follow it to Mitsutoge station, use the Pay-All card to board the train to Shinjuku, then follow the rest of the directions. If she didn't understand, then she was to ask someone. At least she knew what a *densha,* a train, was. She had seen many just yesterday, in Tokyo, with Peter.

Peter!

She must hurry, there was so little time. She walked faster, almost running.

The train!

She should follow it to the station, it wasn't far, less than thirty minutes distance. She had several times made the long journey to Kamakura with her father, so even if something should go wrong, she could walk to Tokyo in the remainder of the day.

As she rushed onwards, she remembered...

***

Nene stood by the door to the room and listened. It was totally quiet.

Calling the man 'our visitor' was father's way of making her feel less afraid, she now realized. And, yes, she had been afraid. In her all life she had never seen such a thing; the air opening like a whirlpool of light, and then something - a man

- falling through and collapsing to the floor right in front of them.

She hadn't screamed. Father had not brought her up to be that way. Afraid in that instance, yes, but fearful, no. Nevertheless, he had held her close, his strong, powerful arms protecting her from this apparition, this ghost, this being, this... man.

"Courage," he had once told her, *"is not the absence of fear. Instead, we must learn to control this with our daily practice. That is the way of the samurai!"*

Father hadn't made her practice *Bushido*, at least not like he did, but he had taught her how to defend herself. Which is why she was now carrying his *tanto,* its short, *tamahagane* blade still sharp and deadly, despite decades of non-use.

Nene pressed her ear to the door. There was still no sound. The man must still be sleeping.

"He will bring you no harm." Father's words echoed through her mind. What was he not telling her? He knew about this man, yet why did he not say anything? And why did she feel such a powerful compulsion to open the door? It was as if a voice was calling within her: *Go inside, my child.*

She had to know, had to find out for herself. Nene set the weapon down on the floor. It would stay there until she needed it.

She removed the wooden bar and slid the door open.

***

"Do you need help, my child?"

Nene turned around. The offer had come from an *Obasan,* an old, old lady. A farmer's wife, Nene thought, judging from the way she was almost bent double from years in a rice field.

"I do not know how to use this," Nene said, holding the small Pay-All card.

"Well, that depends on where you are going," the old lady replied.

She looks so much like grandmother.

"To Tokyo," Nene said. "Shinjuku station. But I've never been on a train before."

"Oh, it's so easy," the old lady chuckled. "Just 'one-touch' and off you go. I'll go with you, show you how it's done."

The old lady led the way through the gate. "Put your card here," she said, touching her own card to a black square. "Like this."

The gate opened. Nene followed suit and held the *Obasan's* arm to help her walk.

"I remember when the new station was built," *Obasan* said as they headed to the moving stairs. "Eighty-three years ago. Just ten years after I was born!"

Nene resisted the temptation to say that she was born two hundred years before that.

***

Nene knelt in the doorway and glanced down at the *tanto*. It was hidden from his view, and she could get to it quickly if needed.

The man was sitting on the futon. "It's all right, Nene-san," he said. "There's no reason to be afraid."

"How is it you know my name?" she replied, just about managing to conceal her astonishment. She'd thought he had said 'Nene' when he had arrived so suddenly earlier that day, but she had dismissed it as just as sound, a fight for air, no more. She'd been wrong, and now she found herself fighting to control the shock.

The man didn't reply.

"Who are you?" she said, recovering composure.

"My name is Peter. And I'm a traveler, from a faraway place."

"A traveler? How did you journey here?"

"It was a mistake," he said. "I did not mean to come here."

"That is not what I asked."

Nya-Nya padded into the room and brushed herself against Nene's ankles before skipping across the tatami to rub her neck on the man's legs.

"Pebbles, is that you?" he said, stroking her back.

Nene glared at the man, her stare demanding answers.

"I come from a different world, a different future," he said. "Three hundred years from now, we have machines that can create tunnels through time. I... fell into one and ended up here."

"A tunnel through time?"

"It's difficult to explain. But yes, a tunnel through time, from my world to yours."

"I cannot believe you."

"But you saw me appear in front of you, out of nothing."

"A magic trick, by a demon."

The man pointed to her wrist. "The winds of the heavens shift suddenly, as does human fate. It's written there, a message from your mother. In Chinese."

"How can you know this?" she said, this time unable to conceal her bewilderment.

"I have studied the history of your family. That's why I am here. Why couldn't you remember any of this?"

"Remember this?"

She was too astonished, too dumfounded, too taken aback to say any more. Was this a dream from which she would soon awake? She stared at him, this man, this visitor, this... mystery who claimed to be from another world. How could he know these things about her? He was an *akuma*, a devil, an evil spirit, a ghost come to haunt them.

"Nene-san," he said, "I need to use the, I mean, do you have a bathroom?"

"A bathroom?"

"Yeah, I need to, you know. Go."

"You wish to have a bath? To go to an o-sento?"

"No, I mean I need to use a, what is it, a *kawaya*?"

Nene suppressed a laugh. She had never heard anyone ask for such a thing in her home. Even if it did mean he was not a demon, how should she answer such a request?

Nene suddenly had the fleeting impression that she knew this man, this traveler from another world. The notion had come from far away, as if a distant echo of a forgotten whisper, then it was gone, carried away like a feather on the breeze.

The sound of the *genkan* door sliding open broke through the silence and snapped her back to room.

"Nene!" her father called out to her.

"I am here, father."

Nene stood as her father entered the room.

"You are waking," he said to Peter in English. "Good. Now we go." He turned to Nene. *"Later I will explain,"* he said in Japanese. *"But first he must change clothes."*

Eighteen

There was no time to waste, not one second.

Peter had shocked Nene by telling her he was a visitor from the future, but he'd figured there was no other thing for it. He *had* to tell her; Nene was the key. He must plant into her mind everything she needed to know, so that she would remember and pass the message on three hundred years from now, either to him or to those who created the ERG. They *had* to know, and he had to find a way to tell them.

He'd made her smile, though, by asking to use the loo. The sudden request had thrown her off balance, but he'd had to do something to force a way through Nene's natural resistance to his strange appearance in front of her. It had worked better than he'd expected, and the *kawaya* itself wasn't as primitive as his twenty-first century brain thought it might have been.

There was still so much more he needed to tell her, but at least the path ahead was relatively clear. And now that was done, he'd had time to consider several scenarios.

He was back in Edo, that much was obvious, and it was before Nene's journey forward in time. The wormhole that had brought him here wasn't the one that had brought her to the cave in Mount Nyukasa; that was still yet to happen. If he could nudge the order of events so that Nene would know what to tell him when she arrived in 2019, then he could introduce corrective actions, somehow. The trouble with that idea was, although it was currently in her future, it was in his past and he would surely have some recollection of her saying something over the kitchen table.

Had she? He searched his mind, running over all the conversations they'd had. He couldn't identify anything. The point was to change that, starting here, this day.

What about other alternatives? He could head to Mount Nyukasa and leave a note in such a way that the construction teams of the future would find it. Not a bad idea, and it might work, if he could get himself there.

He'd thought through several other options while lying on that futon and vomiting his guts out into that damn bowl, none of which involved walking through the night streets of Edo, disguised as a Japanese, his face half covered with some kind of cloth, and with Nene's father leading the way.

So, where were they going?

"Too tall, need down," her father said, pushing Peter's head.

Peter bent lower. He had been tall enough in modern Tokyo, but in early eighteenth-century Edo he stood out, literally.

"Where are we going?" Peter whispered.

"Meet the friend," her father replied.

"I see."

He didn't see, not yet, but it was clear that her father knew something that Peter didn't. It was almost as if he'd been expecting this strange gaijin to drop in one of these days.

And that, Peter thought, was of extreme interest.

***

The old lady got off the train at Tachikawa station and waved to Nene through the glass as the doors closed. Nene waved back.

She really did look so much like grandmother.

Nene opened Peter's 'Stylish Backpack' - she'd found the name on a label - and pulled out the letter. Shinjuku station, the old lady had told her, was another thirty minutes away. There was a number-clock on the small TV above the door, together with a map and a sign that showed where the train was, so she would know.

If Peter were with her, perhaps Nene could marvel at such things, but she was on her own in a strange city that she did not recognize, in a world that she barely understood. She wouldn't let herself be afraid, though. If the young boy in the seat opposite her could journey by himself, then so could she.

She put the letter back in the backpack. As the train trundled out of the station, she remembered…

Father has taken the visitor somewhere; I think to Sakae-Sensei's residence. I look through the pockets of his blue hakama. There is a small sheet of paper in one of them. It says, "Starbucks Coffee," and has numbers written on it, and a date; October 22, 2019.

It was at that precise moment that she had begun to understand.

***

Peter kept his head down to avoid eye contact with anyone and did his best to walk like a local, which was difficult given the far too small sandals that he had on his far too big feet. He was surrounded by the noise and commotion of the night, none of which he could see. It made him feel like he was wasting an incredible opportunity; *he had just travelled back three hundred years to Edo City,* and yet all he was doing was staring at the ground.

But there were far more important things at stake here, such as the rather non-trivial matter of the death of the universe. He'd known it instantly, instinctively, when the wormhole had opened in the garden – when the uncertainty he'd had the day before had snapped like a collapsing quantum wave function into the realization that whatever was happening was far more significant than a local causality paradox, which might cause the solar system to crunch into a singularity, a black hole, but itself wouldn't be enough to cause the end of everything that ever was or will be…

It wasn't the first time since the cave that he'd found those words inside his head.

He had to figure this out, and he had to warn the people at the ERG.

"This is here." Nene's father stopped outside the front door of a wooden terraced house - Peter didn't quite know how to describe it otherwise - in a quiet, dimly lit residential area somewhere between Akasaka and Shinjuku, though that was no more than a best guess on his part.

The samurai slid back the front door and ushered Peter inside, where a short, bespectacled Japanese man was waiting for him. The man held out his hand, and said, in perfectly accented BBC-English, "Do I have the honour of addressing mister Peter Walker, by any chance?"

Peter was so taken aback he couldn't find the words to reply.

***

They sat cross-legged at a small table on the tatami matting, the room surprisingly well-illuminated by a simple oil lamp, which Peter took to be paper stretched over a bamboo frame. He'd seen one in a museum once, or it could have been that antique shop in Ginza; he wasn't sure. It smelled of fish, too, due to the sardine-oil used for the flame.

"You're a time-traveler, like me, aren't you?" Peter said, as his host poured the tea.

It hadn't been that hard for him to make that assessment. The man spoke perfect English, knew what an iPhone was, and wore modern-looking spectacles made from early eighteenth-century materials, which he must have put together himself. The story behind the glasses, however, could wait.

"A marooned one, sadly. But yes, like you Peter-san, I am," the man replied. "My name is Yujiro Sakae, by the way. Call me Sakae, everybody does. *Yujiro* can be hard to say."

Peter didn't think so, but he wasn't going to argue. "I'd like to say nice it's to meet you, too, Sakae-san. But the way things are going, I'm not so sure about that. No offence."

Sakae smiled. "That's perfectly understandable."

The toll of a bell striking three times echoed throughout the neighbourhood. Peter had heard them earlier and knew what they were. Somewhere in time Mariko probably still had that photo he took of her ringing the one in Zojoji temple.

"Ah," Sakae said as the chimes continued. "The time-bells. It must be eight o'clock." Sakae gestured to his guests. "Dozo."

Nene's father said, *"Itadakimasu,"* and picked up his cup. Like Jane, he had asbestos fingers. Peter would wait until his cooled.

"From what year?" Peter asked.

"You mean when did I travel here?" Sakae said. "Twenty forty-two."

"And how long have you been here?"

"Fifteen years."

"That's a long time."

"It is, indeed."

That didn't sound good. If Sakae had been stuck in Edo for a decade and a half, what were the chances of the same happening to Peter? Shit, things were beginning to look worse than he'd thought, as if that were possible.

"How did you know it was me?" Peter said.

"At first it was just an assumption, but that was confirmed by seeing your face at the door."

"You know my face?"

"Of course. You are famous."

"I am?" Peter said.

"In my world you are, Peter."

Peter had already figured out that the ERG was a key element in Sakae-san's world, but himself being part of that world wasn't what he was expecting.

"It seems we both have stories to tell," he said.

"I believe so," Sakae said. "Perhaps you would like to go first, and then I will follow."

***

"These instabilities," Sakae said. "The wormhole complex, we know nothing of this. All my journeys were as if stepping through an open doorway."

Peter had formed his own opinion on that, which was more of a hunch than a rigorous evaluation. "I think it's something left over from the big bang, connecting a series of parallel universes, if I'm right," he said. "How many trips have you made, by the way?"

"Twelve, including this one."

"Did you ever lose your memory?"

"No. Why do you ask?"

"Because Nene did, when she came to me."

"I don't know, I'm sorry."

Peter had recounted the whole story, from finding Nene in the cave to his arrival at her feet a few hours earlier, three hundred years before she left in the first place. He could see the concern on Sakae-san's face – things were definitely not going as planned, and it was time to find out what those plans were.

"It doesn't matter," Peter said. "At least, not yet. So why did you come here, Sakae-san? What's your part in this?"

Sakae set his cup down.

"It was an experiment. There was, or will be, a terrible fire. Many lives will be lost. My mission was to observe the house where the fire starts so we could extinguish it before it took hold. Then we'd evaluate the impact on the timeline throughout the three hundred years from the event. Well, that was the plan but instead I arrived fifteen years early, at least, and everything went wrong from there."

"And no one came looking for you? Of course not, they don't yet know you've missed your return timeslot. Except they will do, one day. Shit. Didn't you bury a message somewhere for them to find, or something?"

Sakae shook his head. "I wanted to, but where? We had no plan for that. So, I was stranded, and had to survive as a street beggar. Then one day I saw a Dutch delegation touring the city. I spent ten years in Amsterdam in my youth, and my Dutch is rather good. So I started talking to them. From there I was introduced to Shinbori-san and employed as a translator."

"And then became Nene's English teacher."

"Such a privilege to teach one so gifted. And so lovely."

Peter leant back on his hands and stretched out his aching legs. Nene's father was unaffected, as was Sakae-Sensei, both happily still sitting in lotus positions.

How could they not have a contingency plan?

"And now we're both stuck here," he said.

"It seems to be that way. For me, I can survive. But for you, the Dutch delegation from Nagasaki are here paying tribute to the Shogun. So, for a few days you are safe. But after that..."

"An uninvited foreigner in Edo. Yes, I know."

"Prison and probable execution."

"Very reassuring." Peter let that sink in for a while. "So, you're a time-traveling fire-fighter, Sakae-san."

"Actually, I'm a professor of linguistics, and also history. From Tokyo University."

"The perfect man for the job. What were you trying to do anyway, save all mankind?" Peter said it as a joke, but from the way Sakae hesitated he realized it was close to the truth. "Oh, dear God, you are, aren't you?"

"Peter-san, think on it. If we can intervene successfully, we can stop wars, avoid economic meltdowns, provide warnings about famine and disasters. We can save millions of lives."

"You're serious!"

Sakae shushed Peter. "The walls are thin, people will hear."

"Sorry. But you can't just go around messing about with history. How do you know you're not making things worse? For every problem you solve you could be creating ten more."

"We know. That's why we were testing it."

Ye gods, what were they thinking?

"And I don't suppose the fire just happens to start in the Shinbori house, by any chance?" It was a bit of a wild guess, but from the way things had been going, it seemed a good one.

"Yes, it does. So, meeting Shinbori-san like that, when I did, it was an extraordinary coincidence, quite exceptional."

Peter stared up at the ceiling. He was beginning to think coincidences were meant to happen.

"Does he know?"

"We had too much Sake one day. It came out."

Nene's father nodded. Peter wondered how much of their native-speed English he could understand. Quite a lot of it, it seemed. At least it explained why he hadn't been particularly surprised by Peter falling through the portal in his living room.

"And what about Nene? Ah, of course, that's why we're in your house, so she doesn't overhear."

"Yes, it could cause her great confusion."

"You should be a politician. When's the fire?"

"I don't know. I was supposed to be sent back a few days before. I never knew the actual date. At least, I don't think I did. I can't remember, to be frank. But, soon, I fear."

So there was potentially some memory loss associated with time travel. Peter wondered what else Sakae had forgotten. How would he know if he had, anyway? And for all any of them knew, the fire could start tomorrow, or even tonight.

"The thing is, Sakae-san," Peter said, "The past you thought you knew, it's gone. We're in uncharted territory. For all we know our very presence here could have changed world history. And God knows what'll happen if there's a causality paradox forming. Actually, I'm worried there might be something else going on here too, something a lot worse than just a simple little paradox."

Sakae crossed his arms. "There must be something we can do," he said.

"I may have an idea," Peter replied. "But, before that, you said you knew me, you knew my face."

"Of course. You are Peter Walker, the father of modern wormhole theory."

"I am?"

"Our project leader is Tom Mitchell. I believe you know him well."

"Tom? Tom's leading the project? Shit, the bastard stole my ideas!"

"No, Peter-san, he always credited you, and wished you could have been there with him, but you had disappeared."

"I disappeared?" Peter said. "Yes, of course. Disappeared here, to eighteenth century Edo."

Peter stared up at the ceiling again. *Why did he keep doing that?* It wasn't as if anyone had written the answers there. It would be handy if someone had, particularly the one about how Tom had solved the little problem of the exploding wormhole.

He returned his gaze to Sakae-Sensei. "What a mess," he said. "I'm beginning to wish I'd never written that damn paper."

Sakae smiled. "Tom considers it one of the finest papers in the history of scientific thought."

Peter laughed. "That's not what he said last week." He rubbed his knees. "You'd better tell me everything you know about the project. And when I say everything, I mean every fucking thing."

***

Peter listened intently as Sakae told him how their mutual friend Professor Yoshiharu Abe had in fact been a project committee member; how Tom and been given a leading role in Japan's CERN-rivalling particle accelerator project after he'd inquired with the professor about Peter's disappearance; how the cancellation of that project had led to Tom's involvement in the matter-antimatter prototype; how Tom had made the connection between Peter's paper and the now very real possibility of time travel – and how Tom had been able to obtain the now unwanted ring-magnets from the accelerator to build the ERG.

Peter hid his sadness on hearing how Abe-Sensei had passed away from cancer four months before Sakae's trip to Edo, but continued to hang on to every word as Sakae told him how they'd taken small steps, tiny journeys through time of a few minutes, then hours, then days, months, then years; how they'd figured out how to assess the impacts of small nudges to the timeline by 'parking' time capsules in an interdimensional sub-space, a kind of 'spacetime limbo' from where they could retrieve the capsules and compare the contents to the new reality, and how they grew in confidence that interventions could be prepared, planned, and implemented for the greatest good.

Peter did his best not to judge. He understood their intentions, and he'd probably have been a willing team member, leading the project alongside Tom.

Except, of course, he knew now they were wrong about the whole fucking thing.

Nineteen

Shinjuku station was the most bewildering place that Nene had been in her life.

It hadn't been too difficult to find her way off the train; she had simply followed everyone and copied what they did, including touching her card to the little black square that made the ticket gate magically open. No, not magic, she knew that. It was *electricity*, the power that made so many things happen in this world. It was after passing through the ticket gate that Nene became lost. There were so many signs, so many corridors and passageways. Which one to take?

She stood by a large pillar in the center of a walkway. Crowds of people thronged past, all going about their daily business, all going somewhere, all unconcerned about her.

Nene had the letter in her hand.

Once you get out of the ticket gate, look for the east exit taxi rank, it read. Where was it? She couldn't see how to find her way there. She felt the smallest surge of fear, the tiniest start of anxiety that could lead to panic. She shut the feeling down, controlling it with her breathing until it was gone.

"Excuse me, ma'am. Do you speak English, by any chance?"

Nene looked up from her letter. The voice belonged to an elderly, grey-haired foreign man, who was with an equally grey-haired foreign woman, both of whom were rather fat. His accent was different from Peter's.

"Yes, I can," Nene replied.

"Oh, that's wonderful. Sorry to trouble you, an' all, but we're getting ourselves kinda lost. Do you know where the east exit is? Only the signs in this place are leaving a lot to be desired, I can tell you."

"There's a map, honey," the woman said, pointing.

"There is?"

"Over there on the wall."

Both the man and Nene followed the line of the woman's index finger.

"That'll do for me!" the man said. He turned to Nene and tugged at his hat. "Y'all have a good day now, you hear."

He had the loveliest, kindest smile.

"May I go with you?" Nene said. "I'm kinda lost myself."

***

The morning sun spilled through the window straight into Peter's eyes. He was already awake, and had lain there for a while, staring at the ceiling, thinking about everything Sakae-Sensei had said the night before. He shifted his position a little, then realized he'd have to keep doing that as the sun rose further, so he shifted his position a lot.

He'd had a lot to think about, too.

The ERG, the Einstein-Rosen Generator, the name he'd made up in the cave, really was called the ERG, and had been built in early 2041, a year after the matter-antimatter reactor went live. They'd chosen the cave in Mount Nyukasa because it was remote, relatively safe, and unwanted visitor access could be restricted. The Japanese government had sponsored the project, but there was a strong international contingent, with his old friend Tom leading the project.

That much was clear. What wasn't clear was whether the government knew about the ERG. Sakae was vague on that point, leaving Peter with the distinct impression that they *didn't* know, and that the ERG was a secret project within an already semi-secret reactor project, which raised all sorts of interesting questions, not least of which was how they'd managed to keep a bloody great big thing like the ERG hidden from their paymasters. Even if he knew, though, it wouldn't help him much now.

There were two overriding issues for him to find answers to. The first being how Tom had managed to solve the wormhole instability problem. It was Peter's idea and his maths, and he hadn't figured it out himself. Not to say that Tom wasn't capable, but in this arena Peter was the chief gladiator, and Tom was his spear carrier.

It also raised the rather thorny issue of what if Tom hadn't solved it? What if he wasn't even aware? Peter only discovered the exploding portal after he'd sent Tom his paper, when he'd put together the simulation which incorporated changes to the underlying concepts and related expressions that he'd previously missed. That scared him, especially considering the carnage he'd seen when he'd found Nene in the cave.

The other thing that's scared him was Nene herself. The wormhole had carried her away from his grasp to who knew where and when. He'd told her that he would look after her, shield her, protect her from harm – and he'd failed, completely, utterly, totally. Was the portal in his back garden an attempt to find her? Someone must have put it there, that much was obvious, even to thick-skulled twerp like himself. Or was she lost in time, like he was, like Sakae was?

The door to the room slid open. It was Nene.

I could just stay here and be with her, live our lives together.

He dismissed the thought.

Her hair was hanging long and free, she hadn't yet put it into the top-knot assembly that women did in all those Edo-period dramas he had watched when he was trying to learn Japanese. She was wearing a simple yet colourful black and red kimono, and had put on her make-up. Was that for him? No, of course not, it was what women did in Edo. She was up early, too. Or was he up late? He hadn't heard any time-bells; maybe he'd slept right through all of them. In any case, he had no idea what the time was. It didn't matter.

"*Ohayo gozaimasu,*" he said.

"Good morning, Peter-san," she replied.

Nene was smiling, no longer afraid of him. Something had happened, and he doubted it was his visit to the *kawaya*.

***

Nene said goodbye to Ed and Gill, two of the kindest people she had ever met. They were from a place called Texas, in the Americas, and were on their first visit to Japan. She had told them that she was from the countryside, far to the north, and this was her first time in Tokyo, which was why she didn't know her way around.

She watched as they headed towards Shinjuku Gyoen, a park that she had no knowledge of, though it seemed from the map that it may have once been the residence of Lord Naito, the Daimyo of Tsuruga.

Nene looked towards the line of black cars that said both タクシー and 'Taxi' on their doors. She waited, quietly observing as people approached the drivers to ask them for transportation. She had the letter in her hand. It told her to give the taxi driver the address, and to pay with the card. The driver would know the way, and Nene would soon recognize the house – it was almost the same external design as the one from her time.

But before then, there was something she must do; something that would bring Peter back to her.

***

Breakfast was rice, natto and miso soup, a traditional combination that Peter had often enjoyed before, though his preference was egg, bacon and toast, which he rarely - if ever - made for himself. What he'd never done before was enjoy that traditional combination in a genuine Edo period house, in genuine Edo.

They ate in silence, which he assumed was the way things were done in the Shinbori household. It did give him thinking time, as if he needed any more of that.

Here he was, an accidental time-traveler, having breakfast with two people born three hundred years before him, one of which was the woman he would choose to spend the rest of his life with – if there was a rest of anything left when this was all over. And, guess what; they didn't seem too bothered by his presence!

OK, so that was down to Sakae-Sensei, at least it was with Nene's father, whom Peter found immensely impressive. Those Edo period dramas had not quite done him and the men of his era justice. In the flesh he was more than Peter would have expected. But, then again, he wouldn't exactly have expected to be eating *asa-gohan* like this, either.

He turned his attention to Nene. There was so much he wanted to tell her, so much to share, so much to warn her about. What would she say if she knew that 24 hours ago he was kissing her lips, her neck, her breasts, the small of her back, between her thighs, her legs wrapped tightly around his back as they...

Nene smiled at him. Was she reading his mind? Was this their connection that she was always talking about?

Stop it, Walker. Get some focus.

They finished eating. Nene's father gave the slightest of nods to his daughter. "My father was wondering, Peter-san, if you should like to tour Edo," she said.

"I thought foreigners were forbidden in the city," he replied.

"My father has issued a..." Nene searched for the right words. "A foreigner's pass. And there is a delegation from Nagasaki visiting the Shogun, so you will not be noticed."

"Except for being a blue-eyed Englishman, in sneakers and jeans," he quipped.

Nene tilted her head.

"I'd love to," he said.

***

There was a hustle and bustle to Edo city that took Peter by surprise. People were everywhere, going about their daily business, running their shops and eateries, delivering water, carrying goods on their backs or suspended on long poles across their shoulders, the richer women dressed in superb kimonos, the poorer dressed in less extravagant affairs.

Nene's father led the way, with a small but growing group of *boku-tachi*, young boys, following them at a safe distance. Peter tried to figure out where they were, but the lack of familiar landmarks made that almost impossible – except for Fuji-san, clearly visible to the west, its sacred summit covered with a fresh layer of autumn snow, implying that it was now mid or late October. Still T-shirt weather for him, at least.

They headed south, meaning they must have gone past Tameike-sanno, which he knew was named after two bus stops, or something along those lines. That, though, had been a relatively modern development. Modern in his world, that was. Then they moved north east, towards the Emperor's palace, except the palace had not yet been built and was still Edo castle. After that they took a series of twists and turns until Peter had no idea where he was, despite Nene's explanations.

The architecture fascinated him. The streets were wider than he'd anticipated and were lined on each side by both single and double-story buildings that stretched from one end to the other, their tiled roofs and wooden awnings sloping long and low. Flags, lanterns, clothing and the people themselves pulsed with vibrant colours that were the forebearers of modern Tokyo; the ancestors of Ginza, Akihabara, Shibuya.

Street vendors and shops large and small were selling everything and anything; books, medicine, clothing, fish, woodblock prints; even rock-hard biscuits that Nene had insisted he try, but which almost shattered an old filling. The seller had a near heart-attack when he'd looked up from his transportable, one-man street-stand-on-wheels to see this odd-looking *gaijin*, perhaps the first and last he would ever see this close. He soon recovered from that shock and, delighted to be serving someone so unusual, had refused to accept anything – a tale for him to tell his grandchildren was payment enough.

The city air was fresh and clean, too, unlike that of the European capitals of the era. With their open sewers and unwashed populations, the stink would have been overpowering. In Edo, however, public baths, *o-sento,* seemed to be on every corner. As for where all the sewage was, well, he'd leave that question for another day.

Peter took photos with his iPhone as discreetly as he could. It would form part of his message to Tom, provided he could figure out a way to ensure Tom got the message in the first place.

And with each and every step, people stood and stared.

At times Peter had wanted to do the same, especially when it had been a priest with a basket on his head and a *Shakuhachi* flute in his mouth. It was a Zen monk called a *Kumuso* from the *Fuke* school, Nene explained, and the thing on his head was a *Tengai* hood, not a basket, and was there to prevent the manifestation of the *Jiga,* his ego. The monk had walked straight past, seemingly unperturbed by the presence of this man from another world.

At other times, in fact for most of the day, being the center of attention wherever he went had been unsettling, especially when it was fierce-looking samurai, armed with two swords and a distrust of foreigners. It was more than distrust; what they were doing was illegal at best and dangerous at worst. Yes, the Dutch delegation were in the city, paying homage to the Shogun, but even so Peter felt terribly exposed and wondered how much of a risk they were taking. It was Nene's father's presence that mitigated that risk. samurai bowed as they passed, an indication of how important and well-known her father was.

"Sakae-Sensei is leading the delegation on a tour of Edo," Nene explained when Peter asked her about it. "And you have been granted permission. So, there is nothing for you to concern yourself with, Peter-san. You are quite safe with us."

He'd nodded in reply, though it was what he would do after the delegation went back to Nagasaki that he was worried about, albeit a small worry compared to the end of the universe. If he could just grab that thought and examine it, evaluate, explore its message to understand *why* it was inside his thick head. He just knew, but just knowing wasn't going to be enough. And even if he did figure it out, how the hell was he going to let Tom know?

They walked on, now heading south west, based on the position of the afternoon sun.

"My father says you travelled here to study the history of Japan," Nene said.

So, that was why she had lost her fear of him. "Something like that," he replied.

"And yet you said you came here by mistake."

"It was both."

"Sakae-Sensei is also here to study. My father explained everything. The people of your time, the things you can do, it is so hard to believe."

"It's hard to believe for me too, Nene."

"How is it that you know of my family?" Nene asked.

"Sorry?" Peter had been distracted by a young woman walking past who was the splitting image of Mariko. It was so uncannily like her that he'd had to stop himself staring as she went by.

"You said you had studied the history of my family. Are we celebrated in your time?"

That was a good question, for which Peter hadn't prepared an answer.

"You father is well known to historians as a collector of foreign works, books, that sort of thing," he said, rather pleased with himself for figuring out a plausible response so quickly. "Actually, I have a history book in my house, on a bookshelf. That's how I know," he added as a deliberate attempt to seed the idea in Nene's mind.

"I see. And the tunnels, the ones that go through time. How do you make those?"

"Well, it's a bit complicated. But, one day, if possible, I will show you how it's done."

"May I see one, and travel to your world, too?"

Another good question, to which he already knew the answer. "If you do, Nene," he said. "Then don't be afraid. I'll come and find you. All you'll have to do is wait for me."

Nene stood still, staring at him. Shit, he shouldn't have said that; he'd aroused her suspicions and alerted her to an event that hadn't happened yet.

My God, her eyes.

Peter suddenly recognized where they were. Ahead he could see the Hie Shrine, where he and Nene had visited two days earlier, or was it three? To say he was losing track of time was an ironic understatement.

The shrine!

"Do you know the story of Urashima Taro?" Nene said, cutting through his thoughts.

"Sorry?"

"Do the people of your time know Urashima Taro?"

"Er, no. Well, I don't think I do."

They continued walking.

"He was a fisherman," Nene said, "who saved the life of a turtle. Three days later, when he was fishing on his boat, the turtle came back to him, and carried the fisherman to his underwater palace. There he met princess Otohime, who wanted to thank him for saving her friend. He stayed for a while, entranced by her beauty, but then he remembered his mother and father, and wanted to go home."

They stopped outside the gate of the shrine at the same location where they'd stood together on their Tokyo trip. Nene's father shooed away the *boku-tachi,* who had overcome their fears and had been running in circles around him.

Nene continued. "The princess didn't want him to leave," she said, "but she gave him a box, the *tamatebako,* and told him never to open the lid. But when Taro-san returned home, everything had changed. His home was gone, his mother and father were dead. People in his village remembered the name Urashima Taro, who had disappeared three hundred years before. Then he opened the box, and white smoke came out, and then, before he could understand what was happening, he was an old man with white hair and a very long beard."

Peter was listening but was distracted by the realization of where they were.

"Do you not think it is a sad story, Peter-san?"

"In a way, yes," Peter said, searching his memory. Nene had done something significant at the shrine. What was it?

"I think the princess fell in love with Taro," Nene said. "But she lost him forever, as he did her."

Nene was staring at him again, her eyes looking straight through to his soul, just as they had done in Tokyo.

The old tree!

***

The taxi stopped a short distance from Hie Shrine.

Nene handed the 'Pay-All' card to the driver, who touched it to a black square, like the ones on the gates in the train stations, then handed it back.

"Arigato Gozaimasu," he said.

"Arigato Gozaimasu," Nene echoed as the door opened by itself.

The taxi moved away, leaving her at the shrine entrance, just where she had first fallen in love with Peter's wonderfully blue eyes.

Twenty

Peter was alone in the small room, the shutters closed for the evening. A lamp burned, giving him just enough light to see what he was doing.

He was sitting on the floor at a small table, and much like his twenty-first century desk in the foothills of Mount Fuji, this one was covered with wormhole diagrams, space-time calculations, Schwarzschild violations and the framework for the simulation that ran on his Mac. He could remember the entire program but there wasn't enough space or time to write out all the code. Except, if he were back at his desk it would all be done on HP Multipurpose Printer paper, not an early eighteenth-century Japanese scroll.

He did his best to draw the wormhole complex, but artistic skills were in short supply on the day of his birth. He'd just have to hope it would be enough for Tom and his team to work on, to make the connection, to dig deeper to find out what he couldn't; that there was something happening here beyond a causality paradox, something that could wreck the entire fucking universe.

He signed the scroll, 'Peter Walker, accidental time-traveler, Edo, 1732.' He had finally worked out the year, having asked Nene how old she was - she was still 25 - and knowing she was born when Mount Fuji last erupted in 1707, even he could do the maths.

The battery on his iPhone was down to 19%. He de-activated the password and was about to shut it down when the door to the room slid open. It was Nene, carrying a tray.

"I have brought you some tea," she said.

"Thank you." Peter cleared the scroll from the table, placing it on the floor beside him.

Nene placed the tray on the table and kneeled. "Dozo."

Peter picked up his cup. "*Itadakimasu.* Is your father not joining us?"

"There are things that he must attend to. It will be difficult for you to stay here after the Dutch delegation have returned to Nagasaki." She pointed to his iPhone. "May I ask, what is this?"

"It's just a thing from my world."

"What is it?"

"I'll show you."

He pointed the camera lens at Nene and snapped her photo, then moved around the table to sit next to her.

"See," he said, showing her the image. Nene was too stunned to reply. "And there's this, too." Peter showed the views of Edo he had shot during the tour.

"It is amazing me," Nene said, as he swiped through the photos.

"It's amazing me, too."

He picked up the scroll. "Nene, this a message for my friends in the future. I'd like to ask you to hide it in the temple. Together with this."

"In the temple?"

"I mean Hie Shrine, where we were today. There are some stones in the far corner by the big tree, although it's probably not so big at the moment. Do you know the one?"

"Do you mean the old tree?"

"It's already 'old'? Yes, the old tree."

The angle of her neck, the softness of her skin – he struggled to maintain composure.

"But how will your friends know where to find this?" she said.

"I'm hoping someone will remember where to look." For all he knew that damned fire could start tonight, so he added; "But, I'd appreciate it if you could do it right away, if you don't mind. It's quite urgent."

"It is very strange. But I understand what I must do. I will go immediately, while it is quiet outside."

"Thank you," he said, then switched off the iPhone and set in in the middle of the scroll. Would it still be in working order 300 years from now? That was a good question. He should have taken out the battery, but without the small-screwdriver toolkit that wasn't going to be possible. He'd just have to hope the lithium wouldn't degrade and melt the internal electronics, and just have to trust that Nene, wherever the future version of her was, would know to look there. He didn't even know if there was a future Nene. What if she really was stuck in time somewhere, alone, afraid? Or worse.

He put the thought out of his mind. She was here now, with him, in this instance. That was all that mattered.

"Nene, when I appeared in front of you, out of nothing, you didn't scream, you didn't run. Weren't you afraid?"

"Yes, I was. Very afraid."

"But you looked after me, you helped me recover."

She paused for a while, before saying, "I felt, somehow, it was as if I should already know you."

"Perhaps you do," he said.

He leaned closer, until his lips were almost on hers. Nene didn't move, allowing the softest of caresses.

"Tadaima!"

Her father's voice boomed through the house. Neither of them had heard the *genkan* door open, and they both moved back to their original seating positions on opposite sides of the table – their connection re-established 300 years before it had begun.

***

As Nene climbed the steps to the shine, she touched her lips, remembering the kiss – her first.

She arrived at the shrine forecourt; it was almost empty of visitors. She headed towards the old tree, where three hundred years earlier she had dressed herself like a ninja and crept unseen through the dusk to bury Peter's message.

***

The Shinbori household library was a marvel.

There were books from all over the world, or at least the world as it was in 1732. But there was one in particular that had caught his attention; a copy of Principia, in Latin, which he now held in his hand.

Ye gods, it was incredible. Newton had died in 1727, just 5 years earlier, and here was Peter Walker-san holding an original printing of the greatest, most significant work in the history of science. The book was worth a fortune. He should have gotten Nene to hide it under the old tree, too.

He pulled another book off the shelf; *'The life and Strange Surprizing Adventures of Robinson Crusoe of York, Mariner,'* published in MDCCXIX – 1719. And next to it were original copies of Moll Flanders and Gulliver's Travels.

"Incredible. Just Incredible."

He put back Robinson but kept a firm grip on Sir Issac.

The maps on the wall were equally impressive: London, Paris, Amsterdam, all from the early 1700s, and all by Guillaume Delisle. Peter's father had been a collector, but he'd had only one authenticated original by the French cartographer. And there were the two antique clocks, both by George Graham of London, whoever that was. One sat on a small European chest of drawers, the other was a grandfather clock in the corner.

Not antique. Not yet.

But the true work of art in the library was the portrait of a woman dressed in a kimono. She had Nene's eyes and was just as beautiful. The artist had been Dutch, although the almost indecipherable signature looked more like 'Van de Squiggle' than an actual name.

Nene's father came to the doorway.

"I have one of these in my own library," Peter said, holding up Principia.

"From your country. Sakae is translate the book. Nene is not understand Latin languages."

Peter did his best not to smile too broadly. Shinbori-san might have been from an ancient samurai family, an expert in Bushido, an advisor to the Shogun on foreign matters, and the owner of conceivably the greatest - and likely the only - collection of imported books in the country, but his linguistic skills left a lot to be desired. But, then again, it wasn't as if there was a school of modern languages on every street corner.

Peter reluctantly returned Sir Issac to the shelf. "Is that Nene's mother?" he asked, nodding to the portrait.

Peter must have hit a nerve, he could see it in the man's eyes, and immediately regretted asking.

"Nene is come back now," Nene's father said. "It is late time, we eat."

***

Dinner was informal, simple, and delicious.

Peter, ignoring the pain in his knees from the hard tatami matting, struggled not to stare at Nene, beautiful in her blue kimono, her hair falling long, which seemed to be her preference, especially at home.

"Tell me more about your world, Peter-san," she said, breaking the traditional Shinbori family silence at meals. "What is it like there?"

Her father looked at her. *"Nene, now is not the time for that kind of talk,"* he said, gently.

Peter's Japanese wasn't much better than Shinbori-san's English, but he understood. "No, it's OK," he said. "It's different in so many ways, but somehow not so different. One day, perhaps, you will come to know more."

"Perhaps I will," she replied. "How long will you stay with us, Peter-san?"

That was the sixty-four-trillion-dollar question that he didn't know how to answer. If Nene didn't find his letter in the future, if the ERG was catastrophically destroyed beyond repair, if the universe was about to explode or implode – or both... if, if, if.

What if he was stuck in this place forever? That was a bloody great risk her father had taken, giving him the tour of Edo like that. Why had he done that? Peter still hadn't fathomed that one out. Would Nene still travel forward in time someday, leaving him here in Edo, possibly as a guest in one of the Shogun's prisons? Or were they on a new timeline, a new branch of past, present, and future?

"Peter-san?" Nene asked.

He hadn't answered her question.

"I don't know, Nene," he said, truthfully. "A short while, I think, depending on whether my friends in my time will-"

He stopped in mid-sentence. How could he have been so stupid, so slow to see it, to unaware?

Nene was wearing the kimono from the cave.

"Nene," he said, "that Kimono you are wearing."

"It was my mother's. She-"

CRACK! BOOM!

A flash of blue lighting blasted through the air close by, followed instantly by a massive crash of thunder. It caught them all off guard. Peter spilled his Miso, Nene dropped her rice-bowl and Nya-Nya darted to the corner. Even Nene's father, the immutable samurai, reacted, instinctively grabbing the table with both hands.

"Christ!" Peter exclaimed, but not even he was prepared for what happened next.

The house began to shake violently, the thin internal walls clattering against the supporting woodwork like a crazed percussionist hammering a *taiko* drum.

Nene's father said it first. *"Jishin!"*

"That's no earthquake!" Peter answered him. "Hold on to something!"

The air shuddered as a dark, sinister portal opened behind Nene. Unlike the one in Peter's garden this was black as hell, an evil apparition whose imperfect circle pulsated like the lungs of a man gasping for air in the vacuum of space. Nene, the closest to the gravity-well, was dragged backwards.

"Tasukete!" she called out in terror as she grabbed a vertical wooden pillar.

"Hold on!" Peter shouted.

Nene's father was already on his feet, lunging towards his daughter, but he never made it to her. In a microsecond, the vortex intensified exponentially, its awesome power far beyond any earthquake the house was built to resist. A ceiling section collapsed around the valiant samurai, the falling structure pinning him to the tatami flooring.

Peter was pulled forward, slamming hard into both Nene's father and the debris. The three oil-lamps in the living area toppled over, spilling their flaming contents to the floor, the flames instantly fanned by the suction. Nene's grip on the pillar was slipping as the wormhole devoured everything within range; Nya-Nya, cooking utensils, bowls; anything loose was consumed into the guts of its insatiable innards.

"Nene!" Peter shouted above the roar. "Wait for me in the darkness, in the cave. I will find you!"

"Peter!" Nene called out as she let go of the pillar, no longer able to resist. With a scream she was sucked into the portal, which then slammed shut as violently as it had opened.

She was gone.

***

There was no time to stare at the empty space where Nene had been; the Shinbori house was a partial wreck and fire from the spilled lamp oil was growing, fanned by the wind surging through the open windows where the shutters had broken in two.

A collapsed ceiling beam had dealt a glancing blow to Nene's father, leaving his head bloody from a deep cut that had rendered him semi-conscious, and his legs trapped beneath the fallen timber.

Peter extracted himself from the debris pile and tried to lift the beam, but it was heavy, and further weighed down by rubble from the upper floor. He looked around. There was wreckage everywhere, even getting to the front door was going to be difficult, and if he couldn't free Nene's father before the flames really took hold, it would be impossible. He pushed aside the ceiling panels and tried the beam again; he couldn't move it.

"Shinbori-san!" he shouted, but Nene's father was too dazed to reply.

He looked once again towards the door. It was too late; the flames had already taken hold.

They were trapped.

Part Three:

Future

Twenty-One

The Taniguchi house wasn't as easy to find as Nene had thought it would be.

It hadn't moved, of course, but the streets of her childhood had changed enough to cause her to take many wrong turns, despite aiming for the tall red tower near Zojoji Temple, from where she was able to get her bearings. Even then, she still had to sense her way through the back streets of Azabu-Juban.

She could have taken a taxi, the address was on the letter, but she had walked those now unfamiliar streets with Peter and wanted to retrace her steps, to see for herself how the new city of Tokyo was different from both the Edo she had once known and the one she and Peter had seen from his car. But there was so little of her world left, and almost nothing for her to connect to. The air was different, though. It was cleaner, and the cars and big trucks made a softer sound than when Peter had shown her the city.

She liked the way the people dressed and the freedom it gave them to be themselves, but it had taken her a while to realize that the earrings some of them wore were not jewelry, but instead were part of the phones that they used to talk with each other. Despite their freedom, people seemed more isolated, cut off from what was around them, as if their world were now within themselves and their *devices*.

What year was it? She had looked for signs on the big TVs, but still didn't know. Peter's house had been deserted but not derelict - the garden grass was long but not completely overgrown - and there were tall buildings towards the west that she recognized from yesterday. Possibly not too much time had passed since the tunnel had taken her from Peter.

Father!

His face, his form, his beauty, his strength had been clearly visible when the tunnel had opened. He was injured; blood was seeping through the bandage around his head, but he was alive. Where was he now? And what of Peter? She had seen the fire start when the tunnel had swallowed her into its dreadful insides. The ceiling had collapsed, too, but the *wormhole* had closed so fast. Was Peter hurt? Was he with father? Or were they separated in different times and different worlds, as she herself was?

If the machine in the future, the one that created the tunnels, was still functioning and still able to create the 'traversable wormholes' that Peter had told her about, then there was hope. If not, then all was lost.

She opened the iron gate and walked the short distance through the front garden to the house. There was a *deur klopper* on the door, a lion's face with a ring in its mouth. It was the same design she had known since childhood, perhaps even the same *klopper* – a gift from a Dutch trader some 300 years earlier.

Nene grabbed the ring and hammered hard on the door. She heard a familiar woman's voice from inside the house, saying, "I'll get it."

The door opened. The woman looked older. Perhaps twenty years or so had passed since they had last met.

"Hello Jane-san," Nene said.

It took Jane a few moments to realize, to make the connection. "Nene? Is that you?" she said.

Nene nodded.

"Oh my God!" Jane exclaimed. "You came back!"

Jane took Nene in her arms and held her close, tears streaming down her face.

***

"She's crashed out on the sofa," Jane said. "The poor thing's exhausted."

"Good. We should let her rest," Shohei replied. "But this, I think, is not so good."

The parchment was open on the kitchen table in front of them. It was in remarkably good condition, considering where it had been hiding for three centuries.

"It is real, isn't it? I mean, it's not fake, is it?" Jane said.

"No, my dear, it is not fake."

"So he really is there, back in Edo?"

"Yes, I believe he is."

"And all that stuff Nene said, about the wormholes, the time-traveling, the fire, everything going bonkers, all that, it's all true?"

"I believe so. And don't forget, the original house here burnt down in the same year."

"The same fire?"

"It may be." Shohei nodded to the wireless charger next to the rice cooker. "Can you check his phone? It might be charged by now. If it can be charged."

Jane retrieved the iPhone and handed it to Shohei. "Here, you do the honours, Batman."

"It's either twenty-five years old, or three hundred and twenty-five," he said, starting up the device. "Either way, it is still working."

Shohei opened the photo app. "Look at this." He handed the phone to Jane.

She flicked through hundreds of photos of the streets and people of Edo City, clearly taken by Peter, some of which were at strange angles, others were poorly focused, but all were a stunning montage of life 300 years before – a living record of a past that was no longer inaccessible, a history that was no longer confined to books, an era that was no longer the stuff of stories and speculation. Half of the photos were of Nene herself.

"Oh my ruddy God, it really is true! He really is there, was there." Jane looked anxiously at Shohei. "Pete had a thing about causality paradoxes screwing everything up. Is that what's happening here?"

Shohei rested his palms on Peter's document. "It appears it could be, from what he has written."

"That's not good, is it."

"No, it is not good. Not good at all."

"So, what do we do?"

"I have an idea about that," Shohei said. "Starting with the webpage for the reactor project."

***

Nene awoke to find Jane sitting on a chair next to the sofa.

"Hello luv," Jane said. "Welcome back."

Nene sat up. "Hello," she replied, rubbing the soreness from her neck.

"I've got some magic cream for that," Jane said, "Cures everything and anything. But first, how about a nice cup of tea?"

"That would be wonderful."

Nene followed Jane to the kitchen and sat at the table while Jane made boiled water. She looked around; the interior of this modern Taniguchi house was, like Tokyo itself, unrecognizable; although it looked such a comfortable place to live.

"Where is your *go-shu-jin?* I mean, your husband?" she asked.

"In his study, calling everyone he knows. And everyone he doesn't know, too, I expect."

"About Peter?"

Jane poured water into two cups. "About everything." She set the cups on the table. "Here you go, luv."

Jane cradled the teacup in her hands, but it was too hot for Nene to do the same.

"Why do you call me 'love'," Nene asked.

Jane smiled. "I'm from up north, chuck, we all do that there. And we say chuck, too. Well, some of us do. We're all a bit daft, so don't you worry about that."

Nene sipped her tea. "I didn't say thank you, Jane-san, for what you did. For helping me like this, and for writing that letter. Without it, I don't know what I should have done."

"I expect you'd have found your way to Tokyo and dug up Peter's message anyway, pet."

Nene tilted her head.

"We say 'pet' too, luv," Jane explained. "You'll get used to it. In time."

If there is time.

"How did you know we would come back to the house?"

"We didn't, not for sure. But we had to do something. So Shohei bought the land and the house a few months after you both vanished. We were so worried, we thought, what if it was all true? Well, he did. That's why we wrote that letter, and put a new one in every year, too, just in case you did come back." Jane reached out and touched Nene's hand. "I still can't believe you're here."

"Neither can I," Nene replied.

"I'll get that cream for you. Hang on a sec." Jane left the kitchen, then soon returned with a small glass jar. "Here you go," she said. "You won't need much."

Nene took the cream from Jane and rubbed some into her neck. The effect was instantaneous. "It feels so much better already," she said.

"That's why I call it magic cream." The study door opened, revealing Shohei. "Ah, here he is. Any luck?" Jane said.

"I spoke with someone at the project and sent a copy of Peter's document. She said they will send a car later."

Right on cue a car drew up outside the house, its blue lights flashing, though its siren was silent. Jane stood up and watched through the kitchen window as two police officers exited the vehicle.

"Don't hang about, do they, this lot," she said.

***

It wasn't a *Chinook*; Nene could tell by the number of wings that swirled above its head. This had one set, whereas the machine that flew over Peter's house had two. And it was quieter, just like the cars had been in the streets below.

A *helicopter*. She remembered the other word.

Jane and Shohei ducked their heads and climbed onboard, but Nene stood and stared at the machine. She understood now how it flew. The turning wings made a strong wind, like a *taifu*, and that pushed the machine into the air. It wasn't so difficult to comprehend.

What was harder to grasp was how anyone could have made the building they were standing upon. It surely was the tallest in the city, perhaps even the tallest in the world. The sky was completely cloudless, and from where she stood it was as if she could see forever. There was Fuji-san; there the ocean; that must be Tsukuba-san in the distance. And over there, beyond the mountains of the north, was Niigata – and beyond that, China.

In the vastness of all that she was witness to, Nene felt alone, isolated, separated. What if Peter had been right, and the machine that made the tunnels was destroyed?

Is this my fate, to be abandoned in this new world, with everyone I have ever loved lost to me?

Jane was waving for her to board the helicopter. "Nene, come on!" she shouted.

Nene climbed in through the open door and sat by the window next to Jane.

"Put your seat belt on, pet." Jane said. "Like this."

Nene copied Jane's lead.

"Don't worry, luv. We'll find him. We'll find Peter."

Nene nodded, and turned her eyes to the city, so far below.

***

Tom Mitchell sprinted the thirty meters from the roof access elevator to the waiting helicopter, which was in violation of not only the strict safety rules of the building but also common sense. When you're four hundred and sixty-three meters above ground, the last thing you want to be doing is rushing headlong towards a landing pad that hung over the edge of the building itself, especially when there was no fence to stop you from sliding over that edge to certain death.

Nor, for that matter, should you be charging towards a BX-93 with its motor on and its rotors turning, their leading edges more than capable of slicing you in half; although you'd have to be an Olympic high-jumper for that to happen. But, then again, saying Tom Mitchell was 'on edge' would be the understatement of all time.

All time. Now, that was an expression that was about to earn its keep. He jumped aboard the chopper.

"Sorry to keep you waiting," he said to the pilot. "Let's go."

They were airborne before Tom had finished strapping himself in. He turned to his passengers.

"I'm Tom Mitchell. Chief scientist with the project. You must be Shohei."

"Indeed I am."

They shook hands.

"And indeed I'm Jane," said Jane. "Don't I know you?"

Tom nodded. "I think you might. Peter's twenty-first at Cambridge. Remember?"

"Oh yeah. The drunken dickhead."

Tom ignored the quip and faced Nene. "And you must be Nene. My goodness, I am so delighted to meet you, to meet all of you."

The helicopter lurched, caught in a bubble of turbulence.

"Not to worry," said Tom. "It always does this. The air will be more stable once we're beyond the city limits."

"And where are we going, Tom?" Jane asked.

"Our mission specialists would like to interview you all, especially Nene. It might help us to find a solution."

"A solution to what, exactly, Tom?"

"I'm afraid that's classified, Jane."

"Is it, now?" she said.

"Yes, it is, sorry," Tom replied.

If they knew what was going on, they'd hijack the aircraft and force a landing.

His earpiece buzzed. He touched his wristband to accept the call, which automatically set his glasses to accept the incoming transmission.

"Excuse me," Tom said to his new companions. "Yes Yuko?"

Yuko's tense face appeared in his video feed. She was in mission control at the edge of the mountain, which implied they still hadn't gained access to the ERG itself. Superimposed on the feed next to her was the main display. On a normal day it would be an organized series of numbers and key data points, with the live feed from the ERG covering one half, and the reactor monitoring routines covering the other. Everything had been orderly, unchanging, and unspectacular for the best part of a year and a half.

Except today the 'everything' was a jumbled mess of emergency alarms, flashing warnings, blank video feeds and constantly changing figures that were too small for Tom to make out at this resolution. Christ, he really had chosen the wrong day to be visiting Tokyo.

"May I talk?" Yuko asked.

"You may if you wish," Tom replied, their standard code for 'I can hear you, but others are here, so I may not be able to respond.'

"Copy that," Yuko said. "I have the recording of the incident for you Tom. Let me know when you're ready."

Tom had been waiting for this since the first desperate message from Yuko at 09:47 that morning. Only the fact that he was heading to a meeting with both the Prime Minister and his Minister of Energy had prevented him from rushing back.

As it was, he'd make the budget request based on an outright lie. Their matter-antimatter reactor had been up and running for almost two years, but as far as Abe-*Shusho* was concerned they were still ironing out teething troubles and were six months away from going live, but all that investment would soon pay off, not only for Japan, but for all mankind; or so Tom had led them to believe. None of them knew about the ERG. It was the best kept secret since the Manhattan Project, except now everything had gone haywire and the investment was paying off in ways no one could have anticipated.

Tom adjusted his glasses. "Ready now."

"This is the video feed from the ERG," Yuko said. "Fifteen seconds before it started."

The feed in front of his eyes changed to theater-mode, the projection filling his vision as if he were at an IMAX cinema on a Friday night. There were ten cameras in the cave, each strategically positioned to give a view of a defined area. The AI would then compile these into a complete view, choosing which cameras were recording something essential, and which cameras could be safely ignored, or at least were less crucial. The trouble was, there was so much going on the AI was having a hard time keeping up.

It started peacefully. For fifteen seconds everything was normal, as things had been for hours, days, weeks and months beforehand. The crew of six were at their individual stations; a series of semi-holographic consoles arranged in a semi-circle in front of the ERG rings, all monitoring the portal in the Shinbori house – the one he'd authorized to use for the hunt for Sakae. It was only a search, not a physical transfer of anyone or anything; no more than a spyhole into the past, a remote viewing mission that had become a standard, non-critical procedure. As if anything they were doing could be called 'standard.'

Flashes of light pulsed from the reactor access tunnel.

That shouldn't be happening! Of course it shouldn't; that was the whole point.

The power readouts at the edge of his view raced from 28% to 85%.

Impossible!

He'd need to review the footage from the reactor room later, but for now he'd stick with the ERG. The image shook, as if a magnitude 9 earthquake had just hit. The video paused.

"That's when the reactor surged," Yuko said. "They tried to shut it down, but it ran away from them."

"And, er, what caused the spike there, Yuko?" Tom tried to make it sound like an innocuous question for the benefit of his fellow passengers, but the tension in his throat was far from consistent with such innocence.

"Some kind of negative energy spiral, we think."

"Understood," Tom replied, though he was far from understanding anything. "We had one of those yesterday, didn't we?"

"Not like this one, Tom."

"OK. Please continue."

"This is where the shit really hit the fan," Yuko said, as she re-started the video.

Four portals opened in midair, their dark, menacing vortexes surrounding the ERG and its crew. Each opening pulsed like bellows driving a church organ, generating a discordant cacophony that obliterated all other sounds. Tom reduced the volume in his earpiece and watched in horror as the vortexes, driven by the surging reactor, induced gravity wells that drew in everything within range. Chairs, loose paperwork, tablets, unworn lab coats were all sucked inside, like rubbish into a giant vacuum cleaner.

The crew followed. One by one they were dragged into those evil fissures, those rips in the fabric of spacetime that could not possibly be occurring. Their screams, inaudible above the thunderous roar, were proof otherwise. One remained, desperately gripping a console as she fought to commence the emergency shut down. It was Melanie, the team leader.

My God, she is so brave.

A flying chair struck Melanie on her forehead. She instantly lost consciousness and was sucked into a portal. The feed went black. Tom took a moment to compose himself.

"Was that Melanie, there, Yuko?" he asked, still far from being composed.

The view in his glasses changed to Yuko. "Yes, it was," she said. "Melanie reduced power but got hit before she could complete the emergency shut down. At least, that's what we think."

"You think?"

"The interface is down, Tom. Thinking is all we can do."

"I see," Tom said.

"And if it surges again, then, shit, I don't even want to try to think about that."

Nor did Tom. But as project controller, it was his job to do just that. "And the bubble, Yuko? What about that?"

"Stable at the moment."

"I mean, do we know what it is?"

"Suzuki thinks we just invented warp drive."

"You're joking."

"I wish we were, Tom. Whatever it is, it's a wall of... something... about thirty meters in diameter, and right now impenetrable. Ultra hi-frequency radio signals just bounce straight back, so do hardwire signals, which means we have zero remote control capability. But we're working on it."

This was worse than he'd thought. He should have cut short his meeting with the Prime Minister and come back straight away.

"Has Suzuki finished analyzing the message from Peter?"

"He's on it now. You certainly picked a great day to be a beggar, Tom."

"You'd rather they shut us down? God, they probably will after this. We'll be there in forty minutes. Keep me posted on any developments."

"Will do."

Tom hung up and took off his glasses. Jane was glaring at him.

"Won't be long now," he said.

***

Nene could see this man was frightened.

She had sensed it from the moment he'd climbed aboard the helicopter and confirmed it the moment he'd started talking. His glasses had gone dark, too. He'd been looking at something, like a TV, and whatever it was had scared him so much his right hand was trembling.

The helicopter bounced again, just as it had when they'd left the roof of the building, causing Jane and Shohei to flinch. Nene centered herself and stayed calm, though her fear of never being with Peter again was growing.

As they flew like a bird high above Tokyo City towards Mount Nyukasa, she sensed a voice.

Nene, there are things you must know.

She closed her eyes and listened.

Twenty-Two

They touched the ground once more on the side of the mountain not far from where Nene had pulled Peter away from the motorcycle; she recognized the curve of the road and the view down the valley. Everything else, though, looked very different.

The small entrance to the tunnel was gone, replaced by a huge metal gate that stretched across the now much larger opening. The rockface had been excavated, and a long, low building flowed along the side of the mountain, almost reaching the sharp bend five hundred paces away that led down to the valley below. A large sign on the building read: "Energy for the Future."

Two men in blue uniforms came running towards them. Tom jumped out from the helicopter first.

"This way, please, everyone." He had to shout above the noise of the wind from the wings above their heads.

They followed Tom into the building.

***

"If you wouldn't mind waiting in here," Tom said, as one of the guards opened the door marked, 'Interview Room One.'

Jane tugged on Shohei's sleeve, holding him back. "And what is *in here*, Tom?" she asked.

"It's somewhere where you can wait," he answered.

"Wait for what?"

"Someone will come soon, Jane, and talk to you all, especially to Nene. We need to find out as much as we can."

Jane looked at Shohei, then Nene. "Is it me, or do you get the feeling we're unwanted guests?"

"Jane, my dear," Shohei said, reassuringly. "It will be all right. We are here to help them."

Jane gave Shohei one of her looks.

"It will be fine," he said. "Let's do as they ask, and go in."

Nene stepped forward, coming between Tom and the others. "Where is Peter?" she said. "Is he here?"

"We don't know yet, I'm sorry."

"There was a fire. You must help him."

"I promise we'll do everything we can, Nene." Tom gestured to the empty room. "Please, you are our guests here."

Shohei led the way into the room. Jane followed reluctantly, with Nene close behind.

"Do take a seat," Tom said. "We'll be with you soon. In the meantime, can we get you anything?"

"Tea would be nice," Jane said. "And a proper explanation, Tom, that would be nice, too."

"I'll see what I can do."

"Very helpful, I'm sure," Jane replied as Tom closed the door.

***

"Nobody goes in or out without my personal approval."

The guard nodded and said, "*Wakarimashita.*"

Tom wondered how much Kenji Hayashi had actually understood. Of all the members of the security team, his English was the most doubtful. He headed down the corridor a few paces, then turned to say, "Oh, and get the cafeteria to make them some tea, can you please, Hayashi-san?"

"*Wakarimashita.*"

"Tom!" The breathless voice came from behind him. It was Yuko, running in the soft, soundless, anti-static rubber shoes they all wore.

"Yes, Yuko?"

"We need you. Now."

"What's happened?"

"It's easier to show you. In the MCR."

Yuko led the way to the Mission Control Room, with Tom close on her heels.

***

Designed to monitor the MAM, the matter-antimatter prototype, the MCR was a cross between a small-scale NASA-style center and the equivalent room found in a fission-based nuclear power station. Three banks of consoles faced the main display, each manned by a pair of scientists and technicians, more than half of whom were, like Tom, from overseas. The team were dedicated, capable and not prone to panic, although the sea of anxious faces that greeted him when they rushed into the room was an indication that alarm wasn't too far away.

Amita, Yuko's second and thus Tom's third in command, handed him a headset.

"Noriko for you, Tom," she said.

"On screen, please, Amita."

He'd been using that Captain Kirk expression since the day the ERG went live. It had been part of the fun of the exploration, the 'going where no one has gone before-ness' of their mission. All that fun was gone now.

The display changed to the video feed from the central access tunnel. Noriko was there with her team of five. On a normal day the view would show a long, straight and well-lit tunnel that eventually curved its way down to the cave, where both the reactor and ERG had been constructed. Today the end of the tunnel was five meters ahead of Noriko, terminating abruptly in a vast nothingness, a giant wall of black, punctuated by tiny flashes of light. It was moving too, forcing the team to slowly retreat, their spectrum analyzers and other measuring equipment seemingly powerless to stop it.

"Noriko, it's me," Tom said. "What's going on?"

"Bad news, Tom," Noriko replied. "It's starting to expand again."

"Since when?"

"Since about ten minutes ago."

"How fast?"

"A meter a minute, near enough."

"Christ."

"That's what I thought."

One of her team snapped together two sections of a three-meter metal pole, then nodded towards her.

"Stand by, Tom," Noriko said. "We're going to try something." She addressed the team. "Simon, go ahead. Everyone else, take a step back."

Simon positioned the far end of the pole at the surface of the membrane. He looked down at the tablet hanging from his neck.

"No reading," he said.

"Try getting closer," Noriko said.

"I'm already at the surface. It feels solid, but pliable, almost like, I don't know, gelatin, or something."

"Try forcing it," Noriko said.

"Are you sure?"

"No. Your decision, Simon."

"Confirm my decision," Simon replied. "Applying pressure to the sensor tip now."

A blast of blue light abruptly enveloped Simon, sending him flying backwards. The video feed from the tunnel cut out.

"Noriko!" Tom shouted. "Can you hear me?"

The entire MCR stared in silence at the blank screen.

"Noriko!"

There was no reply. Tom turned to Yuko. "Get a backup crew in there, now."

"No need." Yuko responded, pointing. "The feed's back."

Tom returned his attention to the main display, where Noriko's team had surrounded Simon. He looked dazed, but otherwise unharmed.

"Is he OK, Noriko?" Tom asked.

"He's fine, Tom. Just a little shaken up, that's all."

"What happened?"

"Some kind of energy pulse, I don't know, mild lighting, something like that. We're all right, it's just... what's going on here, Tom?"

"Good question, Noriko. Wish I knew. We'll work on that here. You stay where you are, but keep your distance, and let me know if there are any developments."

"Copy that," Noriko replied.

"God, if that thing keeps growing it'll swallow us whole." Tom said. "Yuko, Amita, in my office, now, please. And bring Suzuki-san. Where is he anyway?"

"Where he always is when he needs to think," Amita said.

"Then please go to the cafeteria and get him. And bring us all some coffee, too, if you wouldn't mind."

***

"How the hell did a negative energy spiral happen? I thought it was impossible. And that makes two in two days, too."

Suzuki shrugged. "I think it's due to exotic matter influx from the destabilized portal. But, that's just my estimation."

Tom's opinion of Akira Suzuki hadn't changed one bit since he'd first interviewed him five years earlier. A geek's geek, Suzuki was by far the most intelligent person on the team, even smarter than Tom was. Unfortunately, the man had the social skills of a decaying lump of driftwood floating on an ocean of indifference. That said, Suzuki's 'estimation' was the nearest thing to an established fact that they had to go on.

"Which means we don't know," Tom said, although he doubted Suzuki was too far from the truth. "What about Peter's message. Can we learn anything from it?"

"There is much to learn from a deeper analysis. And if we had known before, we could have taken appropriate action. But, right now, it doesn't help us."

That wasn't what Tom wanted to hear. "Suzuki-san, are you telling me that there's nothing in there?"

"No, I'm not saying that, not at all." Suzuki responded. "He has some ideas that we can explore for post-event analysis, but in terms of a resolution to our current problems, it serves no purpose."

Tom tapped his fingers on the table. "I had expected a little more from you on this, Suzuki-san."

Suzuki crossed his arms. "As I said, it will take time, and I do not think we can spare the time for that."

"Akira," Amita said, trying to diffuse the tension. "At least tell us what Peter's message is saying. Can you do that?"

It was an open secret amongst the ERG crew that Suzuki had a huge crush on Amita, to which there was zero chance of reciprocation. Even so, of all the people in the room, or the building for that matter, she was the one who could get him to reveal what was really on his mind.

Suzuki uncrossed his arms. "You have read my synopsis?" he said.

"Yes, on the way back," Tom replied. "But it's your analysis that we're waiting for."

"Peter Walker thinks," Suzuki said, "without supporting evidence, that there is something more than a causality paradox occurring."

"We know that, it was in your synopsis," Amita said. "We just need to know what he thinks is going on, even if he has nothing to back it up."

"That is my point. It will take time. I cannot simply speculate without a full study of his assertions."

Tom leaned back in his seat. Suzuki was being Suzuki, and he'd have to take his word for it. Shit, the bugger was right, too. They had to resolve the immediate issues of a possibly out-of-control reactor creating the bubble.

"OK, Suzuki-san," Tom said. "We'll leave it there. But Yuko said you think we've invented warp drive. What did you mean by that?"

Suzuki stood up and grabbed a pen. Tom was old-school and preferred analog whiteboards in his office to the more ubiquitous digital variety. Suzuki sketched Mount Nyukasa and added the Main Control Room halfway up the south-west face, with the reactor and ERG in the center of the mountain.

"We're here," he said, "in the MCR. The reactor and ERG are one point oh six four kilometers away, in the middle of the mountain, approximately thirty-five meters below our current position."

He drew a pair of parallel lines. "This is the access tunnel. And this," he added a dotted circle, centered on the ERG, "this is the bubble. Its center is the ERG, and currently is forty-three meters in diameter, growing at a meter a minute. In a little over one thousand and sixty-four minutes, if it doesn't stop, it will expand beyond the tunnel entrance, here. That's seventeen point seven hours, approximately."

Tom had already done the maths. "Yes, we got that," he said. "I just wanted to ask why you think it's warp drive."

"Because it's a bubble of space-time, driven by the MAM, that's why."

Amita raised a hand. "But Akira, that would require enormous amounts of energy. Far beyond the capability of the MAM to provide, even at full theoretical power."

"I know," he said, "That is why it's just my speculation."

"But it could be anything, Akira. A force field, even."

"Same thing."

Amita sighed, a deliberate sign of her growing annoyance. "No, it isn't. It's completely different."

"Well, it's there, whatever it is." Yuko said. "And its growing, and we don't know how to stop it. We don't even know what's going on at the core. For all we know, the MAM could be at full theoretical power already. Beyond, even."

"But Melanie shut it down, didn't she?" Tom said.

"Not shut down, Tom. Just reduced power, remember? We lost telemetry after that."

"Yes, you did say that," Tom acknowledged. "What about that wormhole complex, Suzuki-san. What do you make of that? Or, rather, what does Peter make of that?"

Suzuki pushed his geeky glasses back. "That is my point. I mean, Peter-san's point. He thinks it's the source of the instabilities."

Tom nodded. "Your synopsis said Peter thought it was a kind of hyperspace, a gap between universes. Could that be the energy source that's creating your warp drive-that's-also-but-maybe-not a force field?"

"It may be," Suzuki said. "But, until it's confirmed, I think it's best to say bubble rather than any other hypothetical term."

Tom smiled. It was typical of Suzuki to be noncommittal until he was 100% sure. But, then again, the man's 50% was better than most people's 99.9%.

"Thank you," Tom said. "Please take a seat."

Tom waited for Suzuki, then stood up and went to the whiteboard. He stared at it in silence, considering the actions that they could take, and those that they couldn't. Whatever was going on, they were dealing with the unknown. They had been, anyway, since the day he'd first made the connection between Peter's paper and the phenomenal power of the MAM. What had started as *"Mmm, let's run an experiment and see if Peter was actually on to something here,"* had morphed into *"My God, we can save the planet!"*

They'd taken every precaution, going step-by-step, inch-by-inch; evaluating every method, dissecting every procedure, analyzing in minute detail every reading and each data point. Nothing had given them any adverse indication whatsoever.

Where had they gone wrong?

It didn't matter. Not at this moment, anyway.

"OK everyone," he said, "let's focus on the problem at hand. Whatever's causing the bubble, whether it's a wayward reactor, an unstable ERG or negative energy transfers from a parallel universe, we need to find a way to stop it. So, the question is, what do we do?"

Amita joined Tom at the whiteboard.

"We find a way to transmit through the membrane and regain remote control of the ERG," she said, sketching radio-waves piecing through the membrane. "Then initiate the emergency crew escape. We can use it in reverse and just walk in, and then Akira, or someone, can directly shut down the reactor. Assuming it can get through Akira's bubble, which I think it will."

"That's an idea" Tom said. "But, if you can get a signal through, why not just shut it down remotely from here?"

"We need direct access to the reactor console, Tom. We can't do that from here, remember? To stop anyone remotely detonating the reactor. A precaution in case of terrorist attack."

"Whose bright idea was that?"

"It was yours, Tom," Suzuki said.

"I know that, Suzuki-san. I was being ironic." Tom turned his attention to Amita. "Given what happened to Noriko and her team just now, how do you propose to do this?"

"They were trying to measure the internal density," Amita said. "But we have the surface frequency from the rebounding transmissions. If we can align to that, then we can get through. The problem is, it keeps randomly modulating."

"How long?"

"A couple of hours, maybe more. But we think we can do it, given time."

"Time is one thing we don't have. Whatever you need, ask. I want that reactor cold as soon as possible."

"Come on Akira," Amita said. "Let's get moving." As they exited Tom's office, she added, "You know, it would be nice if you could shift from speculation to actually doing something."

Suzuki's reply was inaudible behind the closing door.

***

"Was I too hard on Suzuki?" Tom asked.

"He's only trying to help," Yuko said.

"I know, I know. But things are pretty fucked up. Or they will be if we don't shut down the MAM."

"I know." Yuko leaned forward and placed her elbows on the table. "Look, Tom, there's something you need to know."

"Oh God, not more crap, Yuko."

"Kind of. People are talking. They think it's dangerous bringing that girl and her friends here. It can compromise security. Add that to how the hell she got here anyway, and it's a disaster waiting to explode in our faces."

It had been on Tom's mind, but he hadn't seen any alternative. "I know," he said. "But we can't have them running around telling everyone they meet. Once the world discovers what we've really got here this whole place will be a security risk, us included."

"What did you tell Tokyo?"

"That we had an urgent medical issue and needed a clinical psychologist and his support team."

"And they believed you?"

"Why not? I am the project director."

"I'll come up with a better story."

"It's not exactly our top priority, Yuko."

Tom pulled Yuko's tablet across the table. Peter's document was still open. He flipped through the fifteen pages that Shohei Taniguchi had scanned. He should read it for himself, but that would have to wait.

"Did you know I used to work with him, kind of?" Yuko said.

"Work with who?"

"Peter Walker."

"Really? Where?"

"At the Kadota research center, down by Fuji-san. Before I came to CERN."

Tom handed Yuko's tablet back to her. "I had no idea, Yuko."

"We were in different departments," Yuko said. "I never spoke to him. But I saw him a few times, in the cafeteria, places like that."

"I bet you never thought you'd be sitting here reading something he wrote in seventeen thirty-two."

Yuko shook her head.

"The thing is, Yuko, what if Pete knows something and can't get a message through?" Tom said. "What if he figured out what to do, but can't tell us?"

Yuko shrugged. "He could have left another message, but I'd assume there isn't one. Otherwise the girl would have found it herself when she dug up that one."

Tom leaned back and rubbed his tired eyes.

"Shit, Peter, where the hell are you?"

Twenty-Three

They were surrounded by fire.

Peter had cleared the debris and managed to move the beam enough to free Nene's father and help him up to his feet, but it had been for nothing. There was no way out.

He considered rushing through the flames, but with Nene's father's still semi-dazed and his arm heavy on Peter's shoulder, he doubted they'd make it. The alternative, however, was to stand there and burn to death. No, not that. Fire victims were first overcome by fumes, then their unconscious bodies were consumed by the blaze. He started to cough; the smoke was thickening. They had no choice – it was try or die.

"Shinbori-san!"

Peter recognized the voice. "In here, Sakae-san!" he shouted. "We're-"

Sakae burst through the flames. He was draped in a soaking wet kimono, with an even wetter towel wrapped around his head, steaming from the heat.

"Are you OK?" Sakae said breathlessly, as he removed the towel.

"No," Peter replied. "We're trapped. And so are you, now."

"The fire crews are on their way. I will let them know."

"Are you going to jump back through all that lot?"

Sakae looked behind him. "I will find the way. Wait here."

Nene's father, still weak from the blow to his head, slumped heavily on Peter's shoulder. "Shit!" Peter said. "Hang on, Sakae-san. Help me with him." Sakae took the other shoulder. "We've got to get him out of here!"

The flames were fiercer now, driven by the gale blowing outside; the remnant of the electrical storm that had not yet fully subsided.

"It's too late, Sakae-san," Peter shouted. "You should save yourself."

"No, we will find the way!"

But there was no way. They were encircled by fire, an intense terrifying inferno with one thing on its mind; to engulf them all. Peter felt himself weakening with the heat. The smoke was thickening. He coughed again; a rasping, phlegm-filled cough from the inner reaches of the smoke-laden alveoli deep within his lungs.

Sakae sensed it first. "Look!" he shouted.

Peter twisted his head. A portal had opened behind them, its dark, sinister doorway the only choice they had.

"Come on!" he shouted.

Together, Peter and Sakae pushed aside the fallen debris and carried Nene's father into the jaws of hell.

***

The swirling vortex tossed them around like dice in a croupier's cup.

Peter smashed multiple times into the wormhole membrane, each time bouncing back from its elastic surface only to be slammed once again onto the opposing wall, each impact knocking the breath further out of him until his lungs were screaming for mercy.

He lost sight of Sakae-san and Nene's father but knew they must be close – there were no intersecting wormholes of the kind that had taken Nene from him.

Stay awake! Observe! Learn!

He grimly held on to consciousness, but the constant battering and intense, pulsating, turbulent roar was taking its toll. This was worse than his journey to Edo. It was pure torture, the universe's way of reminding him how insignificantly pathetic he was.

Hold on!

No longer able to feel, he was drifting, like a cherry blossom on a gentle morning breeze, carried along by fate.

This is my death.

He saw Nene's face.

Please forgive me. This is all my doing, all my fault.

***

"Nene?" Jane said, gently touching her on the arm. "Are you all right?"

Nene realized she had been staring at… nothing.

"It's Peter," she gasped. "I must go to him."

***

The floor was hard and cold, but reassuringly solid. Peter opened his eyes and lay motionless, staring at the ceiling.

That's not a ceiling. And what the hell was that bloody awful noise?

He rolled over on to his hands and knees and threw up the entire contents of his stomach; a revolting pool of undigested natto, rice and boiled fish.

Someone rubbed his back. "Are you all right, Peter?" It was Sakae, shouting above the racket.

"No," Peter answered. He stood up and took a step away from the mess on the floor. "Oh my God."

They were at the ERG, and it was in the same state as when Peter had found Nene. But now that he could see it directly, and not through the shimmer of the portal in the cave, he could comprehend the full extent of the damage.

It was chaos.

Consoles were smashed, chairs flung aside, with smoke billowing from overturned equipment and destroyed machinery. Red emergency lights flashed dire warnings, their accompanying klaxons the source of that awful, brain-piercing sound. And in the center of it all, the cylindrical arrangement of concentric rings that made up the ERG glowed a soft, pale blue.

He looked around. Sakae had gone to help Nene's father to stand, the cut on his head deepened from the turmoil of the wormhole. Apart from the three of them, nobody else was there.

Peter went to help. "Is he all right?" he shouted, his mouth close to Sakae's ear.

"There's a medical kit in the kitchen," Sakae replied.

"Can you get him there? Do you need my help?"

"I can manage."

"OK, you do that. I'm going to deactivate those bloody alarms."

"I think over there." Sakae nodded towards the semi-circle bank of semi-destroyed consoles.

"You don't say."

Peter rushed over. Two of the six consoles had escaped relatively unscathed from whatever had caused the mayhem, one of which flashed [Cancel Alarm] in bright, hard to miss red. Peter hit it. Everything went quiet.

"Well, that was easy enough," he said.

"Peter!"

He swivelled around, expecting to see Sakae struggling with Nene's father. Instead, it was a wormhole, a portal opening, stable yet shimmering, and in the center of that shimmer, surrounded by the darkness of the yet unlit cave, was the image of him holding Nene, her long hair falling to the floor and his mouth open wide in disbelief.

The wormhole closed.

"That was me!" he said, echoing the same disbelief. "The day I found Nene. And those people I saw then, that was us three, here, now."

The look Sakae's face showed that he was equally dumbfounded. "How could that be?" he said.

"Good question." Peter righted an overturned chair and sat down. He hit [Main Menu], then glanced behind. Nene's father was moving, with Sakae's assistance.

"Are you sure you don't need my help, Sakae-san?"

"We are fine, thank you."

"Shout if you need me."

"We will," Sakae said, followed by a tense, "Oh my goodness!"

Peter had seen it too; a light pulsing from a passageway at the far end of the cave.

"What's down there, Sakae-san?"

"The reactor."

The pulses grew stronger, brighter, with increasing intensity and frequency.

"Does it always do that?" Peter said.

"No!"

Peter turned back to the main menu. It was arranged logically by someone who understood the machine/human interface and understood that keeping things simple was the key requirement, even for the most advanced systems and users.

He touched [Reactor].

The display changed to a series of charts and readouts that was far more complex than the main menu. To a trained user it would present no difficulties. Peter was far from a trained user, but he understood the problem all right; it was shouting at him from the center of the screen.

Reactor Surge

"Shit, that must be what caused the wormholes to destabilize. How do I-"

The glow within the ERG changed from pale blue to a deep, intense ultraviolet, the colour of the lightning in his back garden. Simultaneously the light from the reactor solidified into a constant, non-periodic radiance, like a neon bulb that had flashed itself into steady luminosity. The hair on Peter's arms stood on end; the cave was full of static electricity. He looked over his shoulder. The air was shimmering ten meters behind him, the harbinger of worse things to come. And from the way both the chair and console were vibrating, those things were already here.

Peter grabbed the console with both hands. "Hold on to something!" he shouted above the building roar.

It was already too late. A second wormhole opened, then another, and one more, forming around the inner edge of the cave, each equidistant from the next, facing the ERG, dark and foreboding, as if preparing themselves to carry away every loose object in the cave, whether living or mechanical. The air pulsed violently, bludgeoned them like an invisible mallet. With nothing to hold on to, Sakae and Nene's father were dragged across the floor, slamming into a computer bank that was solidly-enough anchored into the rock to resist the pull of the gravity well.

Peter's chair was pulled from under him straight into the gaping mouth of the nearest portal, his tenuous grip on the console the only thing keeping him from being hauled in along with it. He hung on, desperately trying to locate the reactor power controls with his free hand, mere seconds remaining before he would be forced to release his hold.

There!

He found the on-screen slider and reduced the power setting from 85% to below 3%. The wormholes disappeared; the vibration ceased.

"Fuck," he said, as he collapsed to the floor, exhausted.

There really was no other word to describe it.

***

"Was that an earthquake?" Jane said, her eyes wide.

"I think so," Shohei replied, sarcastically.

"Fuck."

"Jane!"

"Sorry, but fuck it, that was a fucking big one."

Nene looked at Jane.

"Don't worry luv," Jane said. "We all speak like that up north."

"What does fuck mean?" Nene asked.

"Never you mind," Jane replied.

***

"Talk to me, people!" Tom shouted. "Was that a seismic event, or the MAM?"

The entire MCR team were glued to their displays, but Suzuki, true to form, had the answer already. "Nothing on the Japan Meteorological site," he said.

"So, not an earthquake then."

"Correct, Tom-san. It must have been the reactor."

"Fuck me."

Everyone looked at him.

"Sorry," Tom said. "Carry on, as you were."

Yuko approached Tom's control console, which was set at the back of the MCR, higher than the others, from where he could view everything.

"Yes Yuko?" he said.

"It stopped."

"I know," Tom said. "I was here."

Yuko ignored his sarcasm. "Aren't you wondering how it stopped?"

"Not following you, Yuko."

"Tom, if the reactor was surging, then either the safeties kicked in, which is possible, or-"

"Or someone is still there, at the ERG, trying to maintain control."

Yuko nodded. "Exactly."

"But everyone was sucked into those portals. There wasn't anyone left behind."

"I know. But what if someone found their way back? Melanie, perhaps."

"Could it have been the safeties?"

"They'll prevent an overload, but they can't reduce the power like that, assuming that's what happened. That needs human intervention."

"Good point." Tom stood up. "Amita, how long until we can get a video feed from the ERG?"

"Working on it, Tom," she replied.

"Can't you go any faster?"

Amita turned around and glared. A reminder that she wasn't prepared to take shit from anyone, including him.

"As soon as you can, Amita," Tom said.

***

Peter got to his feet while Sakae helped Nene's father to stand. "Are you guys OK?" he said.

"I think so. But I need to get him to the kitchen."

"OK. No, wait."

In the chaos Peter hadn't noticed that the displays on the two still-functioning consoles were different. The one he'd used to cancel the alarm was now set to the reactor power control menu, but the second console was showing:

> Emergency shut down protocol. Enter Authorization
> Code _____

"Sakae-san, quickly." Peter gestured for him to come over.

Sakae helped Nene's father sit on one of the few remaining chairs that hadn't been swallowed by a wormhole, then sprinted over.

"Do you know the code?" Peter said.

"I don't, sorry."

"Then we need to find someone who does."

Peter returned to the main menu and began searching.

"There must be people at the MCR," Sakae said.

"The MCR?"

"Main Control Room."

"Yeah, that's what I assumed," Peter said as he opened the Communications menu. He glanced around. "I need a mic. Can you see any headsets, or anything?"

Sakae pointed to a small grill on the console frame. "I think you can use that."

Peter touched [MCR] and leaned towards the mic. "Hello, this is... us, in the wormhole generator area. Come in, please."

The only reply was a strange, ghostly static.

Peter tried again. "Can anyone hear me?"

The static continued.

"So much for that."

"What should we do?" Sakae said.

"Someone will come, they must know something's gone wrong. Or we can walk out. How far's the MCR?"

"At the main entrance, about a kilometer through the access tunnel, over there."

Peter's eyes followed Sakae's pointing finger. The tunnel entrance was sealed by the kind of thick, heavy steel blast door typically found in a nuclear bunker.

"Can we open that from here?" he asked.

"Yes, it's just a switch, on the left panel."

"I see it."

Peter headed towards the doors.

"I'll stay here with Nene's father, and wait for you," Sakae said.

"OK," Peter replied. "But keep your eyes on that reactor, don't let it surge again."

"I will. After I have tended to his wounds."

Peter moved the controller to the 'Open' position. As the door rose slowly into the belly of the mountain, he had a realization.

"Actually, Sakae-san, maybe you should go. I'd better stay here and look after everything, just in case."

"All right. But first, I'll-"

The blast door was still only halfway open, but it was clear that Sakae had seen something that Peter hadn't. He bent low and looked up the tunnel, expecting to see a long, straight, welcoming passage that would lead to sanctuary. Instead, the lights of the tunnel abruptly stopped twenty meters away at a shimmering wall of black, peppered by tiny flashes of light.

"What the fuck is that?" he said.

**

Peter stood as close to the membrane as he dared.

He'd spent the last fifteen minutes that way, while he waited for Sakae-san to sort out Nene's father. Nothing had happened, save for the continuing pulses of light that flickered across the seemingly infinite darkness, like tiny bolts of lightning in a sea of imaginary clouds.

It was moving, too, away from the ERG at around two centimeters a second. The exact rate didn't matter, what mattered was that it *was* moving, and presumably was permeating the rock, too – assuming he was right about it being a bloody great bubble of self-supporting space.

Deciding that it was worth the risk, he reached out and touched the surface. It was solid yet malleable, like the walls of the wormhole, and with a latent energy that he could sense through the glow around his fingertips. He withdrew his hand. Until he understood what this truly was, caution was definitely the better part of valour.

"What is it?" It was Sakae, together with Nene's father, complete with head bandage.

"Shouldn't he be lying down?" Peter asked.

"A small concussion, but he is doing better." Sakae said. "And he is full of nanobots, so he will be fully recovered quite soon."

"I see." Peter turned to the membrane. "I wish I could say the same for the rest of us."

"Is it bad?"

"It may be, Sakae-san. It may be."

"What is it, Peter-san?"

"I think it's an Alcubierre drive."

"A what?"

"Think of it as our own little bubble of space-time. A warp drive, Scotty. And if it is, it's why we can't contact anyone. We're cut off from everything. Completely isolated. Unless you know how to do sub-space transmissions."

"I still don't understand."

"You know what, nor do I. It shouldn't be possible. Unless…" Peter touched the membrane again. "You know, I think I may have an idea. Come with me."

Peter headed back to the ERG, with Sakae and Nene's father close behind.

Twenty-Four

"So much for someone coming along to interview us," Jane said as she finished off the last of her disappointing tea.

"We might have just slipped their minds," Shohei replied. "There must be many things that require their attention."

"Yeah, and we're one of them, remember?"

Nene stood up from the table and tried the door. She had distrusted Tom-san since the moment they'd met, and now her suspicions about his honesty were confirmed. "It is locked," she said.

Jane gave Shohei one of her 'I told you so' looks and said, "You know, Shugs, I think we know too much about their little secret. Next thing you know, we'll be joining the ranks of the illustrious disappeared."

"Jane, my darling, that is an over-reaction, don't you think?"

"No, not really. But, just in case." Jane opened her handbag and half-pulled out the parchment from Peter, then quickly put it back inside.

"You still have his phone in there, too?"

Jane nodded. "They forget to ask, so I'm forgetting to hand it over. Insurance." Jane looked up at the ceiling air conditioning vent. "Come on Tarzan, up you go."

"Up there?"

"Well, you don't expect me to squeeze this great arse through that little hole, do you?"

"And you expect me to?"

Nene couldn't help smiling. Jane and Shohei were like an old couple who had been married for fifty years and would stay married for another fifty if they could. With no small children that required their attention, they could live life to the fullest, and be who they truly wanted to be – provided they could stop their squabbling.

But that life was no longer for her. She'd wanted it once, but that longing was gone now, replaced by a recognition that there was something important that she had to do, a fulfilling of a destiny that she did not yet comprehend.

The feeling started when they had left the outskirts of Tokyo, a city so huge and vast in its reach, yet somehow so insignificant compared to this new realization. Her mother's words had come back to her once again. *'One day, Nene, you shall see such wonders. Don't be afraid.'* Ka-chan had said them a few weeks before she had died giving birth to Kentaro, her still-born baby brother. That day had torn Nene in two. She was only six years old and couldn't understand why *Kami-sama* would want to take everything from her like that.

To prepare you for this day.

She swore she had heard his voice in the helicopter, and could feel his presence even now, in this room, in this place.

She must find Peter.

"What is it? Nene asked.

"It's a ventilation system, pet," Jane said. "Carries air to every room in the building. It might be a way out. Or not. Only one way to find out."

"I see." Nene climbed on to the table, reached up to the ceiling, pushed the air vent open and cautiously poked her head into the ventilation tunnel. She didn't expect to see the same monsters as the ones on Peter's TV, but she wanted to be sure.

"Jane-san is right. We can get out."

"Glad someone around here's got some balls." Jane said. "You go ahead, love. We'll wait here."

"Are you sure?"

"It's all right, pet. The chances of either of us two getting our backsides up through there aren't worth thinking about."

"Then I shall go, and return with Peter."

"You do that, pet. You do just that."

Nene climbed into the tunnel.

***

The MAM was totally different from Peter's expectations.

Naturally, those expectations were informed by the warp core on the Starship Enterprise, and so were partly based on some Hollywood production designer's warped mind, but even then they had seemed rooted in some form of scientific reality. The MAM, on the other hand, resembled some of the wildest visions he had twenty years before, when his schizophrenia was at its height and when his doctors and psychiatrists and nurses and parents and Jane and his brother and his teachers had all been 'worried' about him.

They'd all been missing the point, all of them.

It hadn't been schizophrenia, or hallucinations, or delusions, or brain farts, or anything else that could be controlled by popping little blue pills. He'd always suspected those episodes of his were something else, something different, something beyond the mere unbalanced workings of a chemical soup inside a disjointed network of misfiring neurons – and now he was sure of it.

He'd seen it before!

Which left two possibilities. Either the brain was time independent, and at the age of fourteen he'd been able to access memories that had not yet formed of events that had not yet happened; to 'see' the future that had not yet transpired, because, as Herr Einstein had so aptly put it, *'The only reason for time is so that everything doesn't happen at once.'* In which case, all events were happening simultaneously throughout the universe, and our understanding of the flow of time was simply based on our awareness. That's why time travel was possible; because everything *was* happening at once, at all points, in all reference frames. If we could somehow step back and 'see' the timeline in its entirety, then we'd see past, present and future as one, unseparated, all connected.

The other possibility was someone or something had been feeding him those visions, in preparation for this day.

Peter preferred the first possibility, particularly as it formed the core of the highly convoluted yet soundly logical argument in that damn paper of his.

"Peter-san?" It was Sakae, joining him.

Peter snapped back to the unreal real world.

"Hi Sakae-san. Where's Shinbori-san?"

"He took your advice and decided to lie down for a while."

Peter had been meaning to ask. "Nanobots, hey?"

"Yes, they have become a standard medical treatment over the past few years. My past few years. Before I got lost in time, I mean." Sakae nodded towards the reactor. "Almost unbelievable, isn't it?"

"Yes, it is."

Peter let his scientific mind do the analysis. They were standing in front of a thick, reinforced glass window that stretched across the diameter of the passageway. Behind that the MAM stood in a secondary, smooth-walled cave, smaller than the one that housed the ERG, and excavated specifically for the purpose of housing the reactor, which was officially called the Matter-Antimatter Prototype according to the placard on the wall. The shape of the vessel intrigued him; it was a giant metal torus, like a huge half-eaten, house-sized apple core, and must have been six or seven meters tall and three across at the top, narrowing down to one meter at the middle. Twelve ten-centimeter diameter tubes ran from the top to the bottom, as if they had once been positioned on the surface of the apple and remained in place after the fruit had been eaten away. The tubes themselves were semi-transparent and filled with plasma flowing in opposite directions in adjacent tubes. The north flow was red, the south flow green. Matter and antimatter, he assumed, though which was which was anybody's guess.

The whole assembly was bathed in a blue glow that filled the compartment and was banded into lines that presumably matched the unseen lines of force that extended beyond the reactor, like iron filings surrounding a magnet in zero gravity.

"Do you understand how it works, Sakae-san?"

"In principle, some, but not in detail. Not like you would, Peter."

What would he say if he knew I'd seen it before?

"Who designed it, do you know?"

"A professor at Tokyo University."

"And where did he get his ideas from?"

"I don't know where *she* got her ideas from. But, sadly, there was an accident, and Nakayama Sensei did not live to see her dream become reality."

Peter nodded in silent recognition of the true genius behind it all. When this was all done, when it was all over, and if there was a way, he'd like to step back a few years and ask Nakayama Sensei if she'd ever had the same kind of visions he did.

"Those tubes, are they carrying matter and antimatter?" Peter asked.

"I believe so, but I'm sorry, I cannot say for certain."

"And I suppose you don't know what gas is making that blue glow?"

"A kind of isotope of neon, I think. I'm only an historian, not a scientist."

"Yeah, you already said that."

But there was something that Sakae-san had not told him, something that had occurred to Peter at the warp bubble membrane and formed part of the reason he had wanted to see the reactor for himself.

"You know what all this is?" Peter said. "It's the greatest weapon in history. Go anywhere, anytime, assassinate anyone you choose. Friend or foe. Do anything you want. Ultimate, God-like power. Heady stuff, Sakae-san, which you need to use wisely."

Sakae sighed. "The entire team are sworn to secrecy. Some politicians were calling to shut us down for vastly overspending our budgets. If only they knew what we were really doing. That's why we went ahead, to understand it, its potential, its dangers, before someone else developed the same thing."

"So, all that about changing history for the good of mankind, that was just smokescreen?"

"No, that was our purpose, our whole reason for going ahead, Peter-san. I did not lie about that."

"You didn't tell me the whole truth either, did you Sakae-san."

Sakae removed his glasses and rubbed his eyes. This was just as stressful for him as it was for Peter. "I thought it best, just in case you should return to the future and-"

"Give everything away?"

Sakae shrugged. "I'm sorry, it was not my intention to mislead you."

"It's all right Sakae-san, it's not your fault. But you lot really were playing with fire."

"I know."

"Speaking of the fire, how did you know to come to the house?"

"I remembered the date, suddenly, as if I had always known. I rushed over as fast as I could to warn you, but I was too late."

"Oh, I don't know," Peter said. "I think you arrived just in time."

"And Nene is in the cave, this cave, if I have that right, back in twenty nineteen. Meeting you. At least, that is what I said to her father."

"She is, or rather was. Where she is now though, I have no idea. Did you tell him that, too?"

"I said we would find her, wherever she is."

"I hope so, Sakae-san. I really hope so."

Peter touched the window. The blue glow of the ionized neon isotope formed geometric patterns on the other side of the glass that danced around his fingertips, following each incremental movement like tiny fish chasing breadcrumbs on the surface of a pond.

"Incredible. Just Incredible," he said, and tapped the observation window. The energy pattern responded, almost as if it were alive.

"Oh, my goody goodness."

He tapped again; 3 dashes, a dot, a dash, then four dashes, then two – Pi. The energy dance locked into that pattern and continued when he removed his hand.

"It was me. All the time, it was me."

"Pardon?"

"Nothing. Come on Sakae-san, I think I may have figured out what we need to do."

***

Nene arrived at a four-way junction.

She stopped, closed her eyes, and listened. The faintest of sounds were coming from the second tunnel; she crawled into it.

***

Peter sat at the console, with Sakae standing at his shoulder.

"My idea," Peter said, "is to set up a wormhole at the base of the mountain, in real time, and then you walk through it and get help. I'll stay here and keep an eye on things."

"Do you know how to do that?"

"No, but it's all menu driven. Shouldn't be too hard."

"Will it get through that space-bubble?"

"I think so. We did." Peter leaned forward to look behind Sakae. "Hello, Shinbori-san."

Sakae turned around. Nene's father was approaching.

"Shinbori-san. How are you feeling?" he said, in Japanese.

"I am fine."

Nene's father really was a man of few words, Peter thought.

Sakae continued. *"Peter is looking for a way out of here. It may take some time."*

"I will wait."

Definitely a man of few words.

"Look," Peter said, "it may take me a while. Why don't you go back to the kitchen and grab a couple more chairs?"

"Would you like a cup of tea as well?" Sakae said.

"They have that here?"

"Of course! It's a kitchen. *Come on Shinbori san.*"

Peter watched Sakae lead Nene's father to the kitchen, then turned his attention back to the console. The screen was a large semi-transparent vertical pane of glass-like material; not fully holographic, but a more advanced version of a PC monitor. The interface itself was familiar. It might even have been Windows 25, or whatever the version was in 2042.

His first action was to ready the reactor power controls and park them in a corner of the display. If anything dramatic happened he'd know where to go. As to *why* the reactor was surging, or had surged, that still wasn't clear. All he knew was that the surging was linked to those unstable wormholes, and–

Of course! Idiot!

Why hadn't he thought of it earlier?

Too stupid for this job, apparently.

Peter searched through the sub menus and found:

System Log

He dug deeper, and found:

Operational Log

"Okey dokey. Let's try this one, shall we?"

Peter opened the logs for the reactor and the ERG. A series of charts and graphs populated the screen, together with an event listing, which, like a ship's log, was a record of everything that the ERG crew had done. He found the video log from the in-cave cameras and opened the final entry.

09:17 October 17, 2042

***

Nene had chosen the right tunnel.

She could see down into a room full of people, sitting at electric desks with TVs. Half of them were foreigners, all of them looked tense. Tom was talking to a Japanese woman and looked the most tense of everyone in the room, as if the weight of it all were on his shoulders alone. Peter wasn't there. Of course he wasn't, that's why everyone was so anxious.

Nene shifted her position until she could better see the huge TV on the wall. It was showing a picture of the mountain with a circle centered on the middle part. The circle expanded and shrank, as if to indicate that, whatever it was, it was growing.

She had to find a way to tell them that the actions they were planning would destroy everything that ever was or ever will be. The Earth, the Moon, the Sun, the stars; all life and all things in the worlds beyond theirs would be shattered into non-existence. Everything would end. There would be nothing left, nothing at all. *Kami-sama* had placed this understanding in her heart, in her mind, and made it her purpose. That's why she had travelled through time, why she had met Peter, why their connection had been so strong from the start.

Would they listen to her?

No, they wouldn't listen to her. Why should they pay any attention to this girl from 300 years ago who knew nothing about their world?

Because I see what you cannot see, know what you cannot know. It was given to me to be the herald of caution, the emissary of fate, the vehicle through which the warning could be made. Through me the awareness of what you have done has been made clear. I am the teller of the tale, the sounder of the alarm. I am the door through which the one will come, the one to whom it is given to know, to understand, the one who must find the way to save us all, before everything is lost.

They were *Kami-sama's* words, but she had made them her own.

***

Peter waved for the two of them to hurry up and sit down.

Nene's father was carrying two kitchen chairs. Sakae was carrying the tea, which Peter accepted, but didn't quite feel like drinking. Not just then, at least.

"I'm sorry it took so long," Sakae said. "The water boiler needed some attention."

"No problem. It gave me time to figure things out."

"You have found something?"

"You could say that." Peter pointed to the display. "This is the event log, which is a history of what they were doing, when they were going to do it, and what happened as a result. And that's the date, today, October seventeenth, twenty forty-two."

"The day after my journey to Edo!"

"Indeed. But when you didn't turn up at the pre-arranged time and place for the return journey, well, they went looking for you in the house, using a kind of viewing portal."

"We call it a remote-telescope," Sakae said. "A way of seeing without actually being there."

"They should have used that, instead of sending you there in the first place."

"Tom thought an observer on the ground would be more effective."

"Yeah, well, I'm not sure that was the best idea Tom had all day." Peter moved the reactor power charts to center screen. "Anyway, this is the reactor. That's them sending you back, yesterday. See how it spikes? I reckon that explains why you went back fifteen years too early."

"Yes, of course."

"And then this happened."

Peter expanded the graphic to reveal the morning of the 17th. Compared to the relatively small, single power spike of the 16th, this was mayhem. Multiple peaks and troughs filled the view, like interference patterns on an early radar, or the frequency spectrum of a 100-piece orchestra playing in different keys and different tunings.

Sakae stared in awe. "Oh my goodness. Is that today?"

"Yeah, right when they opened the telescope, or just after. Which is when all this happened." Peter repositioned the reactor power graphic and selected the video feed. "You'd better prepare yourself, Sakae-san, this isn't going to be easy." He started the video.

They watched in stunned silence as four portals opened in midair, surrounding the ERG and its crew, just as they themselves had experienced no more than an hour ago, except those paled in comparison with the ones on the video. Peter had already seen the chaos, but even the second viewing was tough.

What affected him most were the scarcely audible screams of the ERG crew as they were sucked, one-by-one, into those evil portals that led to God knew where. They might have survived, all of them, if they had been taken to Earth at another place and time. But they could equally well have been thrown into outer space and died a lonely death amongst the stars. At least that would have been quick. Except one of the crew had survived, he was sure of that.

Peter paused the video.

"So, basically everything went haywire," he said. "The reactor surged, those wormholes formed, the crew got sucked out, and then one of them took Nene forward from the house, and then came back again to grab us three. It just wobbled around on its space-time coordinates. You know, same space, different time, appearing, disappearing. Damn thing's got a mind of its own."

"You mean the wormhole they set up to find me is what caused the fire," Sakae said. "How could that be? It means the future happened before the past."

"Yeah, well, that's the nature of paradox. But I think there may be more to it than that, Sakae-san. I think the wormholes are intersecting with each other, interfering, a kind of crossover event. I don't know what else to call it. And when that occurs, shit, I can't even begin to think what might happen."

"So, all of this is due to wormholes crossing?"

"It may be," Peter said. "But for that, we, or someone, will need to spend months going through all this data. Years, even. But, before all that, there's one more thing I want to show you. And for this, I think you need to need to be extra ready."

"All right."

"And by that, I mean, really, really ready."

"I will try to be" Sakae said, a doubtful look on his face.

Peter allowed the video to go forward another fifteen seconds, then paused at the point where a woman, the last one of the crew, was bravely holding onto the same console where he now sat.

"I think she's trying to shut down the reactor," Peter said, "but didn't have time to enter the authorization code, just reduce reactor power. Still, she saved the day. God knows what would have happened if she hadn't."

"It's Melanie, my friend," Sakae said. "She is lost, too. They are all lost, all of them. I can't believe it."

Peter stretched the video to zoom in closer to the woman's face. He looked past Sakae at Nene's father. The sadness on his face told Peter that he was right.

"Have you seen the portrait of Nene's mother?" Peter said. "The one in his library, I mean."

"Yes, may times," Sakae replied.

"And you never thought she looked like your friend Melanie?"

"I did, but that was just a coincidence, just ... oh my."

Sakae turned to Nene's father.

"Why didn't you tell me?" he said, in Japanese.

Takeshi wasn't listening. He stretched out his hand and touched the face of the woman once lost to him forever, and now lost again.

Sakae turned to Peter. "Why didn't he tell me? All these years, he knew. Why not tell me?"

Peter shook his head. "I don't know, Sakae-san. I've been thinking about that, too."

"But how did it happen?"

"She must have been taken back to the house, probably by the same wormhole that brought us here. You know, it bounced around on its coordinates and just grabbed her here and threw her back there. Why don't you ask Shinbori-san, see if she just magically appeared in front of him one day, just like I did."

"I will, yes, I will."

"And in the meantime, I'm going to try to figure out the portal creation protocols and see if we can get ourselves out of this bloody place before there's nothing left for us to get ourselves out to."

***

Nene thought she could see a small room with a large glass window. She lay her head flat on the vent to see better. Yes, it was definitely a room, like a library, with a table and shelves with boxes, books and other things that she could not clearly see.

The tunnel ahead branched into four other tunnels, one of which was heading in that direction. She crawled forward as quietly as she could until she reached the junction. The passage leading to the library was narrower than the one she was in. Nene squeezed herself inside, reached her arms forward and found a way to move like a caterpillar who thought she was a snake.

Five minutes later she opened the air vent and dropped silently onto the table in the middle of the library. Keeping low, she crept to the glass window and observed the room. Everybody was facing towards the big TV. No-one had seen her.

What should she do next?

Wait, my child. You must wait.

The voice was her mother's.

Nene sat on the floor, her back to the wall beneath the glass window. After all these years, she could at last remember Ka-chan's face.

Twenty-Five

Sakae stared over Peter's shoulder at the display.

Time Now:	Oct 17, 2042, 15:32:54
Separation:	000 seconds
Location Z:	+500,000m
Location X/Y:	+/- 0000 : 0000
Mass (max):	200kg

"That did not seem so difficult," he said.

"That's because there's a supercomputer over there doing the heavy lifting," Peter replied. "All we have to do is punch in the coordinates."

"What does it mean, location plus five hundred thousand, and all those zeros?"

"They're relative coordinates to where we are now. We're going to open a portal five hundred kilometers above our heads, right now, in real time, and then use that thing," Peter pointed to a small joystick next to the keyboard, "to manually move the opening to the MCR building."

"Why not just position the portal there from the beginning?"

"Because, Sakae-san, I realized I don't know the exact coordinates of the MCR, that's why. This way we fly there, like an eagle, with the wind beneath our wings."

"Very poetic."

"I thought so. Plus, it'll give me some wiggle room if the reactor surges again. Which actually is the main reason."

"You mean to avoid the possibility of crossing over with another wormhole?"

"You catch on fast, Sensei."

"I do my best."

Peter leant forward and positioned his index finger over the [Initiate] button, keeping his other hand next to the reactor power controls.

"When we land, so to speak, you and Nene's father go through. I'll stay here and keep things under control. Just make sure you bring someone back with you before it's too late."

"I will be back as soon as possible."

"Good. Did he say anything, by the way?"

"He said he will tell me later." Sakae said.

Peter looked past Sakae. "Shinbori-san, are you all right?"

Nene's father nodded. When it's all over, Peter thought, we'll grab a bottle of twenty-first century Sake, sit around a campfire and have a come-to-Jesus session where everybody tells their respective stories. And that included Tom, too. No secrets, no hidden agendas, no false narratives – and no accusations either. Just an honest recounting of all that had happened, for the sake of both scientific accuracy and the future of humanity. And for Nene. Especially for Nene.

Will I ever see her again?

There was always hope, but Peter knew that hope wasn't going to be enough. He scratched an eye; better to let them think that he had an itch, rather than a tear.

"Here goes nothing," Peter said, as he hit [Initiate]. "Sakae-san can you monitor the power levels for me? I'm going to need both hands for this portal control."

"Twenty percent," Sakae said. "And steady."

The ERG rings started to glow blue.

"Is that normal?" Peter said.

"I think so."

"Good."

The center of the ERG began to shimmer.

"That is also normal," Sakae said. "It takes about fifteen seconds for the picture to form."

They watched as the shimmer moved through cymatic-like interference patterns into a clear, stable image of a black sky full of stars.

"Oh, my goodness," Peter said, in complete awe.

"Where is it?" Sakae asked.

"*It* is up there, five hundred kilometers high, pointing upwards, straight at the milky way. Incredible, just incredible." Peter moved the view around using the onscreen controller, taking care to point the portal away from the Sun. "Didn't you lot ever think of putting a man on Mars with this thing?"

Sakae nodded. "A woman, next year or the year after. Actually, there is already a NASA crew there, and a small station. But, one thing at a time."

"Melanie?"

"She was the bravest, most adventurous of us all."

"I'm sure she was." Peter scratched an eye again. "OK, let's get this thing back to ground zero."

He rotated the view until Japan filled the ring. It was a cloudless day, and from five hundred kilometers altitude the view was just as extraordinary as the infinity of the universe.

"Our very own private real-time Google Earth," Peter said. "Do you still have that in twenty forty-two?"

"Yes. But, not real-time. Not yet."

"Yeah, that would be quite a thing. How's our reactor doing?"

"Twenty percent, and stable."

"Good, then let's see if we can do this, shall we?"

Peter moved the portal opening downwards towards Mount Fuji, the most obvious landmark.

"Just need to get my bearings here," he said. "That's Fuji-san, so that must be Kofu city. Can you make out the expressway?"

"There," Sakae pointed.

"Oh yeah, I see it." Peter continued to manipulate the portal opening. "We can just follow that up to lake Suwa, and then come down a bit to Mount Nyukasa. You know, this isn't as hard as it looks, but it would be handy if the view had some place names, just like... Shit, what's happening?"

The view, which had been moving north, was now moving south east.

"Aren't you going the wrong way?" Sakae said.

"It's not me," Peter replied. "The controls aren't responding."

The image in the center of the ring continued its gentle glide through the perfectly clear afternoon air towards the Earth's surface. The concrete of Kofu city changed to tree-covered mountains, then to the satin smooth waters of one of the Fuji Five Lakes, the *Fuji-goko*, at the base of the mountain.

"That's Kawaguchiko," Sakae said.

"I know." Peter glanced at the readings.

Time Now:	Oct 17, 2042, 15:36:24
Separation:	-720,320,163 seconds
Location Z:	+3,671m
Location X/Y	-44,230m : -55,236m
Mass (max):	200kg

The glide continued across smaller mountains, passing low over villages and fields, then slowing down before stopping three hundred meters above the farmhouse Peter knew so well. In an instant he understood.

"Oh, my bloody goodness," he said, softly.

"Where is it?" Sakae said.

"My house," Peter answered, "Twenty-three years ago." The image slowly descended towards the garden. Peter could see himself in the cherry tree.

"My detector's acting like a lightning rod, attracting the portal."

My God, I was right. It was me. I did this. All of it.

"That's you!" Sakae exclaimed.

They were thirty meters above the house now, still descending. Nene came out of the back door, carrying two cups of tea.

"And that's Nene-chan!"

Nene's father got up and approached the front of the ring assembly. He stared as the image sank the last few meters to touch the grass. Nene was facing away from him. Then she turned around, as if a sudden sound had attracted her attention.

Peter readied himself as Nene dropped the cups. Her mouth moved, but her words were inaudible. Peter knew them well enough; '*Chichi-ue.*' She turned away, towards him, still in the tree. *'It's my father."*

"Nene!" Shinbori-san cried it out from his soul. His entire life, his reason for being, his whole universe was no more than an arm's length away.

Nene moved towards the portal. Peter watched himself jump from the ladder and race across the garden.

Now, it must be now.

Light pulsed from the passageway that led to the reactor. The power readings fluctuated, then shot up from the relative safety of 20% to a dangerous 85%. Peter dragged the sliders to reduce power, but the response from the reactor was slow. The cave shuddered, as it had earlier, but with a more intense ferocity that shook the solid rock as if it were cardboard.

"Hold to something!" Peter shouted above the roar of the four dark, ominous wormholes now forming within the cave, just as they had done before.

Then everything went black.

***

"It's surging again!" Yuko shouted, although everyone had already grabbed hold of the nearest console, or anything else that was bolted to the floor.

The intense jolting stopped.

Tom came down from his desk. "Did we do that?"

"It wasn't us, Tom," Amita replied, checking with Suzuki, who shook his head in confirmation.

"The control anodes?"

"They must be holding," Yuko said. "Unless it was one of the crew. Either way, we're still here."

"Not if that happens again," Tom said. "Amita, where are you with the frequency alignment?"

"Struggling. We need more time."

"We don't have time," Tom said. "Literally, we do not have time."

***

Nene sat down on the hard floor, her back once again set firmly against the wall beneath the glass window that opened on to the big room.

She'd seen the fear in Tom's face, and that of the others, too. She'd felt it herself, and although the earthquake had stopped as abruptly as it had begun, she knew that they would not survive the next one.

This is it, the beginning of the end.

***

The darkness stretched in all directions through the infinity of non-existence, a complete nothingness formed by the absence of light, of sound, of touch.

He floated, pure consciousness in the eternal void, separated from all that had ever existed or ever will. He held no physical form, his body no longer necessary, his material being no longer required.

A presence. She was nearby.

An image formed in front of him, around him, inside him, through him; multiple wormholes dancing around a giant, translucent sphere, swaying like seaweed caught in an ocean current. The sphere grew larger, expanding beyond the limits of his vision until it was so vast it seemed to fill the universe, to be the universe.

He reached for her – she was so close.

The sphere burst.

The wormholes fell inwards into the resulting abyss, twisting around each other and forming a vortex that spun at the speed of light, tearing open the fabric of space-time before collapsing into a black hole, a singularity of such extreme density, of such ferocious power that all matter, all light, all existence was sucked into its core.

She was gone.

The Earth was gone.

The Solar System was gone.

The Milky Way was gone.

Then the Andromeda Galaxy.

Then the Virgo Cluster.

Then everything else, every last atom, every last particle, every last memory until there was once more only darkness that stretched in all directions through the infinity of non-existence.

Then a massive explosion of brilliant light filled the re-born universe with everything new that ever will be.

***

"Peter!"

He drifted upwards through the void towards the voice.

"Peter!"

He felt himself returning, his form recovering, his being reconstituting from the unbounded energy of thought to the solid reality of the physical universe.

"Peter! Can you hear me?"

The urgency in Sakae's voice finally brought Peter home. He was lying on his side, his left cheek pressed to the cold, hard rock floor of the cave and his back to Nene's father, who was pushing with his thumbs on the *tsubo* points on Peter's shoulders, spine and neck.

Peter raised a hand a few inches to signal he had returned. "I'm OK," he said.

Nene's father pulled Peter into a seating position. *"Daijo-bu, Peter-san?"* he said, vigorously rubbing his back.

"I'm fine," Peter said. "Really, I'm fine."

"Tatte." Nene's father helped Peter to stand.

He surveyed the scene. Whatever had transpired after he fainted had only slightly affected the area, although light grey smoke was floating upwards from a re-smashed console. A fire extinguisher lay on the ground next to it, ready if needed, although its work was done.

"What happened?" he asked.

"I want to ask you the same thing!" Sakae said.

"Did the reactor stabilize?"

"Yes. Apart from the small fire, everything is all right, as much as it can be, except Nene isn't here."

Peter, still dizzy, sat at the console. "I know," he said.

"Shinbori-san is rather upset."

Peter tapped the hand still on his shoulder. "We'll find her, Shinbori-san," he said, knowing it was a lie.

Sakae pulled up a chair. "We were worried about you, Peter."

Peter sat down. "How long was I out?"

"A few minutes, no more."

Peter nodded. "Not so long this time, then."

"Peter?" Sakae needed an explanation. "Please, if there is something we should know."

What was he going to tell Sakae-san? That when he was young he'd had a form of schizophrenia, characterized by deep, dark psychotic episodes with visions so intense, so real, he'd believed them to be the true reality, and that the world upon awakening was the dream? And now, twenty years later, he'd had another, with a warning so abundantly clear, so massively terrifying, so critically urgent… and whether it had been a message from his subconscious or a communication from a fifth-dimensional super-being didn't matter; he understood it now, all of it.

"Are you ill? Sakae asked.

"I'm fine," Peter said. "Just got a bit lightheaded. It happens sometimes."

"Would you like some fresh tea?"

The cup that Sakae had made earlier had spilled on to the floor.

"Please."

"Then I shall get you some."

"Everything really is connected, Sakae-san. Everything." Peter said, as Sakae headed towards the kitchen

"I know," Sakae replied. "I know."

***

"It's Pi!"

Suzuki's ecstatic voice reverberated once around the MCR and twice through everyone's headset.

Amita, standing right next to him, had heard the shout clearly enough, but that didn't mean she had the first clue what he was talking about.

"What is?" she said.

Suzuki turned towards her, his face beaming. "It's Pi!" he exclaimed, for the second time.

Tom came over to Suzuki's console. "What's Pi, Suzuki-san?"

"The membrane frequency modulation," Suzuki said. "It's based on Pi. Amazing!"

"What do you mean, based on Pi?" Tom asked.

"When I was twelve, I memorized the first eight thousand digits. I recognized the pattern in the frequency readouts! It's Pi!"

The entire MCR team burst into applause. Suzuki stood up and bowed, a huge 'I'm the hero of the day' smile on his face.

"OK, everyone," Tom said, his arms extended. "Settle down." The applause died away. "So, what do we do, Suzuki-san?"

Amita answered for him. "We run the membrane modulation pattern through Big Brain, find where in the sequence it aligns to Pi, and then configure our transmission frequencies accordingly."

"How long, Amita?" It was Yuko.

Amita turned to her now-famous colleague. "Suzuki-san?"

"Twenty to thirty minutes." he said.

"That long?" Tom asked.

"Pi is an infinite number series, Tom. Even Big Brain needs time for that."

"Then, you'd better get on it, hadn't you," Tom retorted. "And I thought we all agreed to stop calling our GR-T1X Quantum Supercomputer 'Big Brain.'

Suzuki shrugged – he rather liked the name.

***

Nene crossed her legs, placed her left palm facing upwards in her right, and adopted the *Zazen* meditation posture.

Unlike her father she wasn't a regular practitioner, but the urge to go within was almost overwhelming. She closed her eyes and thought of her mother, her father, her grandmother and all that she had ever known; all gone now, lost in time, beyond her reach.

She let the images pass and waited for her mind to quieten, for her ego to step aside until she reached 無心 - *mushin* - no mind, no thought, a state that she had rarely been able to reach, if ever.

Today was different; she was there in moments.

The void was complete, the darkness total; all form was gone, everything become nothing, nothing become everything.

A voice called gently, "Nene."

"Yes," she replied. "I hear you."

A bright light surrounded her, full of energy and love, bathing her with its warmth, protecting her with its limitless strength.

"Today is only the beginning. There is more to be done."

"What must I do?" she asked.

"Find him after the separation. Then bring him to us."

"How?"

"We will show you the way."

"I don't understand."

"You will," the voice said. "In time."

The light faded.

Nene opened her eyes. She was back in the room, sitting against the wall.

"Peter," she said in a whisper.

***

Peter found the reactor override menu just as Sakae returned with his tea.

"Here you are," Sakae said.

"Thanks," Peter replied, but he was too focused on the task in hand to worry about a hot beverage.

"I'll leave it here, then." Sakae put the cup to one side.

Peter was no longer listening. He moved further down through a series of nested menus until he found it.

Safety Overrides - Proceed with Caution

He touched [Remove Overrides].

"Peter?" Sakae said.

"They should have password protected these too, but they forgot," he said. "Or deliberately overlooked it."

"I meant, what are you doing?"

Peter hit [Confirm].

"We have to wait until the wormholes cross over," he said. "The explosion will dissipate into the vortex and cancel out the singularity."

"Explosion?" Sakae said. "What explosion?"

***

"We're through!" Amita shouted.

Tom was standing right next to her. "Well done!" he said. "All right, everybody, this is it!"

The MCR was already buzzing.

Nene stood up. Everyone was still facing away from her, staring at the big TV, which was coming alive as images began to form.

"We have remote systems control!" Suzuki exclaimed.

The room cheered. This time Suzuki remained in his seat; this wasn't the moment to acknowledge his second applause of the day.

"Listen up," Tom said. The room quietened. "We're going to set up the emergency crew escape portal, right here in the MCR, and use that in reverse to gain entrance to the ERG. I'll go in with Suzuki and shut down the reactor... what the hell?"

The MCR was silent, the whole team staring at the video feed from high in the cave ceiling, just as Tom now was.

"Oh, my fucking goodness," he said.

***

Nene came out of the room for a clearer view.

She recognized the rings and the desk-like TVs, just like the ones in the big room where she now stood. Most of them in the cave were smashed, and several were smouldering, just as they had been when the same image had appeared behind Peter the day he had rescued her from the cave. And, just like her home in Edo, she knew it was the tunnels, the wormholes, that had caused the destruction.

But now she knew who the three figures were, the ones whose faces had been hidden by the haze, whose forms had been lost to her when she had finally slipped into unconsciousness.

They were still alive!

***

"That's Peter!" Tom's yell resonated throughout the MCR. His face was clearly visible, but the others had their backs to the camera. "Who the hell are those two?" Tom said, exerting a modicum of self-control.

One of the men turned towards Peter. They were talking, but their words were inaudible, like an old silent movie.

Amita realized it first. "That's Sakae! But, older."

"Fuck!" Tom said, followed quickly by, "Sorry, everyone."

Tom moved closer to the main display. Peter was accessing the menus on one of the consoles, but the camera was too distant to see clearly what he was doing.

"Can we get another view?" Tom said.

"All the other cameras are down," Yuko replied. "This is the only one."

"Then zoom in closer."

"No zoom, it's a fixed lens."

"Great. What about the desk mics?"

"All inoperative."

"Christ! I need to know what he's doing, people! Suzuki-san?"

Suzuki was focused on the data now pouring onto his screen.

"Suzuki!" Tom shouted. "Tell me what he's doing."

Suzuki looked up from his console. "He's cancelling the overrides, Tom."

"What?" Tom ran to Suzuki's seat to see for himself. "How can he do that? He doesn't have the codes."

"Next upgrade," Suzuki replied. Then the realization hit. "Oh my God, he's going to deliberately surge the reactor."

"Shut it down, shut it down now!" Tom bellowed.

"I can't. We have to make direct interface. You know that."

"Then override his overrides, Suzuki!"

"I can't, not from here."

"Then get us in there!"

"I can give you four hundred kilograms," Amita said. "No more than that. Three minutes."

Tom tapped his multi-function wristwatch, then adjusted his headset mic. "I need the security team here, now!" he instructed, curtly. "Yes, armed."

Yuko looked at him. They all did.

"Just in case," Tom said.

                              ***

Nene stepped back into the shadows. When the moment came, she would be ready.

                              ***

Sakae was beyond worried.

"What explosion?" he repeated the question.

Peter moved the reactor controls to 50% power. "When the power hits eighty percent it'll create unstable wormholes," he said. "You two take your chances in those. You could end up anywhere, but it'll better than staying here."

"But, before you said to shut it down."

"I was wrong. We've opened the door to hell here, Sakae-san, and the only way out is to slam it shut, and for that we need a massive blast of energy. We have to detonate the reactor, there's no other way."

"Are you sure?

"You'll just have to trust me."

"Well I do, but I still don't understand."

Peter pointed to the [Confirm] button.

"I've already hit it once, but if it reappears, which it might, and I'm not around, then push it. It'll release the safeties and send the reactor super-critical. And, if it doesn't, then, well, we're all fucked, anyway."

Peter pushed the power sliders to maximum.

"The winds of the heavens shift suddenly, as does human fate," he said softly.

"Wait," Sakae pleaded. "You're going to blow it up? Why?"

Peter turned to Sakae. "Because, Sakae-san, the universe is too young to die, and we have to… shit!"

The power sliders on the console were moving downwards, back towards the 20% mark. The wormhole generation menu had changed, seemingly by itself.

Time Now:	Oct 17, 2042, 15:54:31
Location:	Channel One, Emergency Crew Escape
Mass (max):	400kg

"What the bloody hell is this?" Peter said, unable to counteract the movement.

***

"We have partial reactor control," Suzuki announced. "Bringing it down to twenty percent."

"Good, good. Well done," Tom said.

Amita entered a series of commands. "I'm initiating the escape portal now, Tom."

"Four hundred kilograms, right?"

"Enough for five people, yes."

Tom turned to the three guards from the security unit. One of them was Kenji Hayashi whom he'd left outside the interview room door. All of them were armed.

"Just follow my lead," Tom said. "And do nothing unless I say. Clear?"

The guards nodded. It was the first time in five years they had been called out, and Tom hoped the long wait hadn't made them trigger happy. But, all things considered, that was the least of his worries.

"It's open!" Amita said.

A circle of light, four meters across, formed in the space between the main display and the first bank of consoles, its bottom edge just touching the MCR floor. Built into the system as an escape route for the crew if something had gone disastrously wrong, it had thankfully never been used. If things had gotten bad enough for the ERG team to be unable to walk out, or to prevent the fast reaction team from getting to the cave, then an emergency exit wouldn't have been any use anyway – or so Tom had always thought. He was glad to have been wrong.

"OK, let's go," he said. "You too, Suzuki-san. Amita, keep the portal open as long as you can. But, if it destabilizes, shut it down. We'll sort things out at the ERG."

"Copy that."

***

The image in the circle began to solidify as the shimmer faded. Nene could see Peter, her father and Sakae-Sensei staring back at everyone in the room, their faces distinct despite the lingering haze. She moved closer, risking someone seeing her, but it was too late for that. She would have to be quick and get through before anyone could hold her back.

Tom and the four men entered the tunnel.

Nene raced passed TVs, desks and people in white coats, and leaped into the portal just as a voice cried out, "Hey, stop her!"

As Nene slipped through the opening into the cave, she heard another voice shout, "Overmass!"

***

The indistinct shadows in the ring morphed into the solid shapes of five men walking towards them, looking for all the world as if they were on morning stroll.

Sakae was delighted. "They've gotten through! We're saved!"

Peter was less convinced. "Hello Tom," he said, as the figures solidified into flesh and blood, three of which had pistols in their hands. They stepped from the ERG on to the cave floor.

Then he saw her.

"Nene!" he cried.

"Peter!"

The four men turned around. Nene was standing right behind them.

"What the hell's she doing here?" Tom said.

Interpreting that as a clear instruction, the nearest guard grabbed Nene forcibly by the arm.

"It will be better for you if you should let me go," she said calmly.

"Don't," Tom said, and turned his attention back to Peter, as did all three guards. Behind them, the image in the center of the ERG ring began to shudder.

This is it.

"You'll need to step away from the console, Pete," Tom said.

"Let Nene go, Tom."

"I can't do that Pete, not until we have rectified the situation."

"You can't shut it down Tom, anything less than a full detonation will precipitate the formation of the singularity."

"What the hell are you talking about? Now, please, Pete, move away."

"Can't do that, Tom."

"Pete. They have orders to shoot, for God's sake. Now stand aside, please."

Peter stood his ground.

"Pete, come on, don't be ridiculous, man!"

***

The grip on Nene's arm tightened. It hurt, but not unbearably so. It mattered not – Chichi-ue was moving silently, unnoticed by the others, and in his hand was, of all things, a teacup.

She closed her eyes.

Peter, my love, do as they ask. Trust it. Trust yourself.

***

Peter stepped back from the console.

He could have sworn he'd heard her voice.

"Suzuki-san," Tom said.

The smallest of the five approached, and with a polite "Excuse me" slipped himself between Peter and the console.

"Hello Sakae-san, it's nice to see you again," Suzuki said.

"Hello, Suzuki-san." Sakae replied, unsure of which side to take.

Peter motioned for Sakae to stand back, just as Nene's father move clear of the console bank, unobserved by Tom and the others.

Suzuki opened the reactor controls. "I'll need a few minutes here, Tom," he said, "for a controlled shut-down."

"Just get it done, and quickly, Suzuki."

Tom positioned himself between the translucent display and the ERG rings. Two guards joined him. Hayashi stayed where he was, Nene still firmly in his grasp.

"Jesus Christ, Pete, just what the hell do you think you were trying to do?"

"We need to blow it up Tom."

"We need to shut it down, that's what we need to do."

"You'll kill us all Tom, every last one of us."

"You're the one that's about to kill everyone. If that thing goes up it'll take half of Japan with it."

"We're in our own private universe here, Tom. The blast energy will be dissipated far into the cosmos."

"Like hell it will."

***

Nene opened her eyes.

This is not the end, my love, it is merely the beginning. But you must stop him, before it cannot be undone.

***

"Initiating shutdown," Suzuki said as he entered the authorization code.

"Tom, think about it," Peter urged. "Why is the warp bubble growing? What's driving it to expand?"

"Phase one complete." Suzuki navigated through additional menus. "Moving to phase two."

"There are multiple wormholes attached to the portal, Tom," Peter said. "It's attracting them, like a giant magnet. I saw them. They're feeding it with exotic matter, not only from our universe but from other universes, too. The whole thing's balanced on a knife edge. If you shut it down, the portal will collapse, the wormholes will crash right through, and if they intersect, if they crossover, it'll rip space-time to shreds and form a singularity right here, right in this cave. And when it does, everything you've ever known, or ever loved, or ever will love, will be, just... gone."

Do not despair, my love. There will be a time apart, but we will find each other once again.

Suzuki looked up through the display. "Phase two complete, Tom. Ready for your final confirmation."

"Confirm shutdown." Tom said.

Suzuki hesitated.

"Well, go on then."

"But, Tom, what if Peter-san is right?"

***

Yuko shouted into her headset. "Tom, Tom!"

"He can't hear you, Yuko," Amita said.

"Damn!"

"I'm shutting down the escape portal now, before it collapses completely. We have no choice."

"OK, OK." Yuko slumped to her seat. "Shit."

***

"Do you really think the entire universe cares how a tiny little fire got started? No, you're wrong on this, Pete. Not this time." Tom gestured to Suzuki. "Keep going, Suzuki, shut it down."

"For God's sake, Tom," Peter was almost begging. "Can't you see? It's not about the bloody paradox, it's the physics of the different universes, they're not compatible, we can't let them mix, it'll be catastrophic."

"Shut up Pete, will you, for God's sake. Suzuki, complete the shutdown, now! And that's a fucking order!"

"But, Tom," Suzuki replied. "I think he might be right."

"Jesus, give it to me!"

Tom rounded the console and shoved Suzuki aside so hard he tumbled out of the chair.

"Tom, don't!" Peter didn't mean to hurt his friend, but with the power of desperation he wrapped a forearm around Tom's throat and pulled backwards with all his strength. They fell together, their destinies entwined, their journeys fused by urgency, their stories as entangled as the unstable, unforgiving wormholes they were trying to defeat.

Nene's father chose that moment to hurl the teacup straight at the guard holding Nene. She was ready and ducked as the ceramic missile struck the man on his temple. Instantly unconscious, he released his grip and fell to the floor.

A pistol fired. The second guard didn't mean to – it was a reflex, a natural, subconscious reaction to perceived danger. The bullet struck Nene's father in the shoulder before he could spin out of its path. But it's hard to put a man down with a single shot, especially one as powerful and determined as a samurai warrior who had spent years preparing for this day of reckoning, this instant, this culmination of everything he had dedicated his entire life to; the protection of those he loved, the ultimate sacrifice his warrior code demanded. He sprang forward and was upon both guards in an instant; Jiu-Jitsu against iron, flesh against lead. In the resonant chamber of the cave, the sound of gunshots echoed like exploding firecrackers.

Nene instinctively ducked to the floor and covered her ears. Peter leaped around the console. She was only a few meters away and he was on her in an instant, shielding her from the mayhem that was her father defending them against the madness.

Bodies thudded to the floor. First one guard, then the other. Then, when those he would give his life for were finally safe, Nene's father sank to his knees and toppled on to his side, his chest drenched in blood.

***

"Get us in there, now, Amita!" Yuko screamed.

Amita was an island of calm in the storm of panic that the MCR had become. "I'm re-configuring the portal," she said. "Three minutes."

***

"Chichi-ue!"

Nene came out from under Peter's protective shield and hurried to her father.

"Chichi-ue," she cried, her hands on his wounds, her heart tearing apart. "Chichi-ue."

Twenty-Six

In all his life, Peter had never felt so helpless.

Sakae-san was dead. A chance bullet had smashed into his forehead, killing him instantly. Tom lay motionless on the floor of the cave where the back of his skull had crashed hard onto the unforgiving rock. It had been unintentional, but Peter knew he would live with the guilt for the rest of his life, and for Sakae too – for everything, in fact. For all this, every last part of it, was his doing.

To make matters worse, if that were even possible, Nene's father lay dying on the floor, and there was nothing he could do about it, nothing that he could say that could possibly comfort her.

He tried anyway. "Nene, I'm so sorry," Peter said, laying a hand on her shoulder.

She touched his fingers with her own. In that second, that instant of unspoken communication, he felt her forgiveness, although her sorrow would surely last as long as his remorse. But there was more to be done, and he was the one who had to do it. He returned to the console. Suzuki, unharmed, rose from his hiding place under the adjacent machine.

"Are you OK, Suzuki-san?" Peter asked.

"I'm OK."

"You know what we have to do, don't you?" Peter said, as he cancelled the reactor shutdown routine and reset the power sliders to maximum.

"Yes, I know. And you are right, Peter-san. I believe you," Suzuki said. "But I reset the safeties, so you'll need to deactivate them again. I will help you."

"Good, then you have control." Peter stood and let Suzuki take his place.

Nene's father was stroking her hair. His injuries were perhaps not as immediately life threatening as they had first appeared, but without medical attention he stood little chance. *If this didn't work, none of them stood a chance anyway.*

Peter went once again to her side. "Nene, you have to go," he said, although he hadn't yet figured how to make that happen.

"I cannot leave him."

"You must go now, before this place is destroyed. I will bring your father."

"No, Peter. I will stay with you."

"I will be with you soon, Nene, but you must go. Now."

"Peter, I cannot."

Her father tried to make the decision for her. "Nene! Go!"

"No, father, I will not."

The ERG rings started to glow blue. Multiple outlines of people rushing towards them shimmered through the central haze.

"See," Peter said. "They're on their way. Go with them, we'll follow."

"Not with them, my love," Nene said. "We must go to a different place."

"What different place?"

He didn't get to find out. The shimmer inside the ERG abruptly disappeared, leaving in its wake a circle of nothing, an empty space devoid of light, a total vacuum, a connection between universes that heralded the beginning of the end of both. The hair on his arms stood on end, as if the air had suddenly chilled.

"Fuck-a-duck," Peter said, instantly understanding that it was already too late.

Suzuki stood up. "It's starting!" he shouted.

Light flashed from the reactor area. The cave shuddered as the warp bubble, still extended as a giant sphere within the core of the mountain, pulsed in sympathy with the reactor.

"Get ready, Suzuki-san!"

"Seventy-three percent power."

"Wormholes will form at eighty, better grab hold of something!"

"I already am!"

Peter grabbed Nene's hand. "Stay with me, and do not let go," he said.

"Always with you, my love," she replied. "For all time."

The first wormhole opened behind Suzuki. Driven by the surging reactor and inherently unstable, its gravity well sucked at him like a tornado. Suzuki gripped the desk, fighting the pull.

"Eighty-two percent!" he called out. "I'm disabling the safeties now."

"OK!" Peter acknowledged above the roar.

The prostate forms of Sakae-san and Tom were sucked into Suzuki's wormhole. A second wormhole opened, then a third, followed by a fourth. Along with the first, they formed a semi-circle around the three time-travellers and their unconscious guards. The suction from each was tremendous, but due to their equidistant positioning the overall effect was nullified, close to neutral.

Peter tightened his grip on Nene's hand. "We'll need to escape in one of those," he shouted in her ear. "Wait for my signal." Peter looked across at Suzuki, grimly holding on to the console. "After you release the safeties, let go," he shouted, unsure if Suzuki could hear him over the cacophony. "It'll be better than staying here."

Suzuki raised a hand to signal that he understood. It was a mistake – the wormhole behind him was too powerful for a single handhold to resist. With an animal-like yelp he was sucked into the void.

"Oh Christ! Nene, come with me!" Peter, hand firmly gripping Nene's, crawled across the floor; he had to confirm the safeties had been released.

"Wait, my father!" Nene turned, but her father was already following, dragging himself as best he could, stoically ignoring the pain of his wounds.

Peter and Nene made it to the console, the change in their relative position to the surrounding wormholes now exposing them to different levels of pull from their dark, insidious mouths.

"Hold on here!" Peter told Nene. "And keep low."

Nene gripped the base of the console. Her father positioned himself on her back, a layer of protection for his daughter.

Peter stood and took hold of the display, jamming a leg tightly in the gap between the console and the one adjacent to it. He had no desire to follow Suzuki-san. Not yet, at least. As for the hapless guards, their fate was in the lap of the gods.

The power levels were at ninety two percent, but the safeties were still on. He continued the procedure, knowing that once he released them the power would keep climbing to one hundred percent, and from there the reactor would exponentially surge to God knows what level until it exploded with the force of a hundred thousand Hiroshimas. If he were right, the anomaly would be destroyed, the blast would be absorbed within the infinity of the two parallel universes, and they'd all be saved.

And if he was wrong – well, then he'd never feel a thing. But he couldn't risk letting that happen to Nene. He chanced a glance behind him. The wormhole was close, its menacing opening no more than five meters away, revealing flashes of countryside as it swirled around in spacetime. Where and when it was, he had no way of knowing; but it represented safety, sanctuary, hope. He leaned down and pulled Nene up by the hand, wrapping his free arm around her waist, pinning her to his chest.

"You must go. Save yourself," he yelled, barely able to make himself heard above the pandemonium.

Nene saw it too; green fields flashing in and out of view as the tunnel danced.

"Don't make me leave you!"

Peter kissed her. "I love you!" he shouted. "Wait for me!"

He released his hold. Nene grabbed on to his outstretched hand, but the pull from the wormhole was too strong. She looked into his eyes, then slipped from his grasp. She was gone.

"I love you!" he shouted it again.

Peter hauled himself against the suction towards the screen and its insistent demand.

Remove Overrides - Confirm Y/N

He reached forward, but the negative pressure from the portal was almost overwhelming. The wormholes were drifting towards each other. In a few seconds they would begin to crossover.

It had to be done now!

He fought desperately to touch the one, simple on-screen red button that would save everything that ever was or ever will be.

His fingers were millimeters away.

A vice-like hand gripped Peter's wrist. Somehow, Nene's father had managed to stand and brace himself against the console.

"Find Nene!" he commanded.

"No wait-"

Nene's father tugged hard and hurled Peter into the wormhole.

***

Takeshi Shinbori, samurai, chief advisor to the Shogun on foreign matters, a student of science, a collector of works from all corners of the Earth, husband of Mei Mei, the beautiful woman from the future who had become the mother of a child from the past, took the last action of his fifty-three years of life – the destiny he had been waiting more than twenty years to fulfil.

He touched the glass and held on tightly as an incredibly bright light filled the cave, extinguishing everything in its path.

Twenty-Seven

The explosion tore through the mountain as if it were paper.

The plasterboard ceiling of the MCR partially collapsed as the shockwave blasted against the external, hardened walls of the two-story building. Consoles tumbled over and short-circuited as aftershocks rattled the solid rock of the foundations, but the structure held firm.

"Put that fire out!" someone shouted.

Amita grabbed an extinguisher and sprayed the flames with foam. The fires subsided.

"Anybody hurt?" Yuko called out.

One by one the MCR team stood and signalled they were all right, though several had nasty looking cuts.

"Better get to surgery," Yuko said.

Amita put the extinguisher down. "They bloody did it," she said. "They bloody blew it up."

"I know," Yuko replied. "I know."

***

Jane took off Shohei's shirt and pressed it to the deep gash on the back of his head.

"What happened?" he said, grimacing through the pain.

"I don't know," Jane answered, although the ceiling panels lying around were a pretty good indication. The earthquake, if that's what it was, had also managed to knock the door half off its hinges.

"Come on you, let's get our ourselves out of here."

Jane gave the door a hefty shoulder barge and sent it crashing to the floor, then helped Shohei into the corridor.

They followed the rest of the walking wounded out through the main doors into the sunlight.

"Oh, my ruddy God," Jane said.

Smoke was pouring from a huge hole in the east side of the mountain, as if a volcano had erupted and left a vast, dust-clouded crater in its wake. Fallen trees littered the slopes, broken off at the base of their trunks like blades of grass mown by a scythe. A debris field of rocks and boulders reached as far as the valley below, the aftermath of a huge landslide that had obliterated the approach road and dammed the river running through the gorge towards Fujimi City.

They stared in bewilderment at the devastating scene.

"What happened, Shugs?"

"An explosion, I think."

"Christ. Nene was still in there. Wait here, I'll go and find her."

"No Jane. It may be dangerous."

"I can't just leave her, you know that."

Shohei nodded, then sat himself down on a boulder as Jane threaded her way through the other evacuees back into the building.

It wouldn't make any difference. He already knew, deep within his soul, that they would see neither Nene nor Peter ever again.

Aftermath

Nene

Nene stood by the window watching Kentaro play in the garden with Ji-chan.

She marvelled, as she always did, how Ji-chan could look so youthful, considering he was twenty years older than Chichi-ue had been when Nene was Kentaro's age. He was much like her father too; strong, kind, resourceful, and although he was a simple farmer, he embodied the true samurai spirit. If he hadn't, then he might well have abandoned her in his rice field the day she mysteriously and magically appeared right in front of him.

Instead he had adopted Nene, and together with his wife looked after her throughout the birth of Kentaro and the six years that followed. She knew why; their own daughter had died at the age of three, more than forty years earlier, and to them Nene had been a gift from the mountain goddess. And when Fuji-san had erupted on the day of her birth and ash fallen deep upon the farms and fields, their first thoughts and actions were for their friends and fellow farmers, rather than for themselves. Yes, Nene thought, Ji-chan and Ba-chan are good people. She would be sad to leave them, to be separated from their warmth, their protection. But the time had come. She could wait no longer.

Nene returned to the main living area of the farmhouse and knelt at a *tsukue*, the small table she used for writing. The *washi* was still there, as it had been all morning, waiting patiently for her to begin. She picked up a *yatate*, carved from bamboo by Ji-chan, and started to write.

***

Nene used a small *suki* to dig a hole in the earth beneath the old cherry tree by the small rivulet that delivered water to the largest of Ji-chan's rice fields.

The tree couldn't have been the same as the one Peter had climbed the day the tunnel, the wormhole, had appeared in the garden, and Ji-chan's farmhouse was, of course, long gone by then, lost to the ravages of nature and time. But it was the same place, the same plot of land where they had spent those few short days together, still more than three hundred years in the future, yet seven years in her past.

One day she would ask Peter; had he known the tunnel would bring her here? She smiled. He would say it was coincidence, and she would say it was her destiny. Then she would tell him, in all the years they'd spent apart, it was his beautiful blues eyes she had missed the most.

"Why are we burying the box, mama?" Kentaro asked.

"So that Papa will know where to find us," she answered.

You have your father's eyes, Kentaro. I pray the day will come when he will see them for himself.

"What's inside the box?"

"A letter for Papa. Now, help me put the box in the hole, and then we'll fill it in, shall we?"

"Hai."

Nene watched Kentaro place the box at the bottom of the hole, then together they pushed the dirt back in with their bare hands. When they were done, she picked him up and held him close as the sun set slowly behind Fuji-san, its golden rays flooding the valley with a benevolent, warm radiance.

"When will Papa come for us, mama?"

"Soon, Kentaro. Very Soon. I promise."

We are here, my love, at the house. Come to us. We are waiting for you, and long to be always with you, for all time.

Nene turned and carried Kentaro inside.

Peter

Somewhere south of the equator, most probably in the Pacific if his best-guess astronomical meteorology was accurate, Peter Walker strode slowly along his favourite stretch of the roughly fifteen kilometers of sand that surrounded Crusoe island.

He christened it that way because he had been stranded there for four long years, still twenty-something years short of the actual Robinson Crusoe, who had an actual island named after him somewhere off the coast of Argentina; although at this rate it wouldn't be long before he beat that record. Well, twenty-something-ish years, to be more precise.

At least all those years alone had given him plenty of time to learn how to fish, but more importantly it had given him time to think.

The first year he'd thought about Nene, all day, every day. She filled his waking hours and soothed him in his sleep. But without her there beside him and without knowing her fate, coupled with trying to keep himself alive, he'd slept very little. He'd heard her voice though, as he had in the cave, echoing through time and space: *Always with you.*

By the second year her voice was a memory that he kept locked in his heart as he worked on making Crusoe island his home.

It was at the start of the third year, when the abandoned Chinese Junk had drifted on to the rocks at the south of the island, coupled with the realization that there were no satellites visible at night, no aircraft lights, no funnel smoke from distant cargo vessels, nor sails, nor any sign whatsoever of the modern world that he'd come to understand he'd moved backwards through time to a place where his only hope of rescue was from Robinson Crusoe himself.

It was then that he began to really think, to evaluate, to dig deeper into the underlying causes and to unravel the hidden impossibilities of what had truly occurred in the confusion and chaos at the ERG

And now, as his fourth year was drawing to its end, he understood it, all of it. It had taken time, solitude, loneliness and seclusion – but he had finally begun to understand the meaning of the vision he had received in the cave.

It wasn't the one paradox - there must be others out there in the furthest reaches of space.

It wasn't the one singularity - it was bigger than that.

It wasn't even the incompatible physics of the two intersecting universes. It was a lot, lot worse than that.

Nene had said so herself – it was just the beginning. The beginning of the end of everything that ever was or ever will be.

The only remaining mystery was why his wormhole had chosen to dump him in the middle of nowhere and nowhen. Perhaps that was the one thing he'd never be able to figure out.

He stared at a storm on the horizon, the swirling clouds pierced by the same strange blue lightning he'd witnessed at his house, and at Nene's house, too.

"Definitely not over," he said.

And there wasn't a damn thing he could do about it.

Investigation

The International Energy Authority report on the 'Mount Nyukasa Incident' was inconclusive, returning an open verdict, at least on the motives behind rogue-operator Akira Suzuki's borderline-insane detonation of the MAM reactor.

As for the role of the Japanese government in concealing the true nature of a matter-antimatter prototype that could solve all humankind's current and future energy problems, on that aspect the report was clear; "Just what the hell were they thinking?" Although the authors did tone that part down a few notches.

Had they known about the ERG, had they known about Peter Walker's involvement and his white paper on wormhole creation, had they had an inkling of the existence of the membrane and its strange connection to Pi, the authors may well not have toned anything down.

But the IEA didn't know, primarily because the ERG team maintained their oath of secrecy. They had to, they'd concluded in a clandestine meeting a few days after the event, because the evidence was clear; messing around with time can screw everything up, literally everything. And even if they hadn't fully understood Peter's motives, they were determined to never let it happen again. So they'd created a smokescreen, deleted the relevant data, gained the reluctant cooperation of Jane and Shohei Taniguchi – and outright lied to the investigating commission, along with blaming everything on their colleague, but not before the whole team had gathered at Akira's grave and begged his spirit for forgiveness.

Had they known that the MAM explosion was equivalent to a two thousand megaton nuclear blast, and ninety-eight percent of that energy had been channeled away from the Earth through a five-million-year-old interconnecting series of Einstein-Rosen Bridges that spanned the entire galaxy, they might have changed their minds.

They definitely would have changed their minds if they'd known that the resulting inter-dimensional shockwave had blown shut a gaping chasm in the fabric of space where two opposing universes had collided, but not before billions of tons of matter had surged through the fissure and mixed in a swirling cocktail of instantaneously annihilating particles and anti-particles, initiating an unstoppable, universe-destroying chain reaction that couldn't be negated by a puny one thousand nine hundred and sixty million tons of TNT-equivalent hiccup.

They had no idea.

Nobody did.

Except Peter Walker, and there wasn't a damn thing he could do about it.

Or so he thought…

Answered Prayers

On her seventy-eighth birthday, exactly a year to the day that Shohei breathed his final sigh, Jane Taniguchi decided to demolish the dilapidated old farmhouse and sell the land.

She'd held on as long as she could for Peter and Nene to return, but she had realized that she needed to let go – they weren't coming back. None of them were. Everyone she had ever loved was gone.

She didn't even have any children to leave the Taniguchi house to, so it would go to Shohei's younger brother, whom she didn't care for. Never mind, her nieces and nephews would benefit, and she liked them very much.

But everything was different now – her whole world was upside down, back to front, inside out.

It had been that way since the *takkyubin* had arrived at ten that morning, three days after the workmen and begun their work at the farm. The delivery driver, their usual man, had handed her the small box found when someone had pulled up the old, dead cherry tree in the garden.

She had asked for it to be sent to her unopened and had waited with trepidation but also with hope. And now that the letter it contained was on the table in front of her, she knew that her prayers had been answered.

She started to read it again, as she would again and again until every word was seared into her overflowing heart.

Peter, my love.

They had survived!

About the Author

Kevin A. Reynolds has lived in Japan for over 30 years, where he spends much of his time teaching leadership and business communication skills at Japanese corporations, along with writing novels and business books.

A brief message from the Author
"I was born just south of London, and have lived in Tokyo since 1989, where I now write novels focused on Japan past, present and future.

Although I cover different genres, there is a core theme that lies at the heart of my work, along the lines of "There are more things in heaven and earth....", with some obvious, some subtle and some hidden linkages across the stories.

I also play guitar, though not particularly well."

Also by Kevin A. Reynolds
Mamoribito - The One Who Protects
www.kevinareynolds.com

THE GIRL WHO FELL THROUGH TIME

BOOK TWO
A UNIVERSE OF STARS

Their Story Continues…

Coming Soon

nanamaru

ONE

The cool evening air breathed through the *sakura* trees and gathered the falling cherry blossoms in its soft embrace before gently laying their petals to the pink-freckled valley floor.

Nene, her long hair caressed by the breeze, raised a hand to shield her eyes as the sun set slowly behind the shoulder of Fuji-san, its golden rays flooding the valley with a benevolent, warm radiance.

Why has he not come?

The thought had been with her every day of the two years since she and Kentaro had buried the message in the garden of the farmhouse that she now thought of as her true home.

We have waited so long, my love. Why have you not come?

Nene understood that centuries must pass before Peter discovered the box under the cherry tree in the corner by the road. But he would know what to do, and would find his way back to them just as surely as the sun would rise again the next morning, and a new day would begin – for everyone.

'What must I do?' she had asked.

'Find him after the separation. Then bring him to us.'

'How?'

'We will show you the way.'

'I don't understand.'

'You will,' the voice had told her. *'In time.'*

In the eight years since the separation, *Kami-sama's* words had sustained her, guided her, comforted her. Yet Peter still had not come, and her fears were growing that they were fated to be apart for all eternity. But surely *Kami-sama* would not mislead her, would not have given her false hope.

'Find him after the separation. Then bring him to us.'

Perhaps she was wrong, and instead of waiting for Peter, she must find the way to him.

"I'm back!"

Kentaro raced along the narrow path between the *tambo* rice fields, leaving Ba-chan and Ji-chan in his wake, then jumped into his mother's arms like a spring-lamb. Nene, strong through years on the farm, held him with ease.

"Welcome home, Kentaro," she said. "Did you enjoy the festival?"

"Mmmm. It was fun!"

"You must be hungry. Mother has prepared your favourite food."

"Natto! Let's eat!"

"We must wait for Ji-chan and Ba-chan. It would not do to start without them."

"Hai."

Kentaro shouted down the path, "Hurry up! Dinner is waiting!"

Ji-chan waved. "We won't be long, Kentaro-kun."

Nene spoke to her son in English. *"You must learn to be patient, Kentaro."*

"But I don't want to be patient, Mother."

"Yes you do." She set him to the ground. *"And you are eight years old, far too big for mother to carry you around like this."*

Kentaro gave her one of his looks. Nene did her best to look stern in reply, but knew she was failing – she always saw Peter in his eyes.

Ji-Chan and his wife reached the farmhouse. Approaching their sixtieth year of life together, they remained young in mind and body. Perhaps that was why they had so readily accepted Nene the day the tunnel of light left her lying in the middle of their largest field, crying like a new-born infant, overcome by the agony of losing both her father and Peter, lost in time, separated from everything she had ever known or loved.

Ba-chan had nursed Nene back to health, but the scars in her heart had not begun to truly heal until Kentaro came into the world. She had wept again that day, but as she held their son close Nene felt in him the promise of a new future, and the tears that flowed down her cheeks were rivers of joy, not despair. And yet there could be no true happiness until they were together again and could be called a family.

Ba-chan took Kentaro by the hand. "Come on Kentaro, let's go inside and wash all that dirt of our hands, shall we?"

"Hai, Ba-chan!"

Ba-chan and Kentaro went indoors, leaving Ji-chan with Nene. Greying, tanned, still fit and powerful despite his long years on earth, Ji-Chan was a study of strength and kindness, much like her own father had been. And like her father, he knew what was in her heart.

"Ji-chan, I…"

"I will wait for you inside, Nene."

He headed inside, leaving Nene alone with her thoughts.

***

"Kentaro, eat properly."

Kentaro, as he often did, was gulping down his rice and natto. Nene knew why - the sooner he finished, the sooner he could have *o-kawari,* a second helping - but where he put it all was a mystery that not even his father would be able to solve.

"Hai," Kentaro replied, and slowed a little.

"Kentaro!"

"Hai."

Kentaro started eating at a more polite pace.

"Kentaro, don't you have something to ask your mother?" Ji-chan said.

"Mmmm."

"It will be all right, I'm sure she won't mind."

Nene put her rice bowl on the small table. "What won't I mind? Kentaro, what have you done?"

"I have not done anything, mother."

"Speak in Japanese, Kentaro."

"I haven't done anything. I just wanted to ask, well, Ji-chan told me, and I wanted to see if I could go, too. Just to see for myself."

"Go where?"

Kentaro hesitated.

"Kentaro?"

"It's just that, Ji-chan told me about the great houses of the Daimyo, in Edo city, and I thought I should like to go and see for myself. Ji-chan will take me."

So, that was it. "No, Kentaro, it is too far."

"But it's only two days walk, and Ji-chan will be there. Please mother, please."

"You are too young, and it is too far."

"I am not too young, and it's not too far. And it's only walking."

"No."

"But mother, please."

How can she resist that look in his eyes? But, going to Edo was out of the question, even for her. Or, it had been, until now.

"I will talk with Ji-chan, and then decide. Now, it is getting late and you must study first with Ba-chan, then to bed."

"But I haven't finished eating yet."

"If you are still hungry after your studies, you may have more. But not until then."

"Yes, mother."

"And speak Japanese at the table, Kentaro."

"Hai."

"I am so sorry for leaving you to tidy everything," Ba-chan said to Nene. "You must be so tired.

"It is fine, Ba-chan, please do not worry."

Ba-chan stood and turned to Kentaro. "Come on, then," she said as she led him by the hand to a small room where they would study *kanji* for the next hour.

Nene watched in silence as the door slid shut.

"Nene?" It was Ji-chan.

She had been staring, she realized, but the *chisai o-heya* was in the same position as Peter's study had been, the one with the *air-con* on the wall that blew cool air and the machine with the strange lights that could sense the tunnels that had brought them together but were now keeping them apart. And each time she went in, whether to sweep the *tatami* matting or to close the shutters for the night, the memories of their time together returned.

The whole house was like that for Nene. Although the one where they had spent a few short days together lay 300 years in the future and was not yet built, it had been the same design, the same plot of land. There was the kitchen where they had taken their first meal; there the bathroom with the *o-furo* that filled by itself; there the window from where she had seen Fuji-san – and there, on the floor, was where they had made Kentaro.

"Nene?"

"I'm sorry, I was… remembering." Nene recovered her focus. "But, I wanted to say, please, Ji-chan, do not make promises to Kentaro like that."

"It is time for him to see more of the world, Nene. He is so very curious about everything. Perhaps it is time to tell him the truth about his father."

"Not yet."

"What harm could it do? And besides, we may hear news."

She stood and cleared the dinner bowls. "He would have come by now," she said. "He would have found a way."

***

Nene knelt beside Kentaro as he lay on the futon in the room they had shared since his birth.

"Did you speak to Ji-chan?" he asked, in English.

When they were alone together like this, they always used that language. It was Nene's way of ensuring that when Peter finally returned, they would quickly become father and son.

"A little, but I have not decided yet. Now, go to sleep. We'll talk more in the morning."

"Is father there?"

"I don't know, Kentaro."

"Do you think he read our magic letter, the one we buried under the tree?"

The simple question cut through to her soul like a knife. "I hope so."

"Then it will not be long before he comes. Yesterday I had a dream about him."

"Did you?"

"I was big and strong, and he was here with us, in this house, and I called him Papa, just like my friends call their fathers. It's Japanese, but I think he would understand."

"That is a good dream, Kentaro."

"Actually, I dream it every day."

Nene ran her fingers through his hair. "So do I," she said, fighting back tears.

***

Nene sat at a *tsukue*, the small table she used for writing, in the main living area of the farmhouse, and began to write.

Peter, my love.

She had started her other letter to him, the one beneath the *sakura* tree, with the same words. This one would be different, and she would place it elsewhere, somewhere where she herself would find it 300 years in the future, on the day she had retrieved Peter's message to the people at the machine in the cave, nine years ago.

Nene hadn't found it then, of course, but she knew actions she made now could change future events. But, more importantly, it gave her hope.

She finished writing, rolled up the parchment and tied the *makio* around the outside. Later, she would put it in her *kome-bukuro* and carry it to Hie Shrine in Edo city – a journey she had not wanted to make, but now saw no alternative.

Nene went outside into the garden, and looked up at the eternal, unchanging stars. She sensed Ji-chan behind her but did not turn.

"He will come, Nene. You must wait, have patience, and believe."

"What is there to believe?"

Ji-chan stood next to her.

"The day you came to us, Ba-chan and I thought you were a gift from the mountain goddess. Who knows, maybe you are.

Even now I still don't understand all this talk of tunnels through time, of worlds where machines fly across the sky. But I know the universe brought you to us for a purpose, Nene. There is a reason you are here, and one day that reason will be revealed to us. And that is why I know he will come."

A *nagare-boshi* burned briefly high above.

"In Edo now," Nene said, "there is a young girl, just six years old. Her mother is carrying her brother, but in a few months from now, when the autumn wind cools the summer, mother and brother will be lost in the agony of birth. And yet I grow older, but by what right? I keep thinking, if Peter comes he can change everything and save us all. But what if he cannot come? What if he is lost, trapped, or even imprisoned? I must go to him, to set him free."

A second *nagare-boshi* flashed across the night sky.

"I'm coming to you, my love. Wait for me."

Made in the USA
Las Vegas, NV
27 February 2022

44671919R00164